Her face smiled into his

She shifted onto her back, and the top sheet settled around her, reshaping itself along her body, at once revealing and concealing. Kyle had never before realized how marvelous a creation a woman's body was. He'd appreciated the female form before, of course, but Roberta's body was so much more. It was one that had both nurtured a child and pleasured him. The faint lines from childbirth were things of unspeakable beauty to him.

Kyle moved closer, as close as he could without disturbing her sleep, and shut his eyes again. Tonight he felt as if he'd shared in another miracle with Roberta, a miracle much different than the last one they'd shared, but no less vital. He wasn't going to let this miracle slip away, as the last one had, before he understood its significance. . . .

ABOUT THE AUTHOR

Judith Arnold says she can't remember ever not being a writer. She wrote her first story at age six and pursued a successful career as a playwright after getting her master's degree from Brown University. Judith, who now devotes herself to writing full-time, also pens novels under the pseudonym Ariel Berk. She and her family live in Connecticut.

Books by Judith Arnold

HARLEQUIN AMERICAN ROMANCE
104—COME HOME TO LOVE
120—A MODERN MAN
130—FLOWING TO THE SKY
139—JACKPOT

These books may be available at your local bookseller.

Don't miss any of our special offers. Write to us at the following address for information on our newest releases.

Harlequin Reader Service
901 Fuhrmann Blvd., P.O. Box 1397, Buffalo, NY 14240
Canadian address: P.O. Box 2800, Postal Station A,
5170 Yonge St., Willowdale, Ont. M2N 6J3

Special Delivery

JUDITH ARNOLD

Harlequin Books

TORONTO • NEW YORK • LONDON
AMSTERDAM • PARIS • SYDNEY • HAMBURG
STOCKHOLM • ATHENS • TOKYO • MILAN

Published May 1986

First printing March 1986

ISBN 0-373-16149-2

Printed in Canada

Chapter One

Everything had changed. Even the beach.

Roberta scanned the smooth white stretch of sand. Some thirty people were lounging on blankets or towels, enjoying the clear, hot August sunshine. Compared to most beaches at this time of year, the small community beach on Madison's south shore was luxuriously uncrowded. But to Roberta it seemed jam-packed. The last time she'd been here, she'd had the entire beach to herself.

That August afternoon, five years ago to the day, had been unseasonably chilly. The fog blanketing the shoreline had been so dense and dank that, standing in the smooth sand not more than two feet from the water's edge, Roberta had barely been able to see the pulsing gray waves of Long Island Sound. Today the water was more green than gray, its gentle surf surging playfully rather than ominously, and the sky was a crisp blue, adorned with a few high, feathery tufts of white.

"Mommy, is this where I was born?" Leah asked.

Roberta gazed down at the slim but sturdy little girl beside her. Even after five years, Roberta still felt a slight thrill at the sight of her energetic daughter, with her thick dark curls and her round, eager eyes. It seemed miraculous to

Roberta that she herself had created a human being like Leah, such a precious, beautiful specimen of life.

At her daughter's question, she smiled and shook her head. "You were born in Aunt Mary's house, Leah. You know that."

Leah pondered for a moment, then asked, "But I *started* to be born here, right?"

Roberta laughed. "I guess you did."

"In this spot?" Leah asked, digging her toes into the sand at Roberta's feet. "This exact spot?"

"I don't remember the exact spot," Roberta replied. "It was very foggy that day.... Somewhere around here, I guess."

"And then Kyle came?"

"Yes." Roberta's voice grew soft and distant. "Then Kyle came."

"When are we going to his house?" Leah asked. "Can I find some shells to bring him?"

"That would be very nice," Roberta agreed. "Give me your sandals, honey, and then you can go and collect shells. We aren't expected at his house for another hour."

"Okay!" Leah yanked off her sandals and darted across the sand, the skirt of her flowered sundress billowing about her coltish legs as she ran.

Roberta watched her daughter weave among the prostrate sun worshipers on the beach, every now and then halting and bending down to examine a shell. Five years ago Leah hadn't even been born. How in the world could Roberta have expected the beach to remain the same, when everything else had changed so drastically?

She tucked a lock of her hair behind her ear, then smoothed the flowing white linen of her skirt beneath her as she sat on the sand. Five years ago her brunette hair had hung long down her back, its weight straightening the natural curls into loose waves. Now she wore it cropped just below her collar and brushed back from her face in a chic, springy style.

Five years ago she was eight months pregnant, bulky and clumsy, strained by the cumbersome shape of her figure. Now she was slender, her waist narrow, her breasts and hips in perfect proportion.

Five years ago she had alternated between believing that she could accomplish anything and fearing that she would fail at everything. Now she was a realist. She knew what she, as a single mother and a professional woman, could and couldn't do, and she accepted both her gifts and her limitations. Now she was practical, no longer swinging between exhilaration and despair but, instead, rolling with the punches, relying on patience and a sense of humor whenever the burden of being both a mother and a father to Leah began to press down too heavily upon her.

Five years ago she would never have imagined that she'd be so strong, so stable, so satisfied with her life today. The universe had seemed far more acute, its rhythms extreme. Now Roberta knew better. She no longer had much faith in her dreams, but she had plenty of faith in herself, which was far healthier.

"Here, Mommy!" Leah scampered to Roberta and dropped several shells onto her lap. "I'm going to go get some more shells for Kyle." Before Roberta could speak, Leah was gone.

Kyle. Fingering the pearly remains of sea life that Leah had given her to hold, Roberta wondered how Kyle might have changed in the past five years. The letters she'd received from him told her a great deal, yet they were somehow circumscribed, reserved, never quite revealing his deepest feelings. Roberta's letters to him had been much the same.

She wasn't certain how their reunion was going to go. Perhaps they'd loathe each other on sight. What they'd shared five years ago had been unspeakably special. But time had altered her, and she knew it must have altered Kyle as well. He wouldn't be a mysterious bearded stranger materializing out of the fog. He would be a man five years older, five years different, and she had to prepare herself for that.

His sudden appearance on the beach that afternoon so many years ago had been a shock. Roberta had been spending the week at her friend Mary's summerhouse half a block from the shore. "You've got to use the cottage," Mary had insisted. "I can't use it this month; I'm facing a deadline. Honestly, Roberta, you should go. Somebody ought to get some use out of it."

"But . . . I don't know. The baby's due at the end of September, and . . ."

"Roberta, if there's one thing I know about pregnant women, it's that they should never spend August in New York City. Ten'll get you twenty your doctor will say the same thing."

He hadn't said it quite like that, but he'd given Roberta permission to spend a week on the Connecticut shoreline. "Your pregnancy has proceeded uneventfully all along; I don't foresee any problems," he'd reassured her. "We generally advise against traveling when a woman is less than four weeks from her due date, but you've still got six weeks to go. And you'll be only two hours from the city. The fresh air will do you good, Mrs. Frankel. I think you should accept your friend's invitation."

Mary Grinnard was more than a friend to Roberta—she was a sister, an aunt, a mother and a guru rolled into one. Mary was a successful writer of children's books, and Roberta's husband, Lee, had illustrated many of her books.

After Lee's death, Mary had taken Roberta under her wing and given her the courage to see her pregnancy through. Mary had even attended the Lamaze childbirth-preparation classes with Roberta, volunteering to be Roberta's birth coach during the delivery.

Mary's summer cottage in Madison was lovely, and as soon as Roberta arrived, she was glad that Mary had talked her into using it. The compact, shingled house boasted views of the water from its parlor windows, and the shore breezes floated through the house day and night, infiltrating it with a fresh sea-tinged perfume. The house's walls were white, its furnishings wicker, its curtains and spreads featuring floral patterns in pastel shades. The cottage had an atmosphere of lightness, which Roberta found an excellent antidote to her own awkward heaviness.

She spent her week reading, sipping tall glasses of skimmed milk on the porch, and taking long, aimless walks on the beach. Because many of the area's homeowners were New Yorkers with city jobs and could use their cottages only during the weekends, the beach was never too crowded. On the Friday before Roberta was to return to her SoHo loft in lower Manhattan, the thick fog that descended onto the shore rendered the beach totally empty.

Roberta dug her hands into the pockets of her denim maternity jumper as she strolled barefoot along the damp sand. She didn't mind the cool weather and she appreciated her solitude. Solitude was something she knew she wouldn't have once the baby was born. She wanted to enjoy what little time alone she had left before her life was invaded by a demanding infant.

She walked the entire length of the curving beach, perhaps a mile, and then turned and retraced her steps, feeling a mild strain in her lower back each time her heels sank into the pliant sand. In spite of the chilly air, the sand was warm, as if it had absorbed the week's sunshine, storing it for just such a sunless afternoon. Roberta's toes molded the gritty powdered surface of the beach, leaving distinct impressions of themselves. At least pregnancy hadn't altered the size or shape of her footprints, she noted as she ambled along the shoreline.

When she was half the distance back to Mary's cottage, she felt the first cramp. She halted.

It didn't actually hurt. It was more a tensing of her abdomen than a genuine pain. She wasn't alarmed. Last month she'd suffered cramps in her lower back, the month before, cramps in her enlarged breasts. Cramps, she'd learned, were par for the course when one was pregnant.

She flattened her hands against the hard, round swell of her belly and waited for the cramp to subside. Then she resumed her walk. Within a couple of minutes, she felt another cramp tightening her abdomen. Like the first, it didn't hurt, but she felt more comfortable squatting down until the tension passed. Once it did, she tried to stand. But her body was so unwieldy that she lost her balance and fell with a graceless plop onto her rear end.

She pushed at the sand, attempting to hoist herself up onto her feet, but she couldn't seem to get her legs beneath her. The one time she came close the fetus began to kick, causing Roberta to giggle and collapse onto the sand again. She supposed she could crawl back to Mary's cottage if she had to....

"Can I give you a hand?" The voice was disembodied, a soft, deep whisper in the fog. She turned in time to see a shadowy figure approaching her, becoming clearer as he moved toward her through the mist.

"Where did you come from?" she blurted out, amazed to discover another person sharing the beach with her. She'd walked all the way from one end of the beach to the other; how could she have missed seeing him?

Noticing her perplexed scowl, he grinned and extended his hand. "I just pulled up in my boat," he explained.

"Your boat? I wouldn't exactly call this a great day for boating," Roberta observed.

"I wasn't boating," he clarified, wrapping his fingers about both her wrists and easing her to her feet. "I was checking my lobster trap."

"You're a lobsterman?"

He laughed and shook his head. "I've got one trap, and it was empty. Doesn't sound like much of a career, does it?"

Roberta studied him through the gray haze. He *looked* like a lobsterman, she thought—or, at least, he looked like what she'd expect a lobsterman to look like. He was tall, ruggedly built, with unkempt dark blond hair and a trimmed beard covering the length of his square jaw and extending into a mustache beneath his prominent nose. He was clad in an old white shirt with its sleeves rolled up and a pair of well-worn khaki trousers, also rolled up above his bare feet. His skin had been darkened by the sun, and his gray eyes were framed with laugh lines. He looked, if not like a lobsterman, like a beach bum, Roberta decided.

He examined her as she examined him. His gaze took in the thick, dark tresses waving down her back to her waist, her large heavily lashed round eyes, her narrow nose and thin lips, the denim jumper stretched smooth across her bulging abdomen, her slender suntanned legs and sand-caked toes. His eyes rose from her feet to the watermelon-shaped swelling beneath her jumper and his smile faded. "Are you all right?"

"Of course I'm all right," Roberta replied briskly. "I'm just a little klutzy these days. Which is only to be expected, considering."

The man stared through the fog toward the rows of houses beyond the beach. "Do you have far to go? I'll help you home if you'd like."

"I'm not an invalid," Roberta protested good-naturedly. Then another cramp began, this one more intense than the last. Her face twisted in a grimace as she waited for the pain to recede. She let out a slow breath, then relaxed and managed a smile. "I'll be okay," she reassured the man.

He was clearly unconvinced. "Why don't I just walk you home?"

"That would be a long way to walk," Roberta joked. "Home is New York City. I'm just visiting in Madison for a brief vacation."

"A vacation?" He brushed his hair back from his high brow and appraised her critically. "I admit I don't know much about these things, but are you supposed to take vacations when you're—"

"Pregnant?" she supplied the word.

He smiled bashfully. "I mean, so far along and all."

"I'm not due for six weeks," she informed him. "My doctor assured me the baby would be perfectly safe if I got away from the city for a few days."

"Then what . . ." He paused, flexing his lips as he sought the right phrasing. "What was that that just happened to you? You looked like you were in pain."

"Just a cramp," Roberta said breezily. "Probably a Braxton Hicks contraction."

"A what?"

"False labor. Lots of women have that in their last month. It doesn't mean anything."

"But it hurts," he guessed.

"Not really," Roberta insisted. "It feels a little strange, but it's perfectly normal, and—"

"I'll walk you home," the man declared decisively. "Wherever it is you're staying, that is."

She peered up at him. He stood over half a head taller than she, his broad, muscular shoulders at a level with her ear. He was apparently determined to accompany her to Mary's cottage, no matter how stubbornly she insisted that she was completely capable of getting herself there safely. Seeing no reason to argue with him, she shrugged and started down the beach. The man fell into step beside her.

"What's your name?" she asked him.

"Kyle Stratton. Yours?"

"Roberta Frankel." She stuffed her hands into the pockets of her jumper and tried not to sway too much when she walked. "Are you vacationing here, too?"

"No, I live in Madison," he replied. "There are a few of us year-rounders mixed in with all the summer folk from New York."

"It's a lovely town," Roberta noted. "I wouldn't mind living here." She veered toward the sand-dusted asphalt leading to a block of houses. Kyle kept pace with her. She pointed out Mary's cottage. "That's where I'm staying," she said.

"Nice place," he commented, sweeping the compact cottage with his discerning gaze. The shingled outer walls had been recently whitewashed, the porch was in excellent repair, and the six-pane windows were open, allowing the cool sea breeze to flutter through the lightweight, flowered drapes behind the screens. "How long have you owned it?"

Roberta shook her head. "I don't," she told him. "It belongs to a friend." She gripped the porch railing and clumsily lifted first one foot and then the other to wipe the sand from them. "Mary Grinnard. I don't know if you'd know her. She's another New Yorker, but she summers here."

Kyle followed Roberta onto the porch. "We year-round people don't know too many of the summer people," he commented. She unlocked the front door and Kyle held it open for her. "Are you going to be all right?" he asked, peeking past her into the empty parlor. "Would you like me to stay here with you until your friend gets back?"

"She's not in Madison," Roberta said. "I've got the cottage to myself for the week."

Kyle considered that news and rubbed his beard thoughtfully. "Maybe...maybe you shouldn't be alone. I'll keep you company until the labor stops."

"It isn't labor," she corrected him. "It's false labor." As if on cue, another cramp seized her, and she gripped the doorknob and took a long, steadying breath. Once the cramp ended, she released the doorknob and turned away so Kyle wouldn't see any hint of pain in her face. She didn't want him worrying unnecessarily about her.

"Look, Roberta—" he spoke softly, hesitantly, as if he wasn't sure that he had the right to impose himself on her "—I don't know whether these things are false or true or what, but let me just stay with you for a little while. For my own peace of mind, okay?"

She smiled. Although she was pretty certain her cramps didn't signify anything, she was touched by his concern. "Maybe you'd like a drink," she suggested, gesturing him into the house. She felt safe with him, not only because he'd behaved chivalrously thus far but because her body was so grotesquely swollen that she couldn't imagine any man wanting to take advantage of it.

He followed her into the bright kitchen. His gaze immediately latched onto the antiquated leaded-glass cabinet doors. "Wow, these are great!" he enthused, swinging one door open. "Nice work. Do you have any idea who built them?"

"None at all," Roberta answered, surprised by his interest. She didn't care much about kitchens one way or the other. "I suspect they were put in before Mary bought the house."

Kyle swung open another door, testing its hinges. "Very nice," he remarked, then grinned. "I'm a carpenter," he explained. "When I see good craftsmanship, I get carried away."

Roberta entertained a private smile. She had a weak spot in her heart for artists and artisans. Lee had been an artist. She herself dabbled in art. Her SoHo loft was currently cluttered with watercolors and pastels she'd recently completed. "Do you build cabinets?" she asked.

Kyle shook his head. "Furniture, mostly," he replied as his gaze took in the ordinary kitchen chairs arranged around the rectangular pine table. He turned one chair around and straddled it, resting his chin on the back of the seat. "Thank goodness I'm better at carpentry than at lobstering...."

His voice trailed off as he noticed the sudden darkening of her brow. She bit her lip and tried to work through the ache with an even breath. When the pain finally faded she sagged weakly against the counter.

Kyle stood and crossed the room to her. His hand hovered near her shoulder in an appealingly shy way. Even though he was inside the cottage with her, he still seemed extremely cautious about imposing on her. "This isn't false anything, is it," he murmured.

"I—I don't know," Roberta stammered, trying to hide her fear. What had earlier felt like a mild cramp now seemed much too severe to be treated lightly.

"Maybe you ought to call your husband," he recommended.

"I haven't got—" she began, then faltered. Kyle's attention was riveted to her, and she realized that her statement would lead him to believe that she was an unwed mother. But if she told him the truth—that Lee had died just weeks after she'd found out she was pregnant—she'd sound as if she were protesting too much, as if she felt she had to defend her position as a single mother to Kyle.

It didn't really matter, she realized. She was an artist, a free spirit; she and Lee had lived together for two years before they'd gotten married, and their wedding had been simply a matter of practicality. She didn't have to explain all that to the friendly stranger who'd insisted on seeing her safely home. If she did try to explain, he probably wouldn't believe her, anyway.

Or worse yet, if he did believe her, he might pity her. He was already much too concerned about her. She didn't want his pity, too.

His eyes remained on her, their gray as soft and mysterious as the swirling fog outside. "Who should we call, then?" he asked.

Roberta was pleased by the lack of condemnation in his tone. A carpenter, she mused. Another free spirit. Someone who didn't give a hoot what her marital status was. "I guess I should phone my doctor in New York," she said. "I'm sure he'll tell me that these are just Braxton Hicks contractions and I've got nothing to worry about."

Kyle nodded. "While you do that, I'll go and get my truck. I've got it parked a few blocks down, near where I pulled in my boat."

"Won't it be safe there?" Roberta asked. Madison struck her as the sort of town where people didn't need to lock the doors of their houses or cars. She locked Mary's cottage whenever she left it only because, after living in Manhattan for years, she wasn't able to break the habit.

"It's safe," Kyle assured her. "But I think we should have it handy, just in case."

"Just in case what?" Roberta asked, laughing.

Kyle only smiled. "You're a pretty brave lady, aren't you?" Roberta wasn't sure whether his comment reflected disapproval or admiration, but before she could question him, he was out the door.

She left the door unlocked for him. She waddled to the bedroom and lowered herself onto the bed. It felt good to sit—not on the beach but on a raised piece of furniture, where she knew she could stand up again all by herself if she wanted. She hadn't realized how tired the cramps had made her.

Her purse sat on the night table by the telephone, and she pulled out her doctor's office number and dialed. The receptionist answered. Roberta identified herself, then told the woman where she was and what she'd been experiencing.

"Dr. Stephens is away on vacation," the receptionist reported. "If you'd like, I can try to have his partner contact you. He's at the hospital, but I can have him paged."

Roberta thanked the woman and provided her with the telephone number of the cottage.

"Your due date is six weeks off," the receptionist noted before concluding the conversation. "And everything has gone just fine so far. I'm sure this is nothing serious, Mrs. Frankel. It sounds like false labor to me, but I'll have Dr. Schroeder give you a call as soon as I can reach him."

After thanking the receptionist again, Roberta hung up. She swung her legs up onto the mattress, rested her head against one of the plump down pillows and sighed. She really couldn't complain about the cramps, which were evidently only a minor inconvenience. As the receptionist had said, Roberta's pregnancy had gone just fine so far. Talking to friends who'd had children and to fellow patients in Dr. Stephens's waiting room, Roberta had heard many horror stories: one woman had endured morning sickness for seven months. Another one had developed such a bad case of varicose veins that she'd had to wear support hose in mid-July, when the temperature teetered toward one hundred degrees. Another one had suffered a pinched nerve in her arm, and her fingers had become numb. One of Roberta's neighbors had stained blood for the first four months of her pregnancy and been confined to bed. Another had started staining toward the end of her pregnancy and spent the last two months in the hospital being monitored. Roberta had never realized that so many things could go wrong in a pregnancy. She was relieved that everything had gone right for her.

Everything but Lee's death, of course.

But at least she had been somewhat prepared for that. They'd been living together for well over a year when a doctor diagnosed the vague collection of symptoms Lee had been suffering from as Hodgkin's disease. "It's a lymphatic disease, related to cancer," the doctor had explained. "We'll treat it with drug therapy and see what happens. I won't kid you—Hodgkin's disease sometimes doesn't respond to treatment. On the other hand, you might live for years and years with this thing. I simply can't say."

"We'll get married, Roberta," Lee had decided. "That way, if something happens to me, you'll be covered by my insurance and all." Roberta had agreed to his sensible plan.

Her parents had been horrified. They'd met Lee only a few times, but what little they knew of him, they didn't like. He was an *artist*, living in a *loft*. Roberta's explanation— that he was a professional illustrator, earning a fine salary, and that his loft was a huge, well-lit floor of a converted building in the currently fashionable SoHo district—didn't sway her conservative parents. They hadn't approved of Roberta's decision to move in with Lee soon after she'd finished college and taken a job sorting slides at the Metropolitan Museum of Art. The few times they'd met him, they thought he looked scruffy and ungroomed. They also didn't care for the fact that he was Jewish, though they never dared to come right out and say so. Instead, they talked unendingly about different ethnic backgrounds, different cultures, the importance of sticking with one's own.

They were appalled when Roberta chose to live with Lee, and even angrier when she and Lee got married—at the Municipal Building, not even in a church. But when she became pregnant, they were apoplectic. "Roberta!" her mother had railed during one of their exasperating cross-country telephone conversations. "This is unbelievably irresponsible. Lee's health is fragile. What in the world are you going to do if he dies and leaves you with a baby?"

"I'm going to love that baby as much as I love Lee," Roberta had replied, her voice as hard and unyielding as tempered steel. "I'm twenty-five years old, and I want a child—Lee's child. He wants a child, too. We can't just sit around waiting. So for heaven's sake, please wish us well and pray that Lee lives to be a grandfather."

He didn't. Yet his courage had inspired Roberta. Even more than before, she was determined to have his child, to raise his child to know its father, the fine, talented man Roberta had loved. She never let herself dwell on the difficulties of raising a child alone. All she thought about was keeping herself healthy for her baby—hers and Lee's.

Lying on Mary's bed, struggling through another cramp, Roberta found herself wondering for the first time whether something might be seriously wrong with the baby. Her doctor had declared the fetus strong and hearty after each examination, and that knowledge had seen Roberta through many lonely days and nights. The baby was a piece of Lee, the healthy, surviving part of him that he himself had been denied. If something went wrong now...Roberta couldn't bear the thought.

"I'm back." Kyle filled the bedroom doorway. Roberta noticed that he'd put on brown leather deck shoes and combed his thick gold-tinged hair. "How are you feeling?"

"A little tired," she said.

"Did you call your doctor?"

"He's on vacation," she informed Kyle. "His partner is supposed to call me back."

Kyle ventured into the room, his attention fully on Roberta. He lowered himself onto the edge of the bed and arranged the pillow more evenly beneath her head. "How do you know the difference between false labor and real labor?" he asked.

"Real labor is more regular, I think," Roberta answered. "And it hurts more. This doesn't really hurt that much. In fact, the nurse I spoke to on the telephone said it sounded like false labor to her, too. She assured me there's nothing to worry about, Kyle."

"I'm not leaving," he declared with finality.

Roberta gazed up at him. He combed his fingers gently through her hair, pushing it back from her pale cheeks. In all honesty, she was glad he wasn't leaving. Maybe she was a pretty brave lady, as he'd claimed, but if something was wrong with her baby, she didn't think she was brave enough to handle it by herself.

"Can I make a call?" he asked, angling his head toward the telephone.

"Of course."

He dialed a number and listened. "Ellie, it's Kyle. I've got to cancel for tonight." Roberta opened her mouth to object. She didn't want him to break a date on her account. But he turned away, tucking the phone more snugly against his bearded chin. "Something's come up.... Yes, it's important. A friend of mine is pregnant, and she's not feeling well.... What do you mean, since when do I have pregnant friends? Don't be that way, Ellie.'' He sighed. ''I'll call you,'' he promised before hanging up.

''You shouldn't have done that,'' Roberta commented quietly.

He twisted to face her, then grinned. ''Why not? You need me more than she does right now.'' He chuckled wryly. ''Frankly, I don't think she needs me at all, but that's irrelevant.'' He rose to his feet and started toward the door. ''I'm going to boil some water.''

Roberta laughed. ''You've been watching too many old movies,'' she chided him.

''What old movies? I want a cup of coffee,'' he returned. ''Can I get you anything?''

''No, I'm not hungry.'' In fact, she felt slightly queasy.

She watched him leave the room. His long, lithe physique made her own body seem even lumpier to her. How she looked forward to a day when she could move gracefully again!

When Kyle returned to the bedroom carrying a mug of coffee several minutes later, he found Roberta lying on her side, hugging her belly and working through another cramp. He quickly set down his mug and knelt on the floor beside her. ''What can I do?'' he asked.

The cramp left her limp and breathless. ''Please—could you rub my back?'' she rasped.

He cupped his hands over her shoulders.

''Lower,'' she mumbled.

He slid his hands down to the small of her back and massaged the taut muscles there. The pressure of his thumbs against her knotted flesh hurt, but it hurt in a delicious, satisfying way. She groaned.

She was very glad he hadn't left. His powerful massage loosened the muscles, easing the ache that spread from the base of her spine down her legs and up toward her waist. He continued to rub her for several more minutes, until she groaned again. Then he let his hands fall to the mattress and examined her now tranquil expression.

"Thank you," she whispered.

He settled on the bed beside her and stroked her hair back from her damp brow. "How long has it been since you called your doctor?" he asked.

"I don't know," she muttered.

"Maybe you should try again."

Roberta nodded and propped herself up with her elbow. Kyle handed her the receiver, then dialed the number for her.

The receptionist answered, and after Roberta gave her name, the woman said that she'd been trying to reach Dr. Schroeder. "He must be in surgery," the receptionist explained, "because he still hasn't answered his page."

Roberta cursed beneath her breath. "Look," she grunted into the phone, "I'm beginning to think maybe this isn't false labor. Tell me what to do."

"Let me try to reach Dr. Stephens," the receptionist suggested. "I've got the name of the hotel where he's vacationing. Maybe I can contact him. You sit tight and start timing your contractions, Mrs. Frankel. I'll get back to you as soon as I can."

Roberta hung up and eyed Kyle. "She told me to time my contractions," she reported.

Kyle scrutinized her contemplatively. He looked not alarmed but, rather, fascinated, perhaps even a bit excited. "You're going to have your baby pretty soon, aren't you?"

"I don't know," Roberta said with a feeble laugh. "I used to think six weeks from yesterday was soon enough. But now..." She winced as a horrid thought crossed her mind.

"Oh, Kyle, I've always heard it's bad to have an eight-month baby."

"Why?" he asked.

"I don't know why. It's just what I've heard. Everybody says it—all the women I know, and their mothers. A seven-month baby is supposed to be all right, and a nine-month baby is, well, perfect. But an eight-month baby—"

"Is also perfect," Kyle reassured her, clearly reading the panic in her wide, dark eyes. "You know more about this than I do, Roberta, but you really ought to try to stay calm, don't you think? There's no sense in wasting your energy worrying about old wives' tales."

"You're right," Roberta agreed with a sheepish smile. She felt the onset of another cramp and gasped, "Start timing," before she closed her eyes and did her best to perform one of the rhythmic breathing patterns she'd been taught in her childbirth-preparation class.

Kyle checked his wristwatch, then slipped around her on the bed and massaged her lower back for her. That he knew to rub it without her having to ask him touched her immensely. Of all the strangers who might have broken through the fog on the beach earlier that day, she was infinitely grateful that Kyle had been the person to enter her world.

She exhaled as the pain ebbed. "Okay," she panted. "How long was that?"

He checked his watch again. "Thirty seconds, maybe."

"Good," she said. "I don't think we're in imminent danger. When you're about to deliver, they last much longer than thirty seconds."

Kyle reached behind her for his coffee and took a long sip. Then he cushioned his shoulders with another pillow and let Roberta rest her head against his chest. His fingers wandered through her long hair. "I wish I could do something for you besides just staring at my watch," he commented.

"You *are* doing something for me," she assured him.

"Rubbing your back?"

"Being here," she said softly. "I'm glad you ignored me and decided to stay, Kyle. I don't think I could have coped with this alone. I don't know who you are, but—"

"I'm a friend," he suggested.

"A good friend," Roberta elaborated. "A friend in need."

He chuckled. "Let's just say I like trying new things," he remarked. "Watching a lady in labor is something I've never done before."

"How about your mother?" Roberta asked. "Do you have any younger brothers or sisters?"

"As a matter of fact, I do have a kid sister, but I was all of two years old when she was born. I'm afraid I don't remember the details." His hand continued to meander through Roberta's hair, running soothingly behind her ear to the nape of her neck, again and again. "How about you? Have you ever watched anyone in labor before?"

"Only in a film," Roberta answered. "In my childbirth-preparation class, the instructor showed a film of a woman giving birth. They made it look like a Sunday-school picnic," she added grumpily.

"I take it you aren't feeling up to competing in the potato-sack race right now," Kyle deduced with a gentle grin.

"The film wasn't bad," Roberta defended it. "But the whole gist of it—of the classes in general—is that you're supposed to view childbirth through euphemisms. You never use the word 'pain,' for one thing. You never say it hurts. Instead, you're supposed to call the cramps contractions and say you're suffering some discomfort."

His lips tightened in a frown of dismay. "It does hurt, doesn't it?" he whispered sympathetically. "If you really are in pain, feel free to use the right word."

She closed her eyes for a moment and nestled her head more snugly against his chest. Yes, it hurt; she was in pain. But compared to the pain of Lee's death, this pain wasn't so terrible. "I can stand it," she said stoically, then managed a smile. "A little discomfort isn't going to get the better of me, Kyle."

"Motherhood's probably going to be tougher," he mused.

She twisted to view his face, her smile expanding. "Do you think so?"

He considered what he'd said, then laughed at his presumptuousness. "Not that I know anything about it, Roberta, but—" his laughter faded "—I've always figured motherhood to be a pretty special job, awfully demanding and all. And to have to handle motherhood all by yourself, without . . ." He drifted off for an instant. "It's none of my business, of course. Forget I said anything."

She focused on his chest, on his strong wrist as his hand reached for her brow and then combed through her hair again. "I don't mind," she reassured him. "Yes, it'll be tough. But I guess I'll have to handle it by myself," she murmured. "I haven't got much choice in the matter."

"You *are* a brave lady," Kyle remarked.

"Brave or stupid." She sucked in her breath. "I'm having another one," she whispered.

He glanced at his wristwatch, then applied his hands to her lower back. She controlled her lungs, squeezed her eyes shut, concentrated on the circles Kyle's fingertips were rubbing into her muscles. The telephone rang, but he continued to massage her back until her body relented and her head sank wearily into the pillow. "Forty-five seconds," he announced. "I'll answer if you want."

"Please," she croaked.

He spoke on the telephone for several minutes, then set the receiver back in its cradle. "That was your doctor," he informed Roberta. "We're supposed to get you to Yale-New Haven Hospital. They've got several obstetricians on call there. He said to tell you not to worry, just to relax and remember everything you learned in your childbirth classes."

Roberta nodded.

Kyle's eyes ran down her body, then lifted to her face again. "What I think we ought to do," he advised, "is call an ambulance to take you to the hospital. It's a half-hour drive, and I don't want to have to pull onto the shoulder of the turnpike so you can have a baby in my truck."

Roberta nodded again.

Kyle searched the shelf of the night table for a telephone book and located the emergency police number. He explained the situation to the person who answered his call and requested an ambulance. Then he hung up.

"I've never ridden in an ambulance before," Roberta said. "I think I'm a little scared."

"Don't be," Kyle consoled her. "Everything's going to be fine."

"Will you ride with me?"

"If they let me," he promised.

She stared at him, his face looming above her. It was an open face, his smile sweet, with just a touch of whimsy in it. His nose had a slight bump in it, she noted. And his eyes were incredibly tender. She hadn't before acknowledged how handsome he was. But perhaps what made him so handsome was his generosity toward her, his kind concern.

"Kyle," she murmured, turning her head to study her huge abdomen. Her voice was suddenly stronger, composed and controlled. "The linen closet is the door next to the bathroom. You passed it on your way here from the kitchen. Maybe you ought to get some clean towels."

He registered the abrupt change in her mood, from fear and exhaustion to resolve and certainty. Roberta didn't see his slight nod of understanding. Taking a deep breath, he instantly matched her calm attitude. "Clean towels," he repeated, starting to the door. "Anything else? Boiling water?"

"Just towels. Lots of towels. And wash your hands."

He nodded again and vanished from the room. She eased the blanket out from beneath her and shoved it off the bed. Dr. Stephens had warned her to remember everything she'd learned in her childbirth classes, and while she hadn't learned much about having a baby arrive six weeks ahead of schedule at a friend's vacation cottage, she had learned to stay sober and alert and to use her mind as well as her body.

Another contraction squeezed her, and she closed her eyes and fought to keep her brain functioning. She was aware of a warm, liquid sensation spreading between her legs, and she bunched her jumper beneath her to protect the mattress. If ever she needed her wits about her, now was the time.

She was out of breath when Kyle returned, carrying a stack of plush white towels. "Under my legs," she panted, waving vaguely at the towels and then tugging off her soaked panties. "Under my bottom. I think—I think I want to push."

"Push what?"

"The baby!"

Kyle scrambled to slide the towels beneath her and over the lower half of the bed. "Can't you hold it in till the ambulance gets here?" he asked with a laugh.

She started to laugh, too. She laughed until a long, elastic tension stretched through her womb, robbing her of everything but the instinctive comprehension that her baby was ready to be born.

Chapter Two

"I can see it," Kyle announced.

Roberta inhaled deeply, then exhaled, trying to rebuild her strength for the next push. "What do you see?" she asked hoarsely. "Do you see the cord?"

"No. Just the head," Kyle replied. He sounded awed, his voice hushed but steady. "Just the top of the head."

"Okay." Roberta gripped her thighs more tightly with her hands and took another preparatory breath. "I'm going to push again. Try to guide the head out."

Kyle bent over her and nodded. "Ready when you are."

Roberta shut her eyes and pushed. She'd been pushing for twenty minutes, and she was utterly drained. But she mustered every last ounce of energy within her body and directed it downward to her child.

Kyle murmured soft words of encouragement to her. "Keep going, Roberta, keep going. A little more, just a little more—" He let out a hoot. "All right! The head is out!"

Roberta released her breath in a soft moan. "Okay," she said, her voice barely above a whisper, her clenched fingers leaving vivid red marks on the skin of her thighs. "You have to direct the shoulders now. Line them sideways, and—" The urge to push overcame her, and she succumbed to it.

"Good." Kyle's soothing voice floated up to her. "You're doing fine, Roberta . . . yes . . . yes. Okay. The shoulders are out—and here comes an arm."

Roberta pushed again, again, her body working reflexively, tapping secret stores of strength. She felt beads of cold sweat forming on her forehead, and her teeth carved dents into her lower lip. But she couldn't stop, she couldn't rest. Not now.

"Oh, my God," Kyle breathed. Roberta dared to open her eyes. Through a blur of fatigue she saw him wrapping a thick towel gingerly around a tiny, squirming creature. "Oh, God, Roberta . . ."

She waited anxiously for him to say more.

"It's a girl," he revealed, his voice hushed, trembling and reverent. "She's beautiful, Roberta. She's the most beautiful thing I've ever seen."

The baby emitted a thin, feeble whine. Kyle dabbed the towel over her little face, wiping her skin clean, and she cried again, a louder, heartier wail. Roberta began to cry, too—tears of relief and happiness. "Let me hold her," she begged, raising her shoulders off the bed.

Kyle rested the baby on Roberta's abdomen, and she cupped her hands around the towel-swaddled infant. The baby seemed so small—small but active, her miniature fingers clawing at the restricting towel, reaching to pinch her mother's belly. Roberta laughed, though she was still weeping.

In the distance she heard footsteps, then a man's voice: "Hello?"

"In here!" Kyle called. "In the bedroom."

Two emergency medical technicians in white uniforms jogged to the bedroom door and stopped. "Looks like we're too late," one of them muttered contritely.

Roberta might have complained that the medics had certainly taken more than enough time in getting to the house. What if something had gone wrong during the birth? What if Kyle hadn't been so capable and confident? What if Roberta had started to hemorrhage, or the cord had been wrapped around the baby's neck, or any other of the countless catastrophes that might have occurred in the interval between Kyle's phone call summoning the ambulance and its belated arrival?

But she was too elated to complain. Her daughter was howling, busily attempting to wrestle her way out of the towel, behaving like a healthy, feisty newborn. Roberta's heart swelled with love and delight. There was no room in it for anger.

One of the medics left the room to fetch supplies, and the other scooped the baby from Roberta's abdomen. "How are you feeling?" he asked Roberta as he gave the baby's face a more thorough wiping and then a superficial evaluation.

"Wonderful," she said. "Is she all right?"

"She's a little fighter," the medic declared. "Small but tough. How early is she?"

"Six weeks," Roberta answered.

The other medic returned with equipment. As the two men clamped and cut the cord, Roberta turned to Kyle. He was standing on the far side of the bed, his expression rapt and his eyes glistening. He caught Roberta looking at him and smiled wistfully. She patted the mattress beside her and he took a seat, taking her hand in his and squeezing it.

"Are you the father?" one of the medics asked him.

"No, just a friend," Kyle replied, shooting Roberta a quick glance. "A good friend."

"You did a terrific job," the medic praised Kyle as he took Roberta's blood pressure. "Have you ever delivered a baby before?"

Kyle shook his head. "I was only following orders," he said modestly. "Roberta told me what to do and I did it."

The other medic had unwrapped the baby and re-wrapped her in a sterilized blanket. "Can I hold her?" Roberta asked.

He started to shake his head, then relented. "Just for a minute," he granted. "You both did an excellent job, but conditions aren't exactly sterile here. I want to get this little bundle of joy to the hospital for a complete check. You, too," he said with a nod to Roberta. He turned to the other medic. "Why don't we go get the gurney?"

The two men departed. Roberta tightened her arms around her daughter and studied her face. The girl's eyes were dark, her scalp covered with thin wisps of black hair, her skin pink, her mouth flexing instinctively. "She *is* beautiful, isn't she?" Roberta whispered, poking her pinkie against the baby's palm and grinning as the baby instantly curled her fingers about it.

"Absolutely," Kyle agreed, his gaze fastened on the baby. "I think I'm in love." He reached out and touched the baby's cheek. She turned her mouth toward him and he smiled. "She's so soft," he whispered. "Her skin is like velvet."

The medics returned, wheeling a stretcher. "Okay, Mama," one of them announced as he pulled the baby out of Roberta's embrace. "The little one gets to ride in a heated basinette, and you get to ride on the gurney."

"Can Kyle come in the ambulance with us?" Roberta asked as the medics lifted her onto the stretcher.

"It'll be safer if he doesn't," one of them replied.

"I'll follow in my truck," Kyle promised. "I'll meet you at the hospital. You don't have to be scared now, Roberta," he pointed out. "The baby's fine and so are you." He gathered up her purse and the house keys. "You'd better take these with you," he said as he passed them to her.

"Thank you." She clung to his hand until they were out of the house, then reluctantly let go of him as the medics lifted her into the back of the ambulance.

One medic remained in the rear of the ambulance with Roberta and her daughter while the other drove. The driver didn't bother with lights or sirens, since the emergency had passed, and the trip to New Haven gave Roberta a chance to think. She thought not only about the delicate little infant lying in a basinette beside her but about Kyle. He was still a stranger to her, a man she didn't know at all. Yet she felt close to him right now, unbelievably close. She couldn't have had her baby without him. She would have panicked, gone into shock. She didn't even want to think about the possibilities. Kyle had saved her life, and her daughter's life as well.

But what Roberta felt for him went beyond gratitude. It was something much less easily defined and much more profound. She recalled the tears she'd seen in his eyes just after the birth and the enchantment of his smile when he'd held the baby in his hands and murmured, "She's beautiful." Roberta wondered if she would ever be able to tell Kyle how much he meant to her.

They arrived at the emergency entrance to the hospital. Roberta was allowed to be with her daughter only long enough for a nurse to string an identification bracelet out of lettered beads for the baby's teeny wrist, and then the baby was taken to the neonatal intensive-care ward. "It's just a precaution," the nurse assured Roberta. "Any baby who's suffered anything at all unusual during birth is sent there for a night of observation. You've got a preemie born in an unsterilized environment. So we want to keep an eye on her tonight. Nothing to worry about."

Sighing, Roberta answered the admitting clerk's countless questions, while an obstetrician examined her and attended to the afterbirth. She was glad Kyle had thought to hand her her purse, which contained not only her medical insurance cards but her personal phone book. She would have to call Mary and her parents. And the hospital would probably want to contact Dr. Stephens's office.

After an hour she was taken to a room on the maternity floor. A nurse helped her out of her wrinkled jumper and into a clean cotton bed shirt. "There's someone here to see you," she told Roberta. "Visiting hours end in fifteen minutes, but he's been waiting for quite a while."

Roberta nodded. "Please bring him in. I'd like to see him," she requested.

The nurse disappeared, then returned shortly, escorting Kyle. He scanned the curtained partition that marked off Roberta's area of the three-bed room before taking a seat on the chair near the bed. He smiled shyly. "How are you?"

"Never felt better," she swore.

His gaze shifted to the table beside her bed. "I should have thought to bring your toothbrush . . . or a hairbrush."

"Don't worry about it," Roberta silenced him. "I'm going to call my friend Mary tonight and tell her what happened. She'll be here in no time flat. Carrying a suitcase containing every kind of brush in the world, if I know her."

Kyle studied Roberta's face, his expression solemn. "So you've got someone to take care of you, then?"

Roberta nodded. She reached for Kyle's hand, which rested on his knee, and covered it with her own. "Kyle, what happened today—"

"Don't say anything," he murmured, his eyes intense, his lips curving in a poignant half smile. "What happened today is too special for words."

Roberta nodded again and ran her thumb along the warm brown skin covering his knuckles. He twisted his hand around and wove his fingers through hers. He studied her hand for a long, silent moment, seemingly transfixed by the contrast of her cool, slender fingers against the thick, slightly callused flesh of his. "I would like..." He sighed uncertainly, then met her gaze. His eyes were still that mysterious gray, welcoming but unreadable. He appeared to be searching Roberta's face for permission to speak.

"Can I ask one thing of you?" he said slowly.

"Anything."

He drew in a deep breath. "After things settle down for you, would you drop me a line and let me know how you're doing? And how the baby is?"

Such a simple request. Roberta wondered why it had cost him so much effort to make it. Despite what she and Kyle had just been through together—or perhaps because of it—he seemed unexpectedly shy. "Of course," she promised, tightening her grip on his hand in a gesture of trust and friendship.

He smiled hesitantly, then released her hand and rummaged in his pockets for a pencil and a scrap of paper. He wrote down his address and placed the paper on the table. "Do you know what you're going to call the baby?" he asked as he pocketed his pencil.

"Leah," Roberta told him. She had decided a long time ago that she would name the baby after Lee.

"Leah," Kyle echoed. "That's a pretty name."

A voice crackled through the public address system, announcing that visiting hours were over. Kyle stood up. "I guess I'd better be going," he said.

Roberta peered up at him, trying to memorize his face. When Leah was old enough to understand, Roberta would want to describe to her the man who had delivered her, who had ushered her into the world, the man who had made Leah's birth a moment of magic, of ecstasy, rather than the nightmare it might have been.

He returned her unwavering stare, as if he, too, was trying to memorize her. Then he bent over the bed and kissed her cheek. Without a word he started to the door.

"Kyle," she called after him. "Thank you."

He turned in the doorway and offered her an enigmatic smile. "Maybe I should thank *you*," he murmured. His smile faded slightly, and then he tore himself away from Roberta and vanished down the hallway.

ROBERTA DIDN'T FORGET her promise to drop Kyle a line as soon as her life settled down. The problem was that her life didn't settle down for quite some time. Once she and Leah had been issued a clean bill of health, they returned to New York City. But Roberta hadn't realized how utterly exhausting motherhood could be—especially without a husband to assist her.

For two months she functioned in a daze of drowsiness, considering her day a success if she managed to get the laundry done—doing laundry had developed into a daily chore, what with Leah soiling several of her own outfits every twenty-four hours and spitting up all over Roberta's clothing. Roberta counted a day as triumphant if she also succeeded in taking Leah outdoors for an airing. Both mother and daughter needed to get out of the apartment, to see the sky every now and then and to view something other than the one-way street and the back alley visible from the loft's windows. But on some days, even a walk around the block became impossible. There was simply too much for Roberta to do, and no one to shoulder the burden with her.

Twice, Roberta's mother-in-law visited from New Jersey to baby-sit so Roberta could do some shopping. But she and

Lee's mother had never been particularly close—Lee's mother, like Roberta's parents, had disapproved of their interfaith marriage. While Roberta appreciated her mother-in-law's willingness to watch Leah for an hour, she simply didn't feel comfortable in the company of a woman who, she knew, harbored a strong dislike for her.

Eventually Roberta had to face the fact that she needed more help than her cold, disapproving mother-in-law could provide. When her parents asked her to live with them for a few months, until she'd gotten her strength back and her life in order, Roberta begrudgingly accepted their offer. She rented out her New York City home and moved with Leah to her parents' sprawling ranch house in suburban San Diego.

Becoming grandparents had had a positive effect on Roberta's parents. As soon as they laid eyes on their adorable granddaughter, they miraculously lost all their animosity toward Lee. He was no longer the *artist* in the *loft*, the long-haired fellow with a different cultural background. Now he was Leah's father, and suddenly that was all that mattered to them. Any man who had fathered such a wonderful grandchild had to have been a good man, they rationalized.

At Christmas, Roberta finally found the time to write to Kyle. She stared at the card she'd bought, unsure of what to say. She hardly knew him. She knew nothing of his interests, his hobbies, his background, his politics. All she knew was that they'd shared something too special for words, as he himself had put it. And that she'd promised to drop him a line.

"Dear Kyle," she wrote, "Season's greetings." She winced. How corny! "As you can see by the enclosed photograph—" she stared at the snapshot she'd taken of Leah to send to him "—Leah is as beautiful as ever. Although her

birth size was small, she's caught up and continues to grow
so fast I can hardly keep her in clothes. She's very sweet-
natured, has the most musical giggle in the world, and seems
quite mischievous and curious about the world. Obviously,
I adore her.''

Roberta reread what she'd written and groaned. There
was a limit to how gushingly maternal she'd allow herself to
sound in a letter. "As you can tell by the return address,"
she continued, "I've moved to San Diego, California. I'm
living for the time being with my parents and planning to
take a couple of courses at the university." Roberta had decided that her degree in art history wasn't going to be of
much use to her if she ever returned to New York. The museum job she'd had before she became pregnant paid a ri-
diculously small stipend, and Lee's life insurance wasn't
going to last forever. The policy had given her enough to
cover her mortgage payments on the loft and her living and
medical expenses for a few years, but for practicality's sake
she decided to take some courses in graphic design and
commercial art in the hope of finding a job in advertising or
illustrating, like Lee's. His New York circle of friends offered her many useful professional contacts. All she needed
was the proper training.

Once again she reread what she'd written. The note
seemed lackluster to her. She wanted to write to Kyle that he
was indescribably important to her and that she owed him
her life and that she wished he could see for himself how
magnificent Leah was. But she didn't know how to put such
thoughts into words. So she ended the letter by writing, "I
hope things are going well for you, and that the new year
brings you the best of everything. Sincerely, Roberta Frankel.''

She didn't hear from Kyle until April. The envelope was
postmarked Boston, and as he explained in his brief letter,

the card she'd sent him months earlier had taken its time reaching him at his new address. He'd moved to Boston to work with a skilled furniture designer and builder. He was learning a great deal, he wrote. He didn't like Boston as much as he liked the sleepy seaside village of Madison, Connecticut, but he felt that his apprenticeship was important, and he'd never been too good at catching lobsters, anyway. He was very glad Roberta had written to him, and he thought Leah looked gorgeous. "She's going to break hearts someday," he predicted.

The next time Kyle wrote was in August, on Leah's birthday. Roberta and Leah had taken their own apartment a few miles from her parents' house at the end of the university's spring term. Although Roberta was getting along with her parents better than she had in years, she wanted to make a real home for Leah and herself. She was twenty-six years old, after all, and she had her own style, her own tastes, her own ideas about how to raise her daughter.

Still, even after moving out of her parents' house, Roberta relied on them a great deal. She enrolled in more courses during the summer session, and one of her professors occasionally farmed out free-lance projects to her, so she frequently asked her mother to baby-sit.

On Leah's first birthday, Roberta hosted a small party, inviting her parents, an aunt and uncle, and a couple of young mothers and their toddlers who lived in the sprawling complex where Roberta rented a cramped two-bedroom apartment. When her parents arrived, they were carrying, in addition to their own bagful of birthday gifts, a parcel the postman had delivered to their home that morning, addressed to Leah.

Roberta opened the package and pulled out a colorful stuffed giraffe and a card. "Dear Leah," it read, "A special happy birthday to a special girl. Love, Kyle."

Roberta promptly took a photo of Leah hugging her giraffe and mailed it to Kyle.

And so their correspondence continued. Roberta's letters to Kyle were primarily devoted to descriptions of Leah: her latest accomplishments, the number of teeth she'd sprouted and the number of inches she'd grown. Usually Roberta sent a photograph of Leah as well. She'd conclude her letters with a brief mention of her own work: "I'm continuing to free lance while I take one more graphics course," she'd write, or: "My current design projects are fairly mundane, but I need the experience, so I can't complain." She'd sign her notes rather formally, "Sincerely, Roberta."

Kyle's letters to her were similar in tone. He'd go on at length about Leah's successes, asking Roberta to congratulate her for him regarding her mastery of the word "Mama" or her conquering of the shallow end of the swimming pool in her grandparents' backyard. Then he'd mention his own work. In one letter he described a project in which he and his associate were working with an architect to design a new interior for a law office. In another, Kyle wrote that he was involved in the refurbishing of some antique furniture at a Beacon Hill town house. He'd comment on Boston's bustle and energy, the variety of restaurants, the vast number of movie houses. Occasionally he'd add nostalgically that he missed the slower pace of Madison, but that Boston was surely a better location for him professionally. He'd conclude his letters by wishing Roberta "all the best. My love to Leah. Kyle."

Every year on Leah's birthday a package arrived from Kyle. On her second birthday he sent her another giraffe, this one carved from cherry wood, varnished and stained, with his initials etched into it. On her third birthday he sent her a magnificent Victorian-style dollhouse constructed of wood. Although he didn't mark it with his initials, Roberta knew instinctively that he'd built it himself. It was much too ornate for a three-year-old to play with, but then what would Kyle know about three-year-old girls? Still, it was a beautiful house, and Roberta and Leah spent many hours creating furniture for it out of empty matchboxes and scraps of cloth.

On Leah's fourth birthday Kyle sent her *real* furniture for the dollhouse, and Roberta again knew he had to have made it himself. The craftsmanship of the tiny dining room chairs and sideboard, the graceful curve of the bed's maple headboard, the working drawers on the bureau—each piece was exquisite. With her mother's assistance, slaving over each awkward crayoned letter, Leah wrote him a thank-you note: "Thank you, Kyle, for my birthday present. They are pretty things. My mommy says you borned me, so thanks for that, too. I love you. Leah."

They mailed the thank-you card, with a photo of Leah, to Kyle at his new address, back in Madison. He'd written to Roberta the previous April that he'd returned to his beloved shoreline town and opened a branch of his Boston associate's custom furniture business there. It was a big step, he'd written, but he'd felt the time was right for it. Many of the architects and designers he'd worked with before he'd left for Boston remembered him, and the Boston company served a national clientele, so whether he was working out of Boston or Madison was unimportant. He was optimistic about his prospects as a semi-independent craftsman.

Roberta had sent him a congratulatory note, wishing him the best of luck in his new enterprise. She tried to imagine the bearded man she'd met on the beach as an entrepreneur running his own business, and came up blank. But then, why shouldn't Kyle have grown in the past four years? Leah had grown from a squawking, flailing infant to a lovely, agile girl who could read and write—with help from her mother, of course—and who could climb trees, swim the width of her grandparents' pool, throw balls overhand and eat more spaghetti in one sitting than the entire population of Rome could devour in a year, as Roberta had once written to Kyle. If Leah could have changed so much, why not Kyle?

Roberta, too, had grown and changed over the past four years. She'd gone from gratefully accepting the few freelance assignments her former professor tossed her way to forging her own way, courting clients with her ever-expanding portfolio and creating jobs and opportunities for herself. Designing billboards for a local radio station wasn't Roberta's favorite sort of work, but it paid well enough, and it brought her ever closer to full independence. With a few more prestigious projects in her portfolio, she'd be ready to present herself to some of the advertising agencies in New York City and perhaps land a job in an art department at one of them. That was Roberta's dream. She wanted to return to her loft in New York, to be back with the friends who had been such a significant part of her life with Lee. She'd met him and loved him in New York. She considered the city her home.

That long-planned return to New York took place shortly before Leah's fifth birthday. Roberta had been offered a position with one of the well-established agencies in Manhattan. The salary would be more than adequate, especially since Roberta already owned her SoHo loft. She'd even be able to afford to send Leah to private school in September.

When she wrote to Kyle that spring about her impending move, he sent her a letter, special delivery. "Once you're all moved in," he wrote, "maybe we could get together. I'd love to see Leah." He included his telephone number and asked Roberta to call him once she was settled in New York.

She suffered a vague apprehension about phoning him, though she didn't know why she should. She'd love him to see Leah, too. She was proud of the job she'd done raising her daughter single-handedly. And Leah had heard the dramatic story of her birth so many times that she greeted the news of Kyle's invitation with an excitement bordering on ecstasy. "He's the man who helped me be born!" she exclaimed exuberantly. "And he made my dollhouse. Let's go see him, Mommy!"

In fact, before Roberta could identify herself to him when she telephoned him one Sunday afternoon a few weeks after they'd moved back into the loft, Leah snatched the receiver from her and squealed, "Kyle! Hello, Kyle! I'm Leah!"

Roberta managed to wrestle the phone from her boisterous daughter. "Hello, Kyle," she said, unable to stifle a laugh at Leah's enthusiasm.

"Roberta," he greeted her softly. He sounded the same, she decided. His voice had been just as soft and sonorous that long ago afternoon. Even after all this time, she would have recognized the sound of it anywhere.

She made a date to visit him for Leah's birthday, which fell on a Saturday. Mary Grinnard would be at her cottage for the month of August; she insisted that Roberta and Leah could stay with her. "I can borrow a cot for you, Roberta," she planned, "and Leah can sleep on the sofa in the parlor. I'd love to have you up here. It sounds like a delightful idea."

Roberta and Leah had arrived at Mary's house the previous night. Leah already knew her Aunt Mary well, since Mary had flown out to San Diego several times to visit Roberta while she was living there. Mary had even dedicated one of her books to Leah, a fact about which the girl was excessively proud.

"I was born here," Leah announced knowledgeably, pointing at the bed in the cheerful bedroom of the cottage.

"That's right," Mary confirmed, tousling Leah's dark curls. A statuesque gray-haired woman in her fifties, Mary Grinnard was determinedly single, but she adored children and felt unusually comfortable with them. She understood the way their minds worked, which was why her books for children were so successful. "Come on, Leah, climb onto the bed—that's right, with your head at the foot of the bed. There," she said as Leah arranged herself on the lower half of the bed. "Now. Does the view look familiar? That's the first thing you ever saw in this world—the foot of my bed. Do you remember it?"

"Nope," Leah replied with a giggle.

"Do you think you'll remember Kyle?"

"Nope," Leah answered.

"I wonder if *I* will," Roberta murmured half to herself as she watched her daughter and her good friend frolic on the bed.

Now, gazing out at the water, inhaling the humid scent of Long Island Sound mixed with the tangy tropical fragrance of suntan lotion emanating from the people around her, Roberta suffered a recurrence of that thought. Would she remember Kyle? Would he remember her? He was no less important to her now than he had been the day Leah was born, but so much had changed—the beach, her daughter, herself. She couldn't deny that she was nervous about seeing him again.

Leah scampered over to her, her hands heaped with shells. "Which ones should I give him?" she asked her mother. "Should I give him all of them?"

Roberta appraised the shells Leah dumped onto her skirt, which was draped between her knees like a hammock. "This one's the prettiest, don't you think?" she said as she held up a perfectly shaped white shell with a smooth, sand-polished edge and an iridescent shimmer along its concave interior.

Leah studied the shell intently. "Do you think I should give him only one?"

Roberta chuckled. "You've got a lot to learn about subtlety," she remarked. "Yes, I think one beautiful shell is a more impressive gift than lots of chipped and broken shells."

Leah appeared doubtful, but she deferred to her mother's judgment. "Okay," she said. "That one's the best."

Roberta stood, dusted off her skirt and handed Leah her sandals. While Leah buckled them on, Roberta adjusted her loose-fitting linen blouse beneath the snug waistband of her skirt. She combed her wind-tangled hair back behind her ears with her fingers and then took Leah's hand. They walked together to the street where Mary's house stood. The car Roberta had rented for the weekend was parked behind Mary's car in the driveway.

After turning on the engine, Roberta studied the map Kyle had sent her, directing her to his house. It didn't seem to be too close to the water, and Roberta fleetingly wondered whether he still kept a lobster trap in the bay.

"Excited?" she asked Leah as she shifted into gear and backed out of the driveway.

"Yeah." Leah turned the single, perfect shell she'd saved over and over in her small palm, inspecting it for flaws. "What if he doesn't like me?"

"He's going to love you," Roberta assured her daughter. "Doesn't he always write 'Love, Kyle' on the birthday cards he sends you?"

"Yeah, but—but I mean, what if he doesn't like me when he sees me?" Leah persisted.

Roberta shot Leah a swift glance and grinned. Perhaps it was her upbringing that made Leah more mature and sen-

sitive than so many children her age. Leah had entered a
world already scarred by loss and had been raised by a single parent struggling to improve her skills and build herself
a career while simultaneously mothering her child. Leah had
learned at an early age that sometimes her mother had to
study, sometimes she had to work, sometimes she couldn't
simply drop everything and attend to Leah's every whim.
She'd learned that her mother had once loved a man very
much and had married him and made a baby with him, and
then he'd died and left her mother all alone. Understanding such things gave Leah an unusual precocity, especially
when dealing with adults.

"He'll love you when he sees you," Roberta promised. As
she considered it, there was a much greater chance of that
than of Kyle's being taken by Roberta. Leah was, almost by
definition, lovable. Roberta was a woman, which complicated matters, though she wasn't sure how—or why.

"Are we there yet?" Leah asked, peering out the window.

"Almost," said Roberta, reaching for the map and scan-
ning it in hasty glances. She steered onto a narrow country
lane lined with low shrubs and, beyond them, dense woods.
The road twisted past a flat, grassy field, then cut through
another grove of trees. She spotted a gray mailbox with
"Stratton" painted on it and turned onto the crushed-gravel
driveway beside it.

A quarter of a mile up the driveway loomed the house, a
large, angular modern structure of wood and glass, surrounded by pine, elm and sycamore trees. Before Roberta
could shut off the engine, Leah had sprung from the car and
was racing to the front door. Remaining in the car, Roberta
watched her daughter rise on tiptoe to reach the doorbell
and press it.

The door swung open and a tall, broad-shouldered man stepped out. The beard was gone, the sandy-blond hair was somewhat shorter and neatly combed; the trousers were well tailored to his lanky legs and his shirt was crisply pressed.

But his eyes were still the same gentle shade Roberta had remembered, the same soft gray, the color of fog, swirling with life and mystery.

Without speaking, he knelt down in front of Leah and wrapped his arms around her.

Chapter Three

Hugging Leah was like holding time itself in his arms.

She was real, solid, strong—strong enough to withstand the crushing embrace of a man with thick muscles and callused hands who stood two inches over six feet tall and weighed one hundred eighty-five pounds. Of course he'd known she would be; he'd known that she was no longer the tiny, fragile creature he'd once taken so gingerly into his arms, with her starfish-shaped hands fisting and flailing and her hair as fine as corn silk. He had over a dozen photographs to go by, and plenty of common sense. He knew Leah wasn't an infant anymore.

But actually seeing her and touching her—that was something else.

Not today, but someday when she was older and more mature, he'd explain to her what she meant to him, how she'd changed him, how her birth had been a kind of birth for him as well. Someday when *he* was older, perhaps he'd be able to make sense of what had happened to him the day Leah was born. He still hadn't worked it all out. He wasn't sure that the change had been totally for the better, but he couldn't deny that he was not the same man today that he'd been before Leah entered his world.

That didn't matter right now. All that mattered was that for the first time in five years he was in the presence of the little girl who had once made all the difference in his life. The little girl and her mother.

He lifted his gaze to locate Roberta, but all he saw was a motionless silhouette through the windshield of the beige Pontiac compact parked in his driveway. Leah's piping voice dragged his attention back to her. "Kyle! Hello, Kyle! I'm Leah! Did you know that? I'm Leah and this is for you." She stuffed a seashell into his right hand. Her bubbly chatter didn't let up for an instant, and in a way, Kyle was relieved. He had no idea what he'd say if Leah gave him a chance to speak. For that matter, he had no idea whether his voice would even function.

"Mommy and I went to the beach," the garrulous little girl continued. "Before we came here, we went to the beach. Aunt Mary lives only a block away from the beach, isn't that neat? Do you know my Aunt Mary? Anyway, Mommy showed me where I started to be born, and then I found all these shells, but Mommy said I should only give you one. I hope you don't mind. This one's the best."

Kyle focused on the small bleached shell in his hand. He ran his thumb over the striated outer surface, then the smooth semicircular edge. Flipping it over, he admired the glossy mother-of-pearl that had been created by the passing irritations of a clam's lifetime. "This is a beautiful shell," he said. The words came naturally, and his voice sounded normal. Could it really be this easy to talk to someone like Leah? A delighted smile lit his face, cutting arching dimples into his clean-shaven cheeks. And more words came: "I wouldn't be surprised if this is the best shell in Connecticut. Your mother was right. One is enough, if it's the best."

"I guess you want to see her," Leah said.

Whether she was being uncommonly perceptive or simply sociable Kyle couldn't tell. But the truth was, he very much wanted to see Roberta. He straightened up and glanced toward the car again. The driver's side door had swung open, but Roberta still hadn't shown herself. "Your mother certainly takes her time getting out of cars, doesn't she," he commented to Leah.

"Sometimes," Leah confirmed with a shrug. "I guess that's on account of she's old." The child slipped her hand into Kyle's and led him down the walk to the car. "Are you old?" she asked him.

He laughed at her refreshing tactlessness. "Getting there, Leah," he replied truthfully. Lately, thirty-four was feeling pretty old to him. "I bet I'm even older than your mother."

Leah stared up at him in disbelief, but he didn't see her frown. His eyes were glued to Roberta—or to the person standing by the car, if that slender, shapely woman was indeed Roberta.

If she was, she wasn't the Roberta he remembered. That five-years-ago Roberta had been the image of softness, roundness, nurturing fullness. In Kyle's mind she'd been a breathtakingly lovely incarnation of a fertility goddess, of Mother Nature, of Mother Earth, her body cradling the most valuable treasure in the world. The thick hair that had once dropped unimpeded down her back had framed a slightly plumper face, he recalled. Now, surrounded by a fashionable halo of curls, her cheeks and chin seemed more sharply defined, more exotic. Her lips, which had been chapped and bitten from her exertion the last time he'd seen her, were now full and pink, shaping not the rapturous smile of new motherhood but, rather, a tenuous, contained smile. The long, lush eyelashes trimming her wide eyes looked familiar to him, but they had a different effect on him today than they'd had the last time he'd seen them. Then, those fan-shaped black fringes had seemed, well, maternal. Now they seemed...seductive.

Not that Roberta was doing anything overtly seductive with her eyes, or with her wonderfully curvaceous body tantalizingly hidden beneath a blousy white shirt and matching skirt that met at her surprisingly narrow waist. But, damn it, she was attractive. He had remembered her as utterly, radiantly beautiful. Not *this* kind of beautiful, though, not the kind of beautiful that made him think about—

He erased that thought before it could come to fruition. Roberta was a mother, for heaven's sake—not just a mother but Leah's mother. Roberta was a friend, an address, a receptacle for five years of rambling letters that had expressed more about Kyle than any words he'd ever spoken to any other woman. She wasn't just a good-looking woman casting him meaningful glances at a party or a bar. She was *Roberta*.

Although she *was* staring at him with more than a little curiosity. Her gaze traveled across his face an inch at a time, studying the square shape of his beardless jaw, the tidier cut of his dark blond hair, the deeper, more permanent laugh lines radiating from the outer corners of his fathomless gray eyes.

Someone had to break the ice, and Leah didn't seem willing to bail out her tongue-tied elders. Kyle drew in a deep breath. "You're looking well," he said in a muted voice.

"So are you," she responded. "I see you've shaved."

"Years ago," he told her, smiling slightly. "And you've cut your hair."

"A mark of maturity," she said with a laugh.

He reached to take her hand, then paused and stared at the shell in his palm. "I gave it to him," Leah boasted. "It was the best shell on the beach, wasn't it, Mommy? I told him it was the best one I found. I told him you showed me where I started being born.''

Kyle peered down at her and his smile broadened. "They ought to put a monument there," he remarked. "A big statue with a sign saying, 'Leah Frankel started being born in this spot.'" The idea delighted Leah, who giggled.

Kyle lifted his gaze to Roberta again. He was intrigued by the sultry warmth in her dark eyes—intrigued and unnerved. He wasn't sure what he ought to be feeling, but what he was feeling didn't seem at all appropriate. "Let's get something to drink," he suggested, turning abruptly toward the house.

Leah continued to cling to his hand as they headed to the front door, and Roberta kept pace on the other side of her daughter. Kyle was both heartened and disarmed by Leah's presence between them. He had a vague urge to send Leah away, yet he didn't know what he'd do if he and Roberta were alone. He wanted to be alone with her; but the mere idea frightened him.

It wasn't at all like Kyle to feel so confused about a woman. But Roberta wasn't just a woman, he reminded himself again. Roberta was . . . Roberta.

They entered the large modern house and passed through an airy living room furnished with low-slung leather couches curved around a freestanding fireplace. Beyond it spread an equally contemporary dining room, which was separated from the well-appointed kitchen by a long counter. The rear outer wall consisted of sliding glass doors opening onto a birchwood deck overlooking the spacious backyard. Kyle had set the house's air-conditioning on low, but he hoped Roberta and Leah wouldn't mind being outdoors, given that he'd planned for a barbecue on the deck. It wasn't too oppressively hot outside, and the sun would be losing much of its fire within an hour or so.

"Would you like some fruit juice?" he asked Leah, who trailed him like an infatuated puppy into the sunny kitchen. "I've got apple juice, grape juice and orange juice."

"Orange juice?" she shouted. "In the afternoon?"

Kyle eyed Roberta quizzically.

"Leah thinks you can only drink orange juice for breakfast," she explained.

He turned back to Leah and grinned. "Well, it's your birthday. Which means you can have orange juice anytime you want it today."

"Okay!" she readily accepted.

While Kyle poured her a glass of juice, he asked Roberta what she wanted to drink. She requested wine, and he filled a goblet with some chilled white. He took a mug of beer for himself, then ushered his guests through a sliding door to the deck.

A built-in barbecue pit filled with glowing briquettes stood at one end of the deck, an outdoor dining table and chairs arranged beside it. Several canvas folding chairs were clustered about a laminated parsons table on the other end of the deck. Kyle set the drinks on the parsons table and gestured for Roberta to sit.

Ignoring her juice, Leah raced from the deck onto the lawn, scampering along its perimeter and surveying the surrounding woods. "All this open space is a big treat for her," Roberta rationalized her daughter's friskiness.

Kyle followed Leah with his eyes. "Is she happy about living in New York City?" he asked.

Roberta smiled. "Yes, she's happy. Everything seems to make her happy. She views life as one exciting adventure after another. New York is one of the most exciting adventures yet."

"She's beautiful," Kyle commented softly. He settled in a chair facing Roberta and raised his mug in a toast. "Here's to your beautiful daughter."

Roberta lifted her goblet in agreement, then took a sip of her wine. Lowering the glass, she discovered Kyle staring at her with the same intensity he'd shown while watching Leah. The shock of actually coming face-to-face with him had waned, and she appraised him reflectively as they sat together in the late afternoon.

There were more profound changes in him than his simply having shaved off his beard, she acknowledged. More profound changes than his having trimmed his hair to a somewhat respectable length and his having replaced his faded and weathered shirt and slacks with clothing that marked him as a civilized, successful man.

The real change was in his eyes. They were no longer as soft and gentle as she had remembered them. There was something guarded about them now, something veiled. Their color seemed more silver than gray, a sharper hue than they'd been the day Leah was born.

But then, everything that day had been foggy—not just the weather but Roberta's thoughts themselves. Perhaps she just didn't remember accurately.

She did remember thinking briefly that Kyle was a handsome man. But she didn't remember how handsome. Maybe he seemed more handsome to her now because of his neat, careful grooming. Or maybe it was because she no longer viewed men from the perspective of a widow loyal to her husband's memory, or a young, struggling mother who simply didn't have the energy for or the interest in pursuing a social life. For the first few years after Lee's death, Roberta had had no particular inclination to become romantically involved with men. During her last year in San Diego, after completing her course work and establishing herself

more securely as a professional free-lance artist, she'd begun to date casually. But male companionship had been
pretty low on her list of priorities.

Kyle was much more attractive than any of the men she'd
dated in California. Perhaps his attractiveness was a result
of her having known him on a peculiarly intimate level. It
wasn't just that he'd seen her half-naked—there was certainly nothing at all romantic about the exposure he'd had
to her body. No, their intimacy was emotional, the outgrowth of a shared miracle. And although Roberta felt an
intimate kinship with Kyle, she truly didn't know much
about him.

"I just can't get over how big she is," he was saying.

Roberta broke out of her reverie to find him watching
Leah, who was hunkering down to pick a handful of the
dandelions sprouting in the grass along the woods' edge.
"She's five years old," Roberta pointed out with a chuckle.
"The last time you saw her she was a newborn."

"But I never realized..." His voice faded for a moment,
and he shifted in his chair to face Roberta again. "She grew
so fast..." His words drifted off again, and he shook his
head in amazement.

Roberta laughed. "What did you expect? A little baby
crawling around in diapers and teething on everything she
could get her grubby paws on? I've been sending you photographs all along."

"It's not the same thing as actually seeing her," Kyle argued. "In my mind...in my mind she was still that tiny pink
creature squirming in a towel, clutching your finger." He
shook his head again and grinned sheepishly.

"In my mind," Roberta countered amiably, "you were
still a bearded beachcomber in rolled-up khakis."

He nodded, his eyes narrowing on her. "And you were
still an Earth Mother in the fog, heavy on your feet and—"

"Built like a walrus," Roberta concluded with a laugh of reminiscence.

"No," Kyle objected solemnly. "Not a walrus."

Her laughter deepened. "Oh, come on, Kyle. I was big and fat and clumsy. Remember how you found me, all sprawled out on the sand? I couldn't even stand up by myself."

"You looked lovely," he insisted softly. "You still look lovely—only different."

"I should hope I look different." Roberta sniffed with pretended indignation.

Kyle smiled briefly, then turned to find Leah approaching the deck with a bouquet of dandelions clutched in her fist. "Look at these flowers I picked," she crowed as she climbed onto the deck.

"Those aren't flowers, they're weeds," Roberta said.

Leah wasn't fazed in the least. "They're pretty, though, aren't they? Here, Kyle, they're for you," she declared, presenting them to him with a flourish and then springing off the deck to explore the woods some more.

Kyle looked at the bunch of scraggly yellow tufts in his hand and chuckled. "Will I hurt her feelings terribly if I don't use them as a centerpiece on the dinner table?" he asked Roberta.

She grinned and shook her head. "Leah's old enough to understand that not everything she does is perfect. I think it's healthy to be honest with kids. If you don't like the flowers, just thank her for the thought and then throw them away. She can take it." At Kyle's dubious frown, Roberta added, "If you gave her something she didn't like, she'd have no compunction about voicing her opinion. Why should you?"

He pondered that notion, then nodded and dropped the wilting dandelions onto the table. "How did you...how did you learn these things?'' he asked, fascinated. "How do you know what kids can take and what they can't take? Is it instinctual? Or does it have something to do with being a mother?"

His genuine bewilderment amused Roberta. Obviously Kyle was a man who hadn't spent much time with children. "I don't know how I learned," she answered honestly. "You live with a kid, you get to know the way her mind works, you pick up on her wavelengths—just the way any two people living together day in and day out pick up on each other's wavelengths. I don't know that it's an instinct, Kyle. It's more a natural learning process, I think."

"I'm really—" he struggled with his words, his smile registering awe "—I'm impressed, Roberta."

"There's nothing impressive about it," she disputed him. "Parents figure things out about their kids, that's all. It comes with the territory."

Leah dashed back to the deck and shouted, "I'm starving. When can we eat?"

"Where are your manners?" Roberta chided her daughter.

Leah meditated for a moment, then said, "*Please*, when can we eat?"

Laughing, Kyle rose and started toward the sliding door leading to the kitchen. "I think the coals are hot enough," he said. "I'll put the steaks on."

Roberta moved as far as the open pane of glass. "Steaks?" she called after him. "I was hoping you'd have some fresh lobsters for us from your lobster trap."

Kyle returned from the kitchen with a tray containing a platter of seasoned steaks and a foil-wrapped loaf of bread. His smile seemed oddly bitter when he commented, "I don't keep a lobster trap anymore."

"Oh?" Roberta asked. "Why not?"

He occupied himself forking the steaks onto the grill. "Too busy, I guess," he said dryly.

Roberta studied him for a long minute. She wanted to question him about his abrupt change of mood, but that wouldn't be polite. To distract herself, she surveyed the stained wood and glass that comprised the rear wall of his house, and his vast yard. The evidence of his professional success only led her thoughts back to his unexpectedly chilly reaction to her friendly teasing about his lobster trap.

"Your company must keep you busy," she guessed.

He nodded.

"I take it there's a big demand for custom-made furniture," she mused aloud.

Kyle gave her remarks careful consideration. Apparently he made the same connection she had made between his business and his abandonment of his amateur lobstering. He issued a pensive smile. "We all mature in different ways, Roberta," he said cryptically. "You cut your hair, and I got rid of the old rowboat and the lobster trap."

Roberta wasn't certain she understood what her hair had to do with his boat. Her decision to cut her hair was simply a matter of practicality. For one thing, the thick, bushy mass of hair was too uncomfortable on her neck in San Diego's year-round heat. For another, as a baby, Leah had taken far too much pleasure in yanking on her mother's free-flowing tresses all the time. And for another, Roberta thought it wise to look chic in her line of work. She was no longer an untrained dilettante artist in her loft. She was a professional career woman with a child to support. She needed to look the part.

But Kyle's getting rid of his rowboat didn't seem professionally necessary to her. If he had enjoyed lobstering, why had he given it up?

She could think of no reasonable way to ask him, so she let the subject drop. Kyle shuttled between the kitchen and the deck, carrying out a large teak bowl filled with a tossed salad, assorted bottles of salad dressing, and a dish of baked potatoes from the oven. As soon as the steaks were ready, he served them onto three plates and arranged them on the table, indicating that Roberta and Leah should sit facing him.

Leah gaped at the full-sized steak on her plate. "Wow, is this all mine?" she asked.

Roberta busied herself cutting half the steak into bite-sized pieces for her daughter. "I doubt you can eat the whole piece," she warned. "Don't try to stuff yourself, okay?" She gave Kyle a reproachful smile. "She's only five years old. This is a portion for a college football player."

"You wrote to me that she could outeat the population of Rome," Kyle reminded Roberta.

"Poetic license," Roberta defended her exaggeration.

"Are we going to have cake for dessert?" Leah asked as her mother served her some salad. "It's my birthday."

Kyle chuckled. "Yes, there's a cake for dessert. It was going to be a surprise."

"That's okay," Leah assured him. "You're *supposed* to have cake on your birthday."

He directed his attention fully to the ebullient little girl. "So, how do you like your new home in New York?" he asked.

"It's not my new home," Leah corrected him. "I lived there when I was a baby. Isn't that right, Mommy? Some other people lived there when we were living near Gramma and Grampa, but I lived there first, before they did. I don't really remember it, but Mommy says I lived there for two months. And my daddy used to live there, too."

Kyle's eyes flickered toward Roberta, their strange silver glow inscrutable to her. It occurred to her that she had never told Kyle about Lee before—that for all he knew, she had never been married. He seemed to be on the verge of saying something, and Roberta held her breath and waited for his question. She wanted him to ask. She didn't know why, but she wanted him to. She wanted to tell him what had happened to Lee.

But before he could speak, Leah asked him, "Did you know my daddy?"

Still staring at Roberta, Kyle answered, "No, I didn't."

"He died before I was born," Leah related, filling him in as Roberta never had. "Mommy's told me a lot about him, though."

"I'm sure she has," Kyle drawled, his expression still totally unreadable.

What was he thinking? Roberta wondered. Mentally reviewing the day Leah was born, she realized that she'd definitely left Kyle with the impression that she was an unwed mother. Undoubtedly he now assumed that Roberta had invented an imaginary father for Leah, and then killed him off, in order to answer her little girl's questions. While Roberta couldn't decipher Kyle's silence, she sensed disapproval in it.

"My daddy was an artist," Leah continued, unaware of her mother's ruminations. "He made pictures for books. What's it called again, Mommy?"

"Illustrations," Roberta said, her eyes still locked onto Kyle's.

"That's right, illustrations. Do you know my Aunt Mary? She's not really my aunt, but that's what I call her. She writes books. My daddy illustrationed some of them."

"Illustrated, not illustrationed," said Roberta, though her thoughts remained on Kyle. The day Leah had been born, explaining to him that she wasn't an unwed mother hadn't seemed important to her, but for some reason it seemed vitally important now. "He died when I was three months pregnant," she stated.

"I'm sorry to hear that," Kyle said slowly.

"You don't believe me, do you?" she challenged him.

Leah eyed her mother and then Kyle. "Of course he believes you," she declared. "If my daddy didn't die, he would have helped me be born instead of Kyle."

"Yes," Kyle said, his gaze shifting to Leah. "I'm sure he would have. So, are you going to start school this fall?"

"I've already been to nursery school," Leah boasted. "This year I'm going to real school. But I already know how to read and write. I did very well in nursery school."

"I bet you did," Kyle praised her.

Roberta sipped her wine and listened with only half her mind to the conversation. The opportunity for her to prove to Kyle that she'd mothered a legitimate child had passed. She tried to fathom why it meant so much to her today to convince him of her marital status, when it hadn't meant a thing five years ago. That day, of course, she'd had more significant worries occupying her. But perhaps her current concern about what people thought of her was another symptom of maturity, she pondered. Motherhood had forced her to abandon many of her free-spirited artist's ways. Nowadays she had to be more sensitive about the impression she made on others.

Not merely on others—on Kyle. She wanted to make a good impression on him. They were meeting now not as strangers whom destiny had brought together on a fateful day, but as a man and a woman who'd endured five years of a bizarre pen-pal relationship. They were meeting as a notably attractive man and a woman who was finally in a position to start paying attention to notably attractive men again.

She gave her head a swift, subtle shake, trying to fend off the idea that she might be interested in anything beyond friendship with Kyle. It simply wouldn't work, not given their complicated history. Certainly there were plenty of available men in New York, if she was looking for love. Once she was completely in the routine of her job and Leah was in school full-time, Roberta would have the opportunity to meet men in traditional, familiar ways—men who could relate to her as a talented, independent woman, nothing more, nothing less.

"Can I, Mommy, can I?" Leah interrupted her thoughts.

"Hm?" Roberta colored slightly, realizing how far she'd drifted from the dinner discussion.

"Can I go in a boat with Kyle tomorrow? He said he could borrow a boat and take me to see where he used to have his lobster trap. I've never seen a lobster trap," Leah babbled, spinning back to Kyle. "I've seen lobsters, though. I've seen them in a store and in a restaurant. Did you know they're green in the store and red in the restaurant?" she asked him. "Mommy says that's because they turn red when they're cooked."

"That's right," Kyle concurred, gazing at Roberta and awaiting her permission. When it wasn't immediately forthcoming, he said, "I'll get a flat-bottomed rowboat. And I'll put a life jacket on her—although according to your letters, she's an excellent swimmer. We'll just take a little trip out and back."

"All right," Roberta granted, "if the weather's nice." Leah bounced gleefully in her seat, and Kyle's lips arched in a satisfied smile. "You can call for her at Mary Grinnard's house—the cottage where she was born. Do you remember where that is?"

"I remember," he said quietly, his tone implying a meaning other than the subject at hand. "Would noon be all right?"

"Noon would be fine," said Roberta. "But you can't take her out for too long. We've got a two-hour drive back to the city tomorrow evening."

"Don't worry," Kyle teased, "I'll get her home before curfew."

He stood up and gathered the dishes. The sun had descended into the treetops during their meal, taking with it the scorching August heat. Roberta watched Kyle through the glass door as he put away the dinner things and then pulled a cake from the refrigerator. He inserted five candles into its creamy chocolate icing. "That's my cake," Leah whispered.

Roberta nodded absently. She felt confused, at odds with herself. She hadn't expected to find herself attracted to Kyle—and she definitely hadn't wanted to be. She sternly reminded herself that her attraction was only physical, since she hardly knew him, and that physical attraction alone didn't count for much. Yet she couldn't deny the comprehension that what she and Kyle shared gave them a unique knowledge of each other.

There was no point dwelling on such thoughts, she realized. Kyle seemed interested in her as a friend—or perhaps only as Leah's mother. Leah was the one he'd wanted to see today—and the one he wanted to see tomorrow. That was probably as it should be, Roberta consoled herself. He had been the very first person to see Leah, to hold her, to bond with her. Their friendship was much more vital than any romantic fling she and Kyle might ever indulge in.

Roberta also admitted that it was far more important for Leah to befriend Kyle than for Roberta herself to befriend him. Leah had no father in her life. If Kyle was willing to become a father figure for her, to take her out in a boat and stick candles into a birthday cake for her, Roberta would never do anything to jeopardize their relationship.

Once the candles were lit, Kyle carried the cake to the table. He and Roberta sang the birthday song for Leah, who sat tall in her seat, placidly absorbing as her due all the attention she was getting. After she'd blown out the candles in one extended puff, he turned on an outdoor light and vanished into the house again. When he returned he was carrying an enormous gift-wrapped box.

"Oh, Lord!" Roberta scolded him for his extravagance as he presented the gift to Leah. "That box is bigger than she is!"

"Help me open it, Mommy," Leah requested, eagerly tearing off the colorful wrapping paper. "You, too, Kyle."

Once they'd removed the paper, Roberta folded back the carton's flaps and Kyle and Leah pulled out a child-size rocking chair. "Oh, wow!" Leah squealed. "Look at this, Mommy!"

The rocker was beautiful in its simplicity. Built of stained maple, it featured rounded arms that arced into the curved runners of the rocker and a semicircular back into which was carved Leah's name. Leah dropped onto the chair, assuming a regal posture, and pumped her feet against the deck floor, testing out the chair's rocking movement.

"You made it, didn't you?" Roberta guessed, smiling at Kyle.

He nodded, clearly pleased by Leah's enthusiastic reaction to the chair. "I don't build many pieces myself anymore," he confessed. "I'm too busy pushing papers these days. But yes, I built this one. And enjoyed every minute of it."

"It's great," Leah declared, leaping out of the chair and giving Kyle a grateful hug. "Thank you! I love it!"

He seemed just a touch embarrassed by her overwhelming joy, though he affectionately returned her hug. "Well, I figured if you were moving into a new home, Leah, you ought to have at least one new piece of furniture just for yourself."

They ate their cake, the adults drinking coffee and Leah a glass of milk, and then, while Leah sat and rocked in her new chair, Roberta helped Kyle clear the table. In the kitchen she rinsed the dishes, and he stacked them in the dishwasher, accepting her assistance as if it were something quite natural. Roberta felt more relaxed with Kyle as they engaged in their domestic chores than she'd felt the entire afternoon. "That was an awfully generous gift you gave her," she commented as Kyle covered the leftover cake in foil and slid it onto a shelf of his refrigerator.

He shrugged. "I wanted to give her something nobody else would give her," he justified himself. "I'm a carpenter; I make furniture. It seemed like a perfect idea."

"She certainly loves it," Roberta observed, spying on Leah through the glass door. She turned fully back to Kyle. "You've always given her such generous birthday gifts, Kyle. Without even knowing her. Why?"

His gaze came to rest on Roberta's upturned face. For the first time since Leah had joined them on the deck for dinner, Kyle seemed to be seeing only Roberta. He carefully mulled over his words before giving voice to them. "Sometimes I feel I know Leah very well," he began, then offered a tentative smile. "From your letters and from seeing her born. I'm glad you wrote to me over the years, Roberta. I used to look forward to your letters so much—" He cut himself off, evidently having a difficult time shaping his thoughts into words. His eyes drifted past Roberta to the darkening sky outside. "Leah is a very special part of me," he attempted. "You both are. I can't really explain it, and maybe I haven't even got the right to say such a thing, but—"

"There isn't a right and wrong about it," Roberta remarked gently, touched by his heartfelt confession.

His eyes returned to her, their gray softening to the sweet, misty hue she remembered. "I'm glad you told her about me," he continued quietly. "I'm glad I'm not just a stranger to her."

Roberta grinned, hoping to reassure him. "Of course you aren't a stranger. You're the guy who always gives her the fantastic birthday presents."

"Maybe that's why I do it," Kyle admitted. "So she won't forget who I am." He glanced through the glass door at the blissfully rocking child. "I'm glad you've moved back east," he went on. "I'd—I'd like to spend more time with her, if that's all right with you."

"I don't see why not," Roberta said, recalling again that Leah needed someone in her life to fill the gaping hole left by her father's death.

Kyle turned fully back to Roberta. "You, too," he added, his tone oddly cautious.

"Me, too, what?"

"I'd like to spend time with you, too."

Roberta believed that his words carried an undercurrent, that perhaps Kyle's interest in her extended beyond the fact that she was Leah's mother. She wanted to ask him to clarify himself, but she couldn't. He seemed shy to her, reticent, uncertain. To push him into stating his feelings more clearly might be presumptuous, and it might threaten his delicate feelings for Leah. "I think," she said, equally cautiously, "it would be nice for us to get to know each other."

"Would you like to come out in the boat with us tomorrow?" he invited her.

She peered outside at Leah and shook her head. "No, that's Leah's special treat. I think she'll enjoy it more if I'm not around telling her to behave herself and nagging at her not to jump up and down in the boat."

He shot Leah a skeptical look. "Is she going to jump up and down?" he muttered. "*I'll* be nagging at her if she does."

"Well—" Roberta smiled and started for the door "—we probably should be on our way. Leah's supposed to be in bed by eight."

"Even on her birthday?" Kyle protested on the child's behalf. "She ought to be allowed to stay up late on her birthday, Roberta."

"How much fun it is to spoil someone else's kids," Roberta remarked wryly as she and Kyle went out to the deck to get Leah. The little girl kicked up a predictable but minor fuss when Roberta announced that it was time to leave, and she calmed down once Roberta reminded her that she'd be seeing Kyle the following day. Kyle carried the rocker to the car for them and wiggled it onto the narrow back seat. He held Leah's door open for her and buckled her seat belt. Then he moved around the car to Roberta's side.

She already had her door open, but he touched her elbow, preventing her from sliding onto the seat. His hand felt warm on her skin, and she detected the smooth leathery calluses on his fingers. Perhaps he spent more time pushing papers than building furniture these days, but he still had the hands of a craftsman.

"I'm glad you came," he whispered.

"We're glad we came, too," Roberta said, speaking for Leah as well as herself. The little girl who had been so reluctant to leave just minutes ago was now dozing on the car seat. "We had a wonderful time."

"I'll see you tomorrow," Kyle murmured. He bent over to kiss Roberta's cheek, then helped her onto the seat and closed the door behind her.

Backing down the driveway, Roberta recalled the last time she'd said goodbye to Kyle. He'd kissed her cheek then, too. That time, lying in a hospital bed and trying to come to terms with the reality of her baby's birth, she'd been too muddled to decipher what his gentlemanly kiss meant.

Tonight, after spending an evening with him, discovering him to be a fascinating, dangerously attractive man, far more complex than she'd remembered, she was just as muddled. And she still had no idea what his kiss meant.

EIGHT-THIRTY. The deck and kitchen were clean, the barbecue briquettes extinguished, the carton and gift-wrapping paper from Leah's rocker deposited in the trash can inside his garage. There was nothing left to do.

He hadn't expected their visit to end so early. Stupid of him, really. He should have known that little children had to be in bed by a certain hour.

He'd hosted plenty of dinners before. Dinners with women guests. They'd have a drink, as he and Roberta had, and then eat, and then maybe enjoy an after-dinner drink, liqueur or brandy—he'd been planning to open the still-sealed bottle of Frangelico for Roberta. And then after the liqueur, after the quiet conversation and the winding down of the evening...

Well, *that* hadn't been on the schedule for tonight, of course. He'd never thought of Roberta in those terms. Even if he had, this party had belonged to Leah. Not to Kyle.

Restless, he prowled to the liquor cabinet in the dining room, reached for a bottle of brandy, and then set it back on the shelf, unopened. Other than an occasional beer on the deck or in front of the television set, he wasn't too keen on drinking alone.

He could call Jerry. Jerry had recently broken things off with his latest girlfriend; he might be free tonight. They could go to Friends & Company, order a round, philosophize. No, if Jerry went to that elegant watering hole with Kyle, he sure as hell wouldn't want to have to leave with him. And the last thing Kyle wanted was to spend the night looking at unattached women in a cocktail lounge and wondering.

Years ago he would have enjoyed that just fine. As recently as five years and one day ago, such an activity would have suited him perfectly. The problem with Jerry—and his greatest attraction as far as Kyle was concerned—was that Jerry reminded Kyle so much of himself at a younger age. They'd known each other ever since Kyle had first settled in Madison about ten years ago, after he'd finished college and grown tired of traveling around the country on his thumb and pondering the Meaning of Life with all the self-importance of so many recent college graduates. Like Kyle, Jerry had been footloose, carefree, defiantly irresponsible.

Only Jerry hadn't changed. Rather than take the nine-to-five job Kyle had offered him at the furniture plant, Jerry preferred to pick up odd jobs wherever he found them, to live from one dollar to the next and worry about nothing. He still lived in the grounded trailer he and Kyle had once shared in a mobile-home park off Route One; he still spoke authoritatively on Kierkegaard and Wittgenstein. There were many times when Kyle found himself envying Jerry, dreaming nostalgically of what his own life had been like before... before Leah.

No, it wasn't Leah's birth that had changed him, he mused. He must have been already ripe for change. Leah's birth had been the catalyst, that was all. Leah's birth, and Roberta. Everything about Roberta.

He stalked to his bedroom and scooped up his keys from the top of his dresser. Then he left the house through the mudroom to the garage, climbed into the truck and backed out onto the driveway.

Within ten minutes he had reached the block of small, cozy beach houses that contained Mary Grinnard's cottage. He'd never forgotten her name, even though he had no idea who she was. He considered himself lucky that she'd never noticed the aged blue pickup that was so often parked across the street from her house, its driver's astute gray eyes gazing at the porch, the door, the flowery curtains rippling in the evening breezes that carried off the water.

Kyle pulled up to the curb and shifted into neutral before surveying the house. Leah's new rocker stood on the porch. The lights were on in the living room. The drapes were drawn, but Kyle could see two silhouettes moving behind them. Leah must be asleep by now, he pondered, and Roberta and her friend were having the nightcap she should have been having with him. Although the windows were open, he couldn't hear the women's voices. Human sounds tended to be muffled and distorted by the sea breezes and by the rhythmic song of the water itself.

He revved the engine, U-turned and drove away. After several blocks, he turned the truck back toward the beach and parked. He removed his shoes and socks, cuffed his pants and jogged down the short stretch of pavement to the sand.

Other than a young couple seated together on a blanket, talking privately, the beach was empty. Kyle ignored the couple and they ignored him. He walked as far as the row of seaweed demarcating the high-tide line, then stared out at the throbbing black water of the Sound.

How had she known? How had she known why he'd given up the boat, the lobstering? Maybe she'd just made a lucky guess.

But even if she hadn't been guessing, Kyle suspected that she didn't know exactly what it was that she knew.

The perennially empty lobster trap had always been a joke with him. And then one day he'd been a party to the birth of a child, and suddenly the perennially empty lobster trap became a symbol of Kyle's life, of its own emptiness and uselessness. What had he accomplished that could even approach the importance of creating a child? What had he done that even remotely indicated that he was an adult, responsible, mature enough to take care of someone else? Being able to take care of himself was hardly a victory. And being able to argue Wittgenstein's theories long into the night with Jerry was only so much garbage.

For several intense hours one foggy afternoon in August, Kyle had been witness to a miracle. Not just the miracle of birth, but the miracle of Roberta. The women he'd known until then had been as frivolous as he was. Their biggest responsibility was in making sure they didn't get pregnant. Roberta hadn't chosen that responsibility; she'd chosen a far greater one.

Kyle had revered her. He had been in awe of her bravery that day, her constant good humor, her willingness to endure without complaining what was obviously a great deal of pain, because she wanted to have her baby. He'd felt privileged to be a part of the experience.

But he'd been more than just a part of it. He'd been essential that day. For the first time in his life he'd taken responsibility, he'd been necessary, he'd lost all consciousness of himself in his concern for another human being. Two human beings, in fact. Nothing would ever be the same for him after that.

After Leah's birth, he'd changed his life. He'd taken on responsibilities; he'd achieved things, accomplished things. Now he owned a flourishing business. He sat at a desk in a glass-enclosed office at one end of the warehouse he'd converted into a thriving plant, and talked to architects in Colorado or Vancouver or Fort Lauderdale who said things like, "It's got to be designed by you, Stratton. My client won't settle for anyone else. Money is no object." When he wasn't sitting at his desk, he was sitting at a drafting bench, drawing tables and chairs and wall treatments that other people—his employees—would build. Then he'd move back to his desk and initial invoices. The only wood that touched his fingers these days was the hexagonally beveled wood of his number-two pencils.

It wasn't enough. He'd known it wasn't enough for some time, but today, seeing Leah, he'd had the truth thrown in his face. Making lots of money, having one's designs in big demand, owning a fancy house, abandoning one's frivolous pleasures wasn't enough. He still hadn't accomplished anything important.

Roberta, however unconsciously, had recognized the truth about him. She had recognized that his career kept him busy but not fulfilled, that a rickety rowboat might be worth more than an elegant house. Roberta was more than strong, more than brave. She was wise. He still revered her.

He wanted her, too. He hadn't expected that part of it, but he wanted her. Merely thinking about her lithe figure, the golden skin exposed above the neckline of her blouse, the graceful line of her throat and the enticing length of her legs, caused his breath to go short.

He turned abruptly away from the water and headed back to his truck. No way could he pursue a woman like Roberta. She was practically a goddess, after all. And he was a fool.

Chapter Four

"He's here!" Leah shouted into the cottage through the open window. She was enthroned in her new rocking chair on the porch, wearing a colorful striped bathing suit and waiting impatiently for Kyle. "Mommy? He's here!"

Roberta slipped on a terry beach jacket over her white bikini and left the bedroom. Mary, dressed in a more conservative maillot, a lacy yellow coverup and a broad-brimmed straw hat, joined her at the front door. Through the screen they saw Kyle's old sky-blue pickup turn onto the driveway. An aluminum rowboat was lashed to its cargo bay.

He climbed down from the cab and strode briskly up the front walk to the porch. Clad in beige cotton shorts, a bright red polo shirt and scuffed deck shoes, he once again looked to Roberta like a beach bum, despite his recent shave. Leah leaped from her rocker and leaned over the porch railing to study the boat. "Are we going in that?" she asked excitedly. "Is it a real lobster boat?"

"It's a rowboat," Kyle answered, chuckling.

"I thought so," Leah said, trying unsuccessfully to suppress a slight pout. Evidently she'd expected him to take her for a ride in a more exotic boat.

Kyle turned from Leah and nodded politely at Mary as she and Roberta stepped outside onto the porch. Mary extended her hand to him and he shook it. "I'm Mary Grinnard," she introduced herself. "And I take it you're Kyle Stratton, Roberta's erstwhile knight in shining armor."

Roberta cringed at Mary's comment, but forced a smile. "I think he's more Leah's knight in shining armor at the moment."

"What's a knight in shining armor?" Leah asked innocently.

Kyle laughed. "A knight in shining armor is a man who takes a little girl out in a rowboat," he explained. Then he glanced at Roberta and presented her with a suitably earnest expression. "What time do you want her back?" he asked.

"Do you believe this?" she muttered to Mary with mock dismay. "Barely five years old, and already she's got older men calling for her on dates." She turned back to Kyle and grinned. "You can keep her for an hour. After that she'll need another dose of suntan lotion. We'll be on the beach, so you can bring her back to us there."

"Fine," he said. Leah was already scampering down the walk to the truck, and Kyle stepped off the porch in pursuit. "I'm going to drive around to a launching place down the beach a way," he called over his shoulder. "I've got a life vest for her, Roberta, so don't worry about a thing."

"I'm not worried," she assured him. "Have fun." She watched him help Leah onto the high seat of the truck's cab. Leah waved energetically through the windshield. She'd never ridden in a truck before, and Roberta couldn't help wondering whether she'd find the drive more thrilling than the boat ride.

Once Kyle had steered the truck around the corner and out of sight, Mary and Roberta gathered their towels, tote bags and beach chairs and strolled down the block to the beach. "So that's Kyle Stratton," Mary remarked, her casual tone failing to conceal her fascination.

"The one and only," Roberta confirmed, scouting the sand for an empty place where they could spread out. She and Mary located an unoccupied stretch of beach and moved to it. They arranged their towels on the sand, and then Mary unfolded the short-legged canvas beach chairs and dug their bases into the sand. Roberta settled herself on one of the chairs, then groped in her bag for a bottle of sunscreening lotion. Her skin was naturally a dark golden hue, but ever since she'd discovered an incipient crow's-foot at the corner of her eye, she'd been acutely concerned about the dangers of overexposure to the sun.

Mary watched Roberta as she slathered her arms, legs and tummy with the shiny lotion. Roberta offered the bottle to Mary, who refused it with a negligent shake of her head. "It's a bit late in the day for me to be worrying about wrinkles."

Roberta grinned and stored the bottle in her bag. Mary was much too modest about her youthful good looks, but Roberta didn't feel like arguing with her about the importance of protecting her skin. She was enough of a mother hen with Leah; she wouldn't subject her best friend to any of her doting concern.

Leaning back in the beach chair, she extended her legs over the towel in front of her and closed her eyes. Although the sun was high and bright, the air was dry enough to render the hot summer day quite comfortable. Roberta lounged motionlessly, feeling the heat permeate her flesh and willing it to relax her. She'd been on edge all the previous night and into the morning, but she had faith in the natural sedative qualities of sunshine, fresh air and the lulling song of the water's tides. As she'd expected, they made quick work of her tension, baking it out of her muscles within several minutes and leaving in its place a delightful languor.

"He's rather handsome," Mary remarked.

"Hm?" Roberta didn't move. She felt too comfortable to acknowledge Mary's comment with more than a grunt.

"Kyle Stratton. He's a very attractive fellow."

Roberta opened her eyes. She gazed for a moment at the water. Its rippling surface caught glimmers of sunlight and threw them blindingly into her face. Pressing her lips together, she pondered whether she wanted to discuss Kyle with Mary. She'd managed to evade most of the older woman's questions last night; fortunately, Mary had been eager to discuss her own dinner engagement with a retired stockbroker who owned a summer house not far from hers, and so Roberta had kept their chatter focused on him.

But there was nothing left for her to ask Mary about Alvin Hemple, and she supposed that it was now her turn to answer whatever questions Mary might pose about Kyle Stratton. Fair was fair.

In response to Mary's observation about Kyle's looks, Roberta shrugged. "I guess he is," she allowed.

Mary gave her friend a long, pointed appraisal. "Funny, you didn't mention that last night," she needled Roberta. "All you said when I asked how he looked was that he'd shaved off his beard."

"He *did* shave off his beard," Roberta retorted. Then she sank deeper into her chair and stared at the horizon. She had no right to be short with Mary, but the last thing she wanted to discuss was Kyle's unquestionable handsomeness. The tranquillity she'd been enjoying beneath the therapeutic warmth of the sun vanished as she was forced to acknowledge the cause of her tension.

Long after Mary had retired the previous night, Roberta had lain awake on the sagging cot in the parlor and tried to work through her feelings about Kyle. Yes, of course, he was a very attractive fellow. No question about it. With his strong, determined features, his virile physique, his beautiful yet puzzling gray eyes, Roberta couldn't help but find him almost irresistibly alluring.

But the more she considered it, the more uneasy she felt about her attraction to him. She didn't know how much of that attraction was a result of gratitude for his having been her "knight in shining armor" five years ago. She didn't know how much of it was a result of his obvious fondness for her daughter. She didn't know how much of it was a result of the fact that she'd just recently begun to pay attention to men.

The entire relationship—if what she and Kyle had could be called a relationship—was simply too strange: one intense, earth-shattering day, one shared miracle and then years of letters, letters that seemed to conceal as much as they revealed. Nothing that Roberta could remember from Kyle's letters had prepared her for the complicated man who had hosted her daughter's birthday dinner last night. During their visit, he'd seemed at times so self-possessed, happily conversing with Leah about boating and school, and then he'd seemed at other times utterly bemused, expressing astonishment over the most basic facts: that Leah had grown, that she was sensible, that she was a more or less typical child. Kyle's ingenuous, affectionate reactions to Leah had touched Roberta deeply. Just thinking about him now caused a velvety warmth to spread through her.

But for her first social encounters with men after five years of voluntary isolation from them, Roberta wanted things to be normal, comprehensible, safe. She wanted to meet a pleasant man through work or at a social gathering, have dinner with him, go to a show or a recital, chat late into the night over espresso, get to know him gradually. She didn't want to become involved with a man who had found her misshapen body collapsed on the beach in a fog and had taken her to Mary's house and delivered her baby. It seemed too complicated, too bizarre.

Besides, she mused, she had no idea whatsoever what Kyle thought of her—or wanted with her. He'd said she was looking well, which fell under the heading of "polite," but mostly his attention had centered on Leah. Leah was the main reason he took an interest in Roberta—which was exactly what Roberta had hoped for before she'd seen him.

"So he and Leah have hit it off?" Mary asked, uncannily cluing in to the subject of Roberta's contemplation.

Roberta forced her attention to her friend. "Yes," she confirmed. "He seems very taken with her."

"She's a lucky girl," Mary commented. "What girl wouldn't want an adoring man in her life, someone to take her out on boats and build rocking chairs for her and all?"

"He's really been so good to her this weekend," Roberta said with a nod of agreement. "The only man in her life at the moment is my father, and he can't be a father figure for her. He's too busy being a grandfather figure. Leah definitely needs to spend some time with someone Kyle's age."

"So that's the plan, is it?" Mary mused. "You're going to let Kyle become a father figure for her?"

Roberta nodded again. Hearing the idea coming from Mary instead of just thinking about it herself made it seem even more appealing to her. Kyle's handsomeness was irrelevant. Roberta would meet plenty of handsome men in New York, but none of them would boast Kyle's current qualifications for father figure. "If he's willing," she told Mary, "I think it would be wonderful for Leah to be able to spend time with Kyle that way—as they're doing on the boat today. Don't you agree? Leah needs Kyle much more than..."

She faltered, then stopped. She couldn't link the words "I," "need" and "Kyle" together in a sentence. She'd needed him once, but that was five years ago in exceedingly unusual circumstances. Today all Roberta needed was what was best for her daughter.

Mary studied Roberta, her piercing hazel eyes attempting to penetrate her friend's skull in search of her thoughts. "Here's my unsolicited opinion," she proposed, her voice hinting at a subtle warning as she mentally completed Roberta's dangling statement. "It's time for you to start worrying a little bit less about what Leah needs and a little bit more about what you need."

Roberta laughed uneasily. "My needs have nothing to do with this," she chided Mary, trying to convince herself as well. "I'm about to start living the swinging life in Manhattan. Don't worry about me."

"You? Swinging?" Mary scoffed in disbelief. "Well, you know I'm not one to give advice, Roberta, so all I'll say is that if you don't have the good sense to find Kyle Stratton one hell of a knockout, then your artistic eye is failing you."

"Why don't *you* go after him?" Roberta teasingly suggested. "You've never been averse to dating younger men."

"Younger, yes. Young enough to be my son, no," Mary distinguished. She pulled a magazine from her bag and opened it, a sign that the conversation had reached its conclusion.

Roberta wasn't relieved. Even if Mary was finished dragging her over the coals, she'd succeeded in reviving all of Roberta's doubt and confusion about Kyle. She thought wistfully of the way she'd felt about him before their reunion. How nice it had been to think of him as a hero, a rescuer, someone she'd been compelled to trust infinitely, someone who had ultimately proved deserving of her infinite trust. How much easier that was than thinking of Kyle as a man.

She scanned the water, searching for his boat. Beyond the narrow cove of the beach, the Sound was filled with watercraft—sailboats, power boats, a few massive yachts that appeared to be ocean worthy. She couldn't hope to find a tiny rowboat in all that clutter.

Yet she did spot it—or rather, she spotted the vivid crimson of Kyle's shirt against the green-gray water, and then the bright orange of Leah's life vest. Roberta couldn't make out their faces, but she was able to follow the course of the red splotch and the smaller orange splotch through the water. A power boat zipped past them, causing their boat to bob in the rough wake. Roberta could imagine Leah squealing with delight at the unexpected bouncing. She was a fearless little girl. Roberta only hoped that Kyle was willing to be firm about not letting Leah stand up in the boat.

They rowed as far as the tip of one of the piled-stone breakwaters bordering the cove, and then Kyle turned the boat around and piloted it back to shore. The closer the boat came, the clearer Roberta's view of it was. After a few minutes she could discern the motion of the oars in the water, the strong pull of Kyle's shoulders and back as he propelled the boat toward the shore.

Eventually they reached the sand. Kyle leaped out and hauled the boat the last few feet out of the water, then gallantly helped Leah out and onto terra firma. She yanked off her life vest before running up the beach to her mother. Kyle followed at a more leisurely pace.

"Mommy!" Leah shrieked exuberantly, her high voice at full volume. "Mommy, here we are! We're back!"

"How good of her to announce that news to the entire state of Connecticut," Roberta whispered to Mary, who chuckled.

Leah reached her mother and dropped onto the towel. "Mommy, it was great. Kyle showed me this lobster trap. It wasn't his, but there was this marker, so we pulled it up to look at it. It was empty."

Roberta lifted her eyes to Kyle, who had arrived at the edge of her towel. He grinned and raised his shoulders in an amiable shrug. "Lobsters must have a sixth sense when it comes to me," he said. "My life's experience in lobstering has been pulling up empty traps. As soon as they sense me approaching, they dive for cover."

"But it was a neat trap, anyway," Leah insisted. "It's like this box, with metal wires on the sides, and it's got this hole in the middle like a door that turns in, with little points on the inside. Kyle says it's very important that it turns in, so the lobsters can crawl into the trap and then they can't get out again. Isn't that right, Kyle?"

"That's right," Kyle confirmed, his eyes still on Roberta, his lips curved in an amused smile.

"Would you like to build a sand castle with me now?" Leah asked Kyle as Roberta pulled away from her beach chair in order to apply some sunscreen lotion to Leah's back and shoulders.

Mary suddenly doffed her hat. "*I'd* like to build a sand castle with you, Leah," she announced. "What do you say we go down closer to the water, where the sand is wetter?"

"Okay, Aunt Mary," Leah rapidly agreed. "You don't mind, do you, Kyle? I like my Aunt Mary a lot, too."

"I don't mind at all," Kyle assured her.

Roberta suspected that Mary had an ulterior motive in dragging Leah off, leaving Kyle and her alone. But there wasn't much she could do about it. She rubbed a little more lotion on her shoulders and legs, then rolled onto her stomach to tan her back. "Do you have to put your boat away?" she asked him.

He dropped onto Mary's towel and adjusted the beach chair comfortably behind his broad shoulders. "Not this minute," he said. "It doesn't seem to be in anyone's way where it is."

His eyes moved from the beached rowboat to Leah. He watched for several silent minutes as the small girl and the older woman knelt down near the high-tide mark and began digging. Roberta twisted to peer over her shoulder. She saw Leah's hands furiously scooping back the sand, flinging it in all directions. Leah's energy astonished her. "Was she well behaved in the boat?" Roberta asked.

"Leah? She was wonderful," Kyle answered. His voice sounded curiously distant, his eyes wandering slowly back to Roberta. "You've raised a wonderful little girl, you know."

She folded her arms beneath her head and angled her face toward him. Even though he was no longer grinning, his eyes seemed to smile. They were filled with the gentleness she'd remembered seeing in them years ago, the soft, tender gray that expressed contentment and pleasure.

Yet the way they ran the length of her bikini-clad body, pausing at the swell of her breasts, flattened against the sand, and at her narrow waist and the rise of her hips, was anything but gentle. His assessing gaze made her feel slightly defensive, and she shifted and drew her legs closer together. "Why are you staring at me that way?" she bluntly challenged him.

He grinned. The boat ride had done wonders for his state of mind. Merely the rhythmic strain of rowing had felt terrific, as had the occasional splash of cool, briny water on his cheeks and the contagious effervescence of his young passenger. Kyle hadn't felt so mellow in ages.

He felt mellow enough right now to permit himself another lazy inspection of Roberta's body. Surely any woman put together as well as she was must know exactly why a man would stare at her. Kyle wasn't staring, anyway, he decided. He was merely... appreciating.

If he'd happened to view so much of her last night, he'd have been overcome by lust. Not today. His appreciation was oddly cerebral. Not that he was unmoved by her shimmering golden skin, her enchantingly lissome shape, the curves and indentations that begged to be touched, and her glowing eyes, which seemed to be daring him, though he wasn't sure exactly what the dare entailed. Roberta, he concluded, was one incredibly sexy woman.

Ironically, her very sexiness was what detached him from her, enabling him to study her without succumbing to his baser instincts. He was frankly amazed to think of Roberta as sexy. Her transformation from the woman she'd been when he'd met her to the woman she was now seemed unreal to him—unreal and almost hilarious.

He shook his head, wondering how he could explain to her that he wasn't ogling her for the obvious reasons. "I'm trying to picture you the way you looked five years ago," he informed her. "It's awfully hard when you're dressed like that."

She snorted, accepting his innocent claim. "Five years ago I wouldn't have been caught dead in a bikini. If you'd run into me on a nicer afternoon that week I was in Madison, you would have had the nightmarish experience of seeing me in my maternity bathing suit."

"Maternity bathing suit?" he asked with genuine curiosity. "Do they have such things?"

Roberta wrinkled her nose at the memory. "Mine looked like something Omar the Tent Maker might have designed. It had expandable bloomers underneath and a baggy top." She lifted herself off the sand enough to trace the shape of the swimsuit in the air with her hands. "Absolutely hid-

eous,'' she described it. ''But then, most maternity clothing is hideous.''

''In what way?'' he asked. In any other context, Kyle
wouldn't have conceived of himself discussing maternity
fashions with someone—let alone being authentically interested in learning about them. But when he was in Roberta's
presence, the subject became fascinating to him. He wanted
to learn about it. He wanted to learn everything he could
about what her pregnancy had been like.

''First of all,'' she complained, ''whoever designs the
stuff seems to think that when a woman becomes pregnant,
her shoulders expand.''

''Her shoulders? What do you mean?'' Kyle asked,
frowning.

''All the blouses always have big, puffy sleeves,'' Roberta explained. ''Or else—even worse—cutesy little bows at
the neck. Maybe the designers think that since a woman is
all wrapped up in thoughts of her child, she might want to
dress like a child while she's pregnant.''

''You weren't wearing puffy sleeves when I saw you,''
Kyle recollected.

''No, I was wearing the Classic Denim Maternity Jumper.
Every pregnant woman I've ever known has owned the
Classic Denim Maternity Jumper. It's mandatory, I think,
like drinking lots of milk. If you don't own the Classic
Denim Maternity Jumper, your kid might be born with six
toes on one foot.''

Kyle's lips arched in a tenuous smile. He didn't know how
to take Roberta's dry humor. He wanted to learn about maternity clothes, but he didn't want Roberta to make fun of
them. He recognized that she was obliquely making fun of
herself, of the way she'd appeared when she was pregnant.
As Kyle remembered it, she'd looked magnificent. He didn't
really remember what she'd been wearing. The clothing

hadn't mattered; what had mattered was her proud bearing, her endearing awkwardness, her life-filled body. He almost resented her for making fun of what he'd found gloriously moving.

He considered scolding her for her ridiculous attitude, but decided not to. He'd never been pregnant himself; he couldn't possibly know how Roberta had felt in her denim jumper and her puffy sleeves and her tentlike maternity swimsuit. To criticize her disdainful tone would be way out of line.

His eyes refused to shift from her, though. They continued to study her, glittering enigmatically.

"What?" she prompted him.

"I don't know." He paused to sort his words, then decided to be as honest with her as she was with him. "When I think of things like childbirth, Roberta, I don't think about... about puffy sleeves."

"That's because you never had to wear them," Roberta suggested.

He shook his head. "No, what I mean is that you looked so..." He paused again, then continued. "So beautiful that day. So absolutely beautiful."

"I looked like a cow," Roberta disputed him.

"Yesterday you said you looked like a walrus," he noted, then smiled gently and shook his head again. "You didn't look like a walrus or a cow. You looked like a woman about to give birth. And I can't think of too many sights more beautiful than that."

He sounded so sincere that Roberta resisted the urge to tease him. She wouldn't dispute that there was something special and lovely about the appearance of a woman with child. But to the woman herself, with her grossly protruding abdomen and her navel stretched into a flat, discolored smudge, to the woman who had to say farewell to her feet when she was seven months along, to the woman being kicked and pummeled from within by an active fetus, to the woman whose sheer bulk made it virtually impossible to find a comfortable position for sleep, being pregnant was frequently not all that beautiful. Roberta was thrilled to have been pregnant and to have given birth to a healthy, happy child, but she'd long ago been disabused of romantic notions about pregnancy and motherhood.

"Maybe you should have sent me a picture of yourself along with all the pictures of Leah," Kyle commented softly. "Then it wouldn't have been such a shock to see you...like this."

His eyes ran the length of her glistening golden body again, following its lean, graceful curves. Roberta felt her cheeks color slightly from his admiring inspection of her. When Kyle looked at her, she didn't feel as if she were being leered at. Actually, she couldn't imagine any man leering at her, given that her body had endured thirty years of wear and tear, not the least of which included the pregnancy that Kyle professed to find so beautiful. But even if some men did consider her leer-worthy, she knew that Kyle wasn't being salacious. He seemed too sweetly confused.

She thought about putting on her beach jacket, but then realized that at this point it would be silly to bother covering herself up. Kyle had already seen her. "Understand," she explained, wishing she could unravel his apparent bewilderment, "that looking like this isn't at all a shock to me. What *was* a shock was looking the way I looked the last time you saw me. I'm used to being thin. I've been thin all my life. Except, of course, for a period of a few months five years ago."

Kyle digested her statement and nodded at its sensibleness. A film of perspiration covered his brow, and he untucked his polo shirt and used the hem to mop his face.

Roberta caught a brief glimpse of his abdomen as he lifted the red cloth away from his torso. His stomach was taut and flat, adorned by a sleek line of blond hair.

Her gaze shifted to his long, muscular legs, also coated with fine golden hairs. For some reason, she was as shocked by his sturdy, masculine physique as he was by her slender, feminine figure. Not because his build had changed over the past five years, but because the last time they were together she simply hadn't paid much attention to his appearance.

Her cheeks darkened with another blush, and she turned her face away from him to give herself a moment to recover. She honestly didn't like the attraction she felt toward Kyle. For some reason she felt threatened by it. It imperiled her concept of Kyle as unique, as an irreplaceable friend, a man to whom she could write page after page of drivel about her daughter knowing that he'd never complain about such maternal outpourings on her part.

From the moment he'd helped her off the sand five years ago, she'd trusted him completely. Being attracted to him endangered that trust. True friends didn't break one's trust, but lovers sometimes did. Maybe her uneasiness about Kyle had nothing to do with his potential as Leah's father figure. Maybe it was simply a matter of her not wanting to risk her ability to trust him.

Furthermore, even if a romantic relationship never developed between them, merely exploring the possibility might put him into a position where he'd feel obliged to reject her. For all she knew, his thorough scrutiny of her underdressed body was exactly what he'd claimed it to be and nothing more. She wasn't a spring chicken; she wasn't a beach bunny. She was, if anything, a recovered walrus, a onetime cow. She mustn't presume that Kyle felt any attraction for her. Even allowing herself to consider that he did could spoil the friendship they had.

"That's quite a castle they're building," he murmured.

She lifted her shoulders off the towel, then turned around to sit. Mary and Leah were engrossed in the creation of an extended sand structure surrounded by a moat six inches deep. "That's not a castle, that's a kingdom," Roberta remarked. "Ever since Leah got that enormous dollhouse you sent her, she's had grandiose ideas about how big and elaborate her make-believe buildings should be."

"Does she still like the dollhouse?" Kyle asked.

"She adores it," Roberta told him. She glanced his way and found him leaning forward, his forearms resting on his bent knees as he watched Leah. His eyes squinted and his windswept hair gleamed with pale blond streaks beneath the sun's unrelenting glare. "You know, Kyle," she remarked, "you never answered my question about that dollhouse."

He turned to her. "What question?"

"After Leah got it, I wrote and asked you if you'd built it yourself. You never answered."

He took a moment to recall the letter, then smiled sheepishly. "That's right," he concurred. "But the way I remember it, you went on for a page and a half about how spectacular the house was, and *then* you asked if I'd built it. If I'd written you that I had, it would have sounded as if I was bragging."

"You did build it, then?" Roberta asked.

"I did."

"Braggart," she teased. He chuckled. She noticed the deep laugh lines accenting the outer corners of his eyes, the dimples cutting into his smooth cheeks. She liked his dimples and the sharp angle of his exposed jaw and the firm, certain lines of his mouth. She decided that she preferred the way he looked without his beard.

But when he'd had the beard, before he'd "matured," he'd been building furniture instead of pushing papers. And

he'd owned a rowboat. She couldn't escape her understanding that in Kyle's case, such maturing hadn't made him
very happy.

Her internal debate about the perilous future of their relationship disappeared from her thoughts, replaced by a
wellspring of concern for him. "Can I ask you a personal
question?"

He eyed her askance and laughed. "Should I brace myself?"

Roberta remained solemn. "Why did you get rid of your
boat?" she asked.

His smile vanished. Roberta wondered whether he was
going to retreat from her. He'd become chilly the previous
evening when she'd commented on his lobstering; he might
react the same way now.

But his eyes didn't grow hard and flinty as they had last
night. They appeared pensive, dense and muted as he shifted
his gaze to the beached aluminum boat not far from Leah's
sand castle. "When I moved to Boston, it was easier to sell
the boat than to bring it with me," he replied emotion-
lessly. "What was I going to do with a rowboat in a crowded
apartment in the Hub?"

"But then you moved back to Madison," Roberta
probed. "Why didn't you buy a new one? Judging by your
house, I'm sure you could afford a dinky little rowboat."

He eyed her coolly, then smiled at her lack of diplomacy.
"It isn't a matter of money, it's a matter of time," he re-
sponded. "I don't have time to go rowing around the
Sound. My business takes a lot out of me."

"But you had time today," Roberta pressed him. "If you
really enjoyed the boating, you'd make time for it. And you
do enjoy it, Kyle, don't you?" Roberta acknowledged silently that her comments were awfully forward, and that she
had no right to give him advice about how to spend his

time—or, for that matter, his money. Still, she couldn't keep herself from concluding, "You ought to make the time for it more often."

Again he gave her a speculative perusal. Why did she keep zeroing in on the subject of his boating? It wasn't as if he were a dyed-in-the-wool sailor, a true-blue Connecticut Yankee who'd been born with a compass in his hand and zinc oxide on his nose. He was a native of landlocked Nebraska who had ventured east for college and decided, ultimately, to settle there. He'd never even tasted a lobster until he was twenty. Why did Roberta go on and on about his abandonment of boating as if he were a lifelong addict in the throes of agonizing withdrawal?

Because, he admitted, because she could read him in a way no one ever had before. Yesterday she'd told him about how, after spending so much time with Leah, she'd learned to pick up on the child's wavelengths. Roberta hadn't spent much time at all with Kyle, yet she picked up on his wavelengths just as well. She was an uncommonly sensitive woman. She knew he was troubled; she knew it had something to do with his having forced himself to outgrow his rowboat and his lobster trap.

"You're right," he said.

Roberta took a minute to digest his terse response to her unwarranted lecture. His failure to resent her pushiness disarmed her, and she began to apologize. "Look, Kyle, it's none of my business—I mean, who am I to tell people how they should—"

"No," he cut her off, his voice quiet but firm. "You're right, Roberta. I should make the time." He turned to watch Leah fill a plastic pail with water from the Sound and carry it back to dump into the castle's moat. He smiled pensively. "People make time for what's important to them. I—I'd forgotten how important rowing out and looking at my empty lobster trap was to me. For some reason, other things seemed more important.''

A breeze rose off the water and ruffled through his thick hair. He fell silent, combing his fingers through the disheveled locks and shoving them back from his sun-burnished face. Roberta wondered what things might have seemed more important than the frivolous but genuine pleasure he'd taken in rowing around the cove. But she bit back the impulse to question Kyle further. If he had wanted to say more, he would have. And she'd already said too much.

"Kyle! Mommy!" Leah hollered across the beach. "Wanna see the castle we made?"

Roberta grinned and started to rise. "In a minute!" Kyle called to Leah before gripping Roberta's wrist and pulling her back down beside him. The sudden gesture surprised her. Her eyes grew round and inexplicably darker as she stared at him.

He was surprised, too. He hadn't expected to do what he'd just done. It had been an act born of near desperation. He wasn't ready to relinquish her to Leah yet.

Her wrist was so slender his thumb and index finger easily met above her pulse. He wondered if he was only imagining the racing tempo of it, or if it was his own rapid pulse he was feeling. He'd held Roberta's hands before, he'd kissed her cheek. Why was this different? Why, after convincing himself that his admiration for the feminine assets her skimpy bikini displayed was strictly academic, did touching her wrist cause his nervous system to spin out of control?

He knew damned well why: Roberta understood him. She knew what he needed. She knew enough to goad him about his boat, to scold him for not keeping his priorities in order. It was no wonder she was such a fine mother, he mused. She read people perfectly. And she had the guts to call him to account. She had the strength to tell him what he'd been unable to tell himself.

And that, even more than the taut swells of her breasts curving teasingly above the edge of her bikini bra, more than the slender sculpture of her abdomen, more than her long, well-toned legs, was what made him want her.

He wrestled with his words for a moment before saying, "Can we get together again next weekend?"

Roberta contemplated his deceptively simple question. Her first thought was that it would be a whole lot easier to get together with Kyle if she didn't feel so physically attracted to him, but she couldn't say that. "What did you have in mind?" she said instead.

Kyle shrugged. "You could come up to Madison again. I suppose I could visit you in New York, but Madison's so much nicer in the summertime—you might prefer to get out of the city for a couple of days. I could probably get hold of the rowboat again. Or maybe even buy one," he added with an impish smile. It faded, and he continued. "I feel...I feel as if we've barely scratched the surface this weekend."

Roberta nodded in agreement. There were still many things she wanted to learn about Kyle. And she didn't doubt that he wanted to spend more time with Leah, or Leah with him. "I'll have to check with Mary and see if she'll mind putting us up again," Roberta said. "After three days, houseguests are supposed to stink like old fish, but I'm not sure whether that applies if the houseguests leave for a few days and you can air the house out."

Kyle laughed softly. "If Mary doesn't want you to stay with her, you can always stay at my house. I've got more than enough room."

Roberta weighed his offer, then refused it. She imagined that she wouldn't feel at all comfortable in his house, knowing him as little as she did and yet feeling so drawn to him. "Thanks, but no," she said. "We'll stay with Mary."

"Mommy!" Leah shouted impatiently. "Hurry! Before it's washed away!"

Roberta shot a glance toward her daughter, and Kyle's hold on her tightened subtly. "I'd like to spend some time with you," he murmured hesitantly. "I mean, just you and me. I think we—we ought to talk some more, learn more about each other. We could go out to dinner or something."

His tone struck Roberta as almost diffident. She didn't know why he should sound so unsure of himself. He couldn't be unaware of the fact that he was an attractive man, rich, accomplished, professionally successful. Certainly he had more than enough going for him. If anything, Roberta was astonished that he didn't have his Saturday nights booked up years in advance.

Maybe he was concerned about destabilizing their friendship with a date. Maybe he was as aware as she was of the risks involved in allowing their friendship to expand into uncharted territory.

Or maybe he was afraid that Roberta might misread his invitation as more than he'd intended; maybe he honestly wanted only for them to learn more about each other over dinner, to review their correspondence and catch each other up on whatever details they'd forgotten to write, and then to devote coffee and dessert to an in-depth analysis of Leah. And then Kyle would drive Roberta home and kiss her cheek, and that would be the end of their relationship.

Whatever the hell their relationship was, she added silently. Maybe Kyle was as confused about it as she was; maybe he wanted to have dinner alone with her so they could try to figure it out. She was all in favor of that. "I'll see if

Mary would mind baby-sitting for us," she said. "If she's willing and available, then we'll have dinner together."

Kyle's smile expanded slightly and he released her wrist. As it was, Leah had run out of patience and was racing across the sand to fetch her mother. Roberta rose as Leah reached her, and she indulgently allowed her daughter to grab her hand and drag her back to the castle, where Mary was standing guard. Kyle accompanied them.

"Absolutely splendid," Roberta pronounced it after a critical examination. "What do you think, Kyle?"

He studied the turrets, the towers, the packed sand bridge constructed across the moat, and nodded his approval. "It's very nicely realized," he declared.

"Realized?" Leah asked. "What do you mean, realized?"

"That means you built it well," Roberta explained.

"Can I make one suggestion, though?" Kyle asked, dropping to his knees to give the castle a closer scrutiny.

"What?"

"Well, you've got this fine moat here, but there aren't any boats on it. Now, suppose the princess who lives in this castle likes to keep a lobster trap in the moat. How's she going to check it?"

Leah pondered that dilemma. "Do lobsters live in moats?" she asked.

"I don't know," Kyle admitted, conceding to the child's hardheadedness in puncturing the fantasy he'd woven for her. "But even if we assume that they don't, the princess might like to unwind every now and then with a little boat ride around the moat." He lifted a thin, slightly concave shell and placed it carefully on the surface of the murky water in the moat. It floated. "There you go," he said.

Leah clapped her hands. "It's perfect, Kyle. What do you think, Aunt Mary?"

Mary Grinnard's discerning hazel eyes shuttled between Kyle and Roberta, apparently trying to fathom why Kyle would have made such a whimsical recommendation. Roberta knew why he'd suggested the boat, and her face lit up with a delighted smile. Seeing Roberta's glowing expression satisfied Mary.

"I think it's perfect," she declared.

Chapter Five

"Venezuela on the line," said Margo.

Kyle could see his secretary through the glass wall separating their offices, and she could see him. They could hear each other only through the intercom line on the telephone, however. The offices occupying one end of the converted warehouse were all soundproof; if they weren't, Kyle would be unable to conduct business over the cacophony of power saws and sanders and lathes, and the constant *bonk* and rattle of lumber chunks hitting the concrete floors.

He'd had to block out the noise, but not the view. Seated in his glass-enclosed cubicle, he could observe the entire length of the warehouse. He could watch his employees, a devoted corps of nine carpenters, as they worked the wood, shaped it, groomed it. He could watch them and feel the wood vicariously.

Only wood working was performed at his North Branford warehouse, which was located in a barren-looking industrial park fifteen minutes from his house. Upholstery was handled at the workshop in North Carolina, and occasionally in the Boston workshop, which also produced most of the metal and glass pieces. When Peter had first invited Kyle to become his partner, there had been only the two plants. Kyle had established the North Branford shop simply because he'd wanted an excuse to return to Madison. It had made sense for that shop to be dedicated strictly to carpentry, since that was his specialty.

He knew how to design upholstered furniture and exotic combinations of aluminum and marble, but he found no satisfaction in executing those designs. There was no tactile pleasure for him in handling cloth, foam, kapok, leather or cold, unyielding metals. He'd gladly let other people build those items.

There wasn't much tactile pleasure in paper, either, he mused as he pulled the order forms in question closer to himself and pushed the flashing button on his telephone console to take the Venezuela call. There wasn't much tactile pleasure in a plastic telephone receiver, in a felt-tipped pen. His eyes latched onto one of his workers who was operating an enormous industrial fine-grade sander, prepping the half batch of imported West Indian mahogany that had arrived at the workshop that morning. The rest of the mahogany was still in transit, and Kyle had spent the better part of the day trying to track it down.

"Jorge!" he greeted his caller, one of his major suppliers. The clients who commissioned Kyle's company to produce their customized furniture wanted him to spare no expense in the quality of the wood he used, and he relied on a few trusted suppliers to ship him the best imports they could find. "Where the hell's my mahogany, amigo?"

"Ay-ay-ay," Jorge groaned. This was his third conversation with Kyle that day. "It's on its way, Keel. Trust me, eh?"

Kyle muttered an oath and eyed the order forms spread across his desk. "It was supposed to come in last week," Kyle reminded him. "I got only half the shipment this morning. An interior designer in Tucson is going to bust my chops if I don't get this dining room set done by the end of

September. So come on, Jorge, you'll have to do better than 'Trust me.' ''

"I can do better," Jorge swore. "It's on a boat right now, okay? New York Harbor tomorrow, trust me."

"Why not New York Harbor last week?" Kyle pressed him.

"Last week it was in—how do you say it?—Mo-bee-lay. On the Gulf Coast."

"Mobile, Alabama?" Kyle asked incredulously. "How did it wind up there?"

"Mistake, Keel. A big mess. Trust me, New York Harbor tomorrow morning. Your shop by sundown. This I guarantee."

"Uh-huh," Kyle grumbled. He couldn't very well erupt in a tantrum; Jorge was still one of his most dependable suppliers, even with "big messes" like this one cropping up on occasion. "All right, Jorge. Tomorrow. Or else."

"I guarantee, Keel," the supplier vowed. "Trust me, eh?"

Kyle hung up the phone and sighed. Haggling with international wood suppliers over deliveries might have seemed glamorously professional to him at one time, but not anymore. He gazed through the glass partition at the worker wielding the sander and sighed again.

Margo buzzed him, and he pushed the appropriate button on his telephone and lifted the receiver. "What's the story, Kyle?" she asked. "Has he found our wood yet?"

"It got rerouted to Mo-bee-lay, Alabama, by mistake. It's slated to get here by tomorrow evening. I'm supposed to trust Jorge."

Margo laughed. "I've got seven volunteers for overtime on Saturday," she reported. "Will that be enough?"

He glanced at his calendar. Once the entire order of wood was on the premises, the work would proceed apace. One Saturday shift might be all it would take to get the project back on schedule. If they were still running tight by mid-September, he'd ask his people to volunteer for another Saturday shift. Or else wire some credible excuses to the designer in Tucson.

"Seven volunteers is fine," he told Margo. "I'll come in, too. Eight of us working together ought to get something accomplished."

"I would hope so," said Margo. "Also, Jerry Griggs called while you were on the phone with Jorge. He said if he doesn't hear from you, he'll meet you at Chips Pub at six-thirty tonight."

"Six-thirty," Kyle echoed. "Thanks, Margo."

He lowered the receiver and turned once again to the glass wall overlooking the workshop. He surveyed the bustle and smiled. Saturday he'd get to join the crew, breathe the sawdust, do *real* work for a change. Far better, Kyle thought, to risk getting splinters than to risk getting paper cuts.

He had planned to spend Saturday afternoon with Roberta and Leah. He'd have to telephone them and rearrange things. Saturday night he'd still have dinner with Roberta, and then he'd spend Sunday with Leah. That ought to work out, he mused.

In fact, it might be for the best if he didn't spend time on Saturday with Leah before accompanying Roberta to dinner. The entire concept of having an evening alone with her struck him as a bit foolhardy. When Leah was around, the adults had a buffer, common ground, a charming child who meant the world to both of them. When Leah was around, Kyle knew he could feel totally at ease. Without her, he and Roberta would be on their own, forced to contend with each other. Which was exactly what he wanted, and exactly what scared him.

Spending the day working with superior mahogany would probably be the best preparation for his evening with Roberta. Crafting things out of wood always put him in good spirits. Even if the bulk of the work was doomed to be such relatively tedious chores as prepping the wood and cutting it down to size, Kyle looked forward to it. It would restore his equilibrium; he'd be in the perfect mood to see Roberta.

He locked up his office at six o'clock, after the last of his employees had already left for the day. Kyle ran things fairly loosely at his plant: no time clocks for his people, no by-the-book bureaucracy. When Peter was still in the business, he'd been a stickler about employee policies, but once he'd retired and Kyle had bought him out, Kyle had adjusted the style of the North Branford workshop of Keane Furniture Design to suit his own personality. His managers at the Boston and North Carolina plants were more rigid than he was and that worked for them. But Kyle preferred surrounding himself with employees who didn't watch the clock, who were willing to put in an extra hour when it was needed and who, in turn, were rewarded with shortened days at full pay when the work load was light. Kyle's crew tended to share certain of his traits—most important, a love of the work itself. If his management practices weren't letter-perfect, well, the productivity of the North Branford workshop and the quality of craftsmanship emerging from it were the best of any of the branches. That was what counted.

He crossed the parking lot to his truck, the only vehicle left in the lot. The warehouse was air-conditioned, and the muggy evening air impelled him to roll the sleeves of his shirt up to his elbows and open a second button below his throat. He wasn't wearing a tie; he avoided proper business attire whenever possible, appearing in his office in a suit and tie only when he was expecting outsiders to drop in. Mostly, he wore oxford shirts and corduroy pants, as if he wanted to believe that he could drop his deskload of papers into the nearest wastebasket, don an apron and goggles, and join the workers in the shop whenever he felt the urge.

He felt the urge quite often. But his forays into the workshop to contribute his manual labor to a project were much too rare. He looked forward to Saturday with great pleasure.

Jerry was already at the pub when Kyle arrived shortly after six-thirty. If Kyle was dressed like an entrepreneur who dreamed of dirtying his hands with physical toil, Jerry was dressed like the genuine article. His overalls were faded to colorlessness, and his shirt had mysterious stains on both its sleeves. His bright red hair was an uncombed mess of curls, and his hands were wrapped around a chilled bottle of Miller beer.

He smiled brightly at Kyle and waved him over to the table. Kyle dropped onto the chair facing Jerry and signaled the waitress. "Another Miller," he requested.

Jerry continued to smile and stare at his friend until the beer arrived. Like Jerry, Kyle ignored his glass and took a swig directly from the bottle. He lowered it and waited for Jerry's inevitable question.

"Well?" Jerry asked, as if on cue. "What was it like?"

"Strange," Kyle confessed.

"That much I gathered," Jerry said, leaning forward and running one hand through his tangled curls. "When you called me Sunday night and said you wanted to get together, you sounded pretty spacey. What happened?"

"It's hard to say," Kyle began, then hesitated. "Actually, nothing happened. They came over for dinner, then they left, and then we got together again on Sunday. I borrowed Tim O'Donnell's rowboat and took Leah out for a ride. Then I talked to Roberta for a while on the beach, and then—" he shrugged "—they left Madison and I went home."

"Heavens, how strange," Jerry gasped. "Strange, indeed. A boat, you say? Dinner and a boat ride? Few things have ever been as strange as the weekend you've just described."

"Give me a break," Kyle complained good-naturedly. "The weekend wasn't strange. I mean—" he peeled a strip of the label from the sweating beer bottle, then took another long sip "—Roberta is gorgeous."

"Uh-huh," Jerry grunted, then frowned. "Set me straight again—Roberta's the little girl?"

"No, Leah's the girl. She's very pretty, too. Roberta's the mother."

"Ah." Jerry nodded knowingly. "And the mother is gorgeous, huh?"

"Stunning."

"I see." He stroked his chin thoughtfully. "Well. As our good friend Hegel would say—"

"Leave Hegel out of it," Kyle silenced him. He and Jerry both had college degrees in philosophy and could quote philosophers with equal aplomb. But Kyle wasn't in the mood to play quoting games with Jerry right now.

Jerry gave him a measuring look. "Okay," he said soberly. "We'll leave Hegel out of it. You're looking stricken, Kyle. Is this another Ursula we're talking about?"

Kyle grimaced at his friend's mention of the woman with whom Kyle had been seriously involved for several years. Although Jerry had only met Ursula a few times on trips to Boston to visit Kyle, he knew enough about Kyle's relationship with the woman to be able to speak authoritatively on the subject. "No, this isn't another Ursula," he assured Jerry. "The woman's a mother, for God's sake. Ursula worshiped at the shrine of modern contraception. You know that."

Jerry nodded. "I didn't mean she was a clone of Ursula, Kyle," he clarified. "I meant, are we talking about another long-term monogamous thing here? Are we talking about Commitment with a capital *C*? Why are you giving me these baleful looks, Kyle? Explain yourself."

"I wish I could," Kyle said. "I lived very nicely for five years thinking of Roberta as some distant image—an idea more than a person. Motherhood incarnate and all that. And suddenly there she was, standing in front of me, flesh and blood. Definitely a person. Definitely a *female* kind of person. I wanted her, Jerry, and I'm not sure that's the way this thing's supposed to go."

"What thing? Is it a thing?"

"It's always been a thing," Kyle pointed out. "It was a correspondence thing. It was Leah's thing." He leaned back in his chair, his eyes circling the crowded restaurant, seeing nothing.

"So, big deal," Jerry concluded. "So, now maybe it'll evolve into a sex thing. Why not? The world doesn't begin and end with the kid, Kyle. If the mother turns you on, why not? You're a good-looking guy; lots of women like you. I bet she does, too."

"I don't know," Kyle said with a vague shrug. He toyed with the shredded corner of his bottle's label and meditated. He'd told Jerry only so much and no more about Roberta and Leah. Jerry knew that Kyle had exchanged letters with Roberta for five years and that he sent the little girl birthday gifts. Jerry knew enough to have nicknamed Roberta and Leah Kyle's "California family."

But he didn't know the profound effect that experiencing Leah's birth had had on Kyle. He didn't know that the reason his drinking-and-philosophizing buddy had gone to Boston to acquire professional skills and then returned to Madison to build a business was that one time in his life, one foggy late-summer afternoon, he'd done something essential, invaluable, immeasurably important, and he'd spent the next five years trying to recapture that sense of significance. Jerry didn't know just how much Leah's birth had influenced Kyle's life.

Jerry was arguably Kyle's closest friend, but there were plenty of things Kyle couldn't confide to the red-haired man who'd once been his bachelor trailer mate in the mobile-home park. There were things Kyle couldn't talk about with anyone. He was a private person, given more to reflection than to confession. Yet for five years he'd discovered in himself the ability to write out his feelings, to inscribe on paper thoughts he could never express verbally. Then he'd fold the pages, slip them into an envelope, and mail them to Roberta.

Maybe if he'd spent those years thinking of her as a flesh-and-blood female kind of person, he wouldn't have been able to write such letters to her. He'd never been able to describe to Ursula what it felt like to take a solitary walk in January along the sand that separated Madison from the water, barefoot and freezing, free to fantasize about the origins of the earth and the life that teemed within the briny world of the ocean when the land was locked in ice. He could write about that sort of thing to Roberta, but he couldn't talk about it with Ursula. Ursula had been a Bostonian, bright and beautiful and as professionally ambitious as Kyle was in those days. How could he explain the epic beauty of a winter beach to someone who believed that the most important thing in the universe was to be promoted to head of the geriatrics department at the social service agency where she worked?

So he'd written to Roberta instead.

"Order up dinner," Jerry broke into Kyle's thoughts. "I'm treating."

"You don't have to," Kyle declined. He knew how precarious Jerry's finances were.

Jerry dismissed his concern with a smug grin. "Hey, this landscaping gig is going to last through the end of October. Come turkey time, you can treat. But tonight I'm flush—as long as you don't order anything over five bucks."

Kyle chuckled and opened the menu the waitress had left with his beer. He decided on a hamburger. "Tell me about the landscaping," Kyle asked his friend once the waitress had taken their orders and left. He was eager to be distracted from his continual thoughts about Roberta.

Jerry obliged. While they ate, he regaled Kyle with anecdotes about the multimillionaire at whose estate Jerry was working as a seasonal employee, about the chief grounds keeper who occasionally reeked of bourbon and reminded Jerry, alternately, of W. C. Fields and Arthur Godfrey, a pairing that Kyle had a difficult time making sense out of. Jerry shared with him the intrigues of the romance between a Costa Rican gardener and a Haitian housekeeper. "The OAS could learn a few things from those two," he remarked.

Kyle listened eagerly to all of Jerry's humorous stories. They reminded him of a time when he was an itinerant laborer, a carpenter invited to pitch in on nonunion projects or tricky restorations where an extra pair of willing, talented hands was needed. There was no security in that sort of work, but then, there wasn't much more security in running a well-reputed furniture design firm. One major recession could bankrupt Kyle's company. Not that he minded. Financial security was never high on his list of priorities. The act of creating, whether one was creating a dining room set or a business—or for that matter, a child—always entailed risks. Kyle liked those sorts of risks.

"Well," Jerry announced, wiping his mouth on a napkin and then hailing their waitress for the check. "It's after eight. I promised I'd stop by Linda's place tonight."

"I thought you two broke up," Kyle said.

"We did. That doesn't mean we still can't enjoy each other's company now and then," Jerry justified himself with a whimsical shrug. "Hey, any woman who worships at the shrine of modern contraception is all right in my book." He pulled his wallet from his hip pocket and flipped out a ten-dollar bill. "As my good friend Sartre would say, being sure beats nothingness. Can you handle the tip, Kyle?"

"No problem," Kyle said, chuckling. He wedged three one-dollar bills beneath his empty beer bottle and accompanied Jerry from the pub. They parted ways in the parking lot, Jerry cruising to his sometime girlfriend's house and Kyle heading for home.

The sky was still clinging tenaciously to the last lavender glow of daylight when he locked the truck in the garage. As was his habit, he entered the house through the mudroom connecting the garage with the kitchen and went directly to his bedroom. He hoisted the telephone from the night table beside the bed, carried it across the room on its long extension cord, and flopped onto the Stratton chair occupying the dusk-lit corner of the room by the door to the side deck. Nothing Kyle had ever lain upon was as comfortable as the reclining chair he himself had designed out of flexible leather-padded slats. Nothing inhuman, at least, he amended as a picture of Roberta's luscious body flickered across his brain.

Not a good thought, he scolded himself as he lifted the telephone and dialed her number. She answered on the third ring. "Hello?"

"Roberta? It's Kyle," he identified himself.

"Oh—hello," she said warmly. "Hang on a second, let me just—" A brief silence ensued, and he expected to hear Leah's squealing voice greeting him as she snatched the phone from Roberta. However, the next voice he heard was Roberta's again. "Sorry," she apologized for the pause, "I'm in the middle of five hundred things here. I had to clear a space so I could sit down."

"Where's Leah?" Kyle asked. The few times he'd telephoned Roberta, her daughter had always stolen the phone from her mother to talk to him.

"She's asleep," Roberta said. "It's eight-thirty."

"That's right," he recalled. "Since I'm not around to spoil her, you got her into bed on time."

Roberta laughed. "Well, if you called hoping to talk to her, you should have known better."

"Actually, I called hoping to talk to you."

Roberta didn't say anything for a moment, and when she did finally speak, she sounded slightly hesitant. "Oh? About what?"

Kyle tried to fathom the subtle change in her tone. Did she think Leah was his only interest, his only reason for dialing the Frankel home phone number? He supposed that such a suspicion on her part wasn't outlandish. Leah *was* a major aspect of the bond between him and Roberta.

As it was, he had called Roberta to discuss Leah, however tangentially. "It's this weekend," he said. "I've got to work on Saturday. My plant is running behind on a project, and we've got to put in some extra hours to catch up."

"Oh." After another pause, she continued. "No problem. We can always get together some other weekend, Kyle."

Clearly she'd misunderstood him and assumed that he wanted to cancel their dinner plan. Before he set her straight, he allowed himself a moment to savor the obvious sadness that rimmed her voice. Whether or not Roberta was as nervous as Kyle was about their spending an evening alone together, she wasn't doing much to hide her disappointment at his breaking their date. She wanted to see him. Realizing that only made him want to see her even more.

"I'm free in the evening," he corrected her. "I was hoping you and I would still be on for dinner. The only change in plans is that I won't be able to spend the afternoon with Leah. Maybe I could take her down to the beach on Sunday, though."

"Okay," Roberta said brightly. "Mary had mentioned something about a craft fair on the Madison town green Saturday afternoon. Maybe she and I can take Leah to that to keep her mind off the heartbreak of not spending the day with you."

Roberta's flippant tone didn't conceal the compliment imbedded in her statement. Kyle wanted Leah to like him as much as he wanted Roberta to like him. In different ways, of course. "She'll enjoy the fair," he predicted, modestly ignoring Roberta's flattering remark. "They're supposed to have clowns there to entertain the kids. Leah'll probably prefer professional clowns to an amateur like me."

Roberta laughed. "When it comes to clowns, Leah doesn't discriminate. After all, she's put up with me all these years."

Kyle joined Roberta's laughter. "Well, all right, then. I'll pick you up at Mary's around seven Saturday night for dinner. And we'll save Sunday for Leah."

"Fine," Roberta confirmed. "Are you sure you want to keep the plan for Saturday night?" she suddenly asked. "Maybe you'll be too tired after an extra day of work."

"Saturday is going to be very pleasant work for me," Kyle reassured her, not bothering to add that the work he'd be doing on that extra day would be far less tiring to him than the work he did every weekday. "I won't be too tired."

"If you're sure—"

"I'm sure," he said with conviction. "I guess I should get off the phone and let you finish the five hundred things you're in the middle of. I'll see you Saturday night, Roberta."

"All right. Goodbye, Kyle."

"Good night," he murmured before hanging up.

ROBERTA STARED at the telephone for a several minutes, an uncertain smile teasing her lips. When, on Sunday afternoon, he'd suggested an adults-only evening for the two of them, she hadn't been sure whether he was talking about a date or just a friendly dinner. She still wasn't sure.

But she knew now that Kyle wanted more than simply to see Leah. Even if they wound up devoting the entire evening to discussing Leah, it was still Roberta he wanted to spend that evening with. She wondered whether it was even possible for Kyle to relate to her except through Leah. Saturday night she'd find out. Maybe.

But she didn't have time to think about that now. She'd been exaggerating only slightly when she'd told him she was in the middle of five hundred things. Every evening after putting Leah to bed, Roberta faced numerous chores. Not only did she have to take care of the usual tasks of running a household, tasks she was unable to attend to during the day while she was at the advertising agency, but she also had to repair the damage Leah and Natalie inevitably inflicted on the apartment during the course of eight hours. Natalie was a fine baby-sitter, active and energetic, happy to take Leah to a museum, the park or the zoo. But she was a slob. Roberta always returned home from her office to find the loft a mess. Leah's toys would be scattered throughout the living room, the kitchen sink would be filled with dirty dishes, the dining table would be blanketed in crumbs.

Roberta couldn't complain; she knew how difficult it was to find adequate day care in the city, especially a day-care worker who was willing to work at the minimum wage and on a temporary basis. But still, the last thing Roberta wanted at the end of a tiring day at her job was to have to wash dishes and wipe the counters clean of smeared peanut butter and dribbled milk.

Besides having to clean up the wreckage Leah and Natalie left about the apartment, Roberta was still dealing with the minor alterations the loft required to become a comfortable home for her once again. Her tenants during the years she and Leah had lived in California were careful people, but the walls had nevertheless required fresh paint and the carpets a professional shampooing before Roberta and Leah moved back in, and Roberta herself took care of washing the insides of the windows, purchasing curtains, hanging pictures and arranging the contents of the kitchen cabinets to her convenience. Because she was working a forty-hour week at the agency, she had to see to the various details of settling into a new residence at night, after Leah was tucked into bed and no longer underfoot.

Roberta also found herself bringing work home from the office on occasion. She was infinitely grateful to her boss for making allowances for her. He'd been an old friend of Lee's, and Roberta knew that that connection had been at least as important in winning her the job as her talent had been. After all, the city was full of talented graphic artists. But Stan had taken pity on the widow of his old friend and selected her for the opening in his art department.

She honestly didn't care that she'd been hired out of sympathy. In the cutthroat world of advertising, one accepted whatever position one could get and didn't ask questions. Roberta knew she'd do an excellent job for Stan. Whatever his reasons for hiring her, she was determined that he wouldn't be disappointed in his decision to give her the chance she needed.

All of which meant that every now and then she lugged her oversize portfolio home with her, spread the contents out at her worktable in the loft's study, and toiled late into the night on letterings and layouts for the newspaper ads with which she'd been entrusted. Stan understood that, with a five-year-old daughter at home, Roberta had to leave the office by a certain time, no matter what. Even after the school term began and Leah would no longer be at home with a baby-sitter, Roberta wouldn't be able to remain at the agency for late meetings. Eventually this might cost her opportunities for advancement, Stan warned. But for the time being, as long as she was able to get her assignments done, he was willing to be flexible about where she did them.

Although having to work at home on her own time was exhausting, Roberta had no grounds for complaint. She'd never expected that moving back to New York and taking on the responsibilities of full-time work would be easy. The struggle was definitely worth it. She couldn't remain dependent on her parents forever. And San Diego had stopped being home to her the day she'd met Lee. Returning east had been returning home as far as Roberta was concerned, and whatever difficulties she faced in surmounting her many duties as a single working mother were more than compensated for in the delight she took in her independence.

Among the five hundred things she'd been in the middle of doing when Kyle had called her was proofreading the layouts she'd finished at her office earlier that day. A minor job, it wouldn't take more than an hour. As she carried her portfolio into the study, she found herself wondering about whether Kyle frequently had to work on weekends.

She assumed not; he hadn't anticipated having to spend the upcoming Saturday at his plant, so such weekend work probably wasn't a regular occurrence.

Even so, she considered the possibility that he was working too hard. If he was too busy to buy a cheap rowboat and paddle around the harbor every once in a while, then he was too busy.

Maybe she'd been unbearably pushy on the subject when she'd been with him. Maybe she ought to stop thinking about it, stop worrying about him, let him cope with the demands of his life in his own way. Who was she to be giving him advice? Who was she to be worrying so much about his well-being?

She was a friend, that was who. She was his good friend.

Kyle had been her good friend the day Leah was born. When the medics had asked who he was, he'd said, unflinchingly, "A good friend."

She would be a good friend to him, too. It had nothing to do with her attraction to him or her confusion about whether anything would blossom from that attraction. If nothing ever did, so be it. She was still entitled to worry about him, to urge him to take better care of his psyche, to find a way to keep his eyes eternally filled with warm good humor and gentle affection. That was what good friends were supposed to do, and she would gladly do as much for him.

Chapter Six

On Friday Roberta sat up late into the night reading Kyle's letters.

She ought to have been asleep, or at least in bed trying to rest. If every day was tiring for her, Fridays were especially so, given that they arrived at the end of a long week of work. The following morning she would be taking the train to Madison with Leah—another tiring day, although she knew the change of scenery and the fresh sea air would restore her strength.

She needed a good night's rest. But, instead, she found herself staying awake, reading.

She'd wanted to reread Kyle's letters ever since she and Leah had returned from their visit to Madison the previous weekend. Every evening when she arrived home from the agency, she'd promised herself to read at least a couple of the letters. But by the time she'd cleaned up the loft and prepared dinner, played with Leah for a while, tucked her into bed and then tackled whatever work she'd brought with her from the office, Roberta had been too fatigued to do anything more strenuous than doze in front of the television.

Friday night, however, she hadn't had any extra office work to finish at home. Settling herself comfortably on the living room couch, she untied the string that held his letters in a neat stack. She had saved every letter from him, as well as the birthday cards he'd sent Leah, figuring that someday Leah might want to read them herself and learn something about the man who'd brought her into the world. It had never occurred to Roberta when she was saving the letters that she might someday wind up back on the East Coast, seeing Kyle for two weekends running.

She read his first brief letter, in which he'd described his move to Boston and his apprenticeship with a furniture designer. She almost didn't have to read it; she remembered it nearly to the word. Setting it aside, she reached for his next mailing—his first birthday card to Leah—and then his next letter to Roberta.

Each letter, she realized, was slightly longer than the preceding one, slightly more descriptive and detailed. Roberta hadn't noticed that before. But then she wouldn't have, since she'd received each letter months after the previous one.

Kicking her feet up onto the coffee table in front of the puffy Haitian-cotton couch, she smoothed the creased pages out across her lap and perused them carefully. In one long letter, Kyle wrote about the special pleasure he derived from working with wood. "It resists, but you can master it. You can cut it, warp it, shape it. Then you sand it until it's as smooth as glass, and you stain it and unlock all its secrets. The grain is kind of like a map of the wood's life. Once you stain it, all the whorls and knots and flaws become visible, and by the time the stain dries you know that wood. It's yours."

In another, longer letter, he wrote about his decision to move back to Madison. "I've reached a point in my life where I need to be on my own," he'd written. "I need to be my own person, not an underling, not a sidekick, but me, answering to myself, accepting full responsibility for what I do. It might have been easier just to stay where I am. I get along well with Peter—'' that, Roberta had learned from an earlier letter, was the name of the artisan with whom Kyle had apprenticed, and who later made Kyle a partner in his business ''—but getting along isn't enough anymore. I need new challenges, new responsibilities.''

Roberta smiled in amazement. She'd forgotten many of the letters, or at least the philosophical and personal digressions they'd contained. What she had remembered was that Kyle wrote a great deal about his work, and that he devoted large portions of each letter to Leah, expressing his delight at her latest accomplishments and remarking that, judging by the photographs Roberta sent him, the little girl was definitely a heartbreaker in the making. Roberta's memory of his correspondence hadn't been mistaken, but it hadn't been quite accurate, either.

Why had she remembered the letters Kyle wrote to her as being detached and impersonal? Probably because when Kyle did get philosophical, he usually wrote about his work, not about himself. Yet his work was obviously a very important part of his life. Maybe his poetic imaginings about staining wood offered glimpses of his soul that Roberta had never before paid attention to.

By the time she'd reread all the letters, it was after one. She trudged to her bedroom, one of the five large rooms into which she and Lee had divided the loft with floor-to-ceiling partitions. She undressed and dropped wearily onto the bed. Sleep came quickly to her, refusing her the opportunity to dwell on the letters, or on the man with whom she'd be having dinner the following night.

LEAH WAS IN AN EBULLIENT MOOD Saturday morning as they boarded the train to New Haven. Riding a train was a rare treat for her. In San Diego, she'd never ridden trains, and the only trains in Manhattan were the subways, which were dark and spooky and noisy. But the train to Connecticut traveled above ground, its windows filled with sunshine and suburban scenery. And if she got restless, she could walk up and down the aisles, something she couldn't do in an automobile.

After pacing the length of their car twice, Leah climbed over Roberta's knees to the window seat and folded her legs beneath her on the vinyl upholstery. "Do you think Kyle will like me as much this time as he did last time?" she asked her mother.

"I'm sure he will," Roberta replied.

"Even if he has to work today? You're always a grouch after work. You're just like the guy on *Sesame Street*, Oscar the Grouch."

"I'm not that bad," Roberta defended herself, then laughed. "If you and Natalie would do a better job of cleaning up after yourselves before I got home, I'd be much less of a grouch."

Leah stared out the window for a while, deep in thought. Then she turned back to Roberta. "I guess Kyle doesn't have to clean up after anyone when he gets home. Maybe he should get a dog, Mommy," Leah mused. "I bet he's lonely, living all by himself."

As she so often did, Leah astonished Roberta with her sensitivity to those around her. Roberta had no idea whether or not Kyle was lonely, although now that Leah had planted the idea in her mind, it didn't seem at all farfetched. In fact, it seemed quite possible. A good-looking single man in a rural town, rattling around in an oversize house set far apart from his nearest neighbors... Of course he might be lonely. Perhaps his loneliness was what caused him to take such an interest in the Frankels.

It amazed Roberta that Leah would have recognized Kyle's loneliness before she herself had. Her daughter was uncommonly perceptive sometimes.

Mary was waiting at the New Haven station for them, and the drive east to Madison was filled with lively conversation. The previous night Mary had hosted an intimate dinner for Alvin Hemple, the stockbroker who'd retired to Madison and taken a fancy to her. She entertained Leah by enumerating all the gourmet leftovers they'd be eating for supper that evening. "Have you ever tasted caviar?" she asked Leah. "I've got a little caviar left, and we can spread it on crackers and pretend we're rich."

"You *are* rich," Leah pointed out. "You don't have to pretend."

"I'm not that rich," Mary protested with a laugh. "People don't get rich writing hot novels about runaway teddy bears and the adventures of little prickly porcupines. However, I am rich enough to splurge on caviar every once in a while. Plus I've got some leftover pâté."

"What's that?" Leah asked.

"It's like chopped liver," Roberta informed her.

The little girl made a gagging noise and screwed her face into a grimace. "Yuck! I hate liver, Aunt Mary! Yuck!"

After a lunch of peanut-butter-and-jelly sandwiches—a meal about which Leah felt much differently than she did about liver—they left Mary's house and headed for the sprawling green at the heart of downtown Madison. Craftspeople and vendors had set up colorful booths all along the perimeter of the green, and swarms of visitors milled about the lawn, browsing, shopping and conversing with friends and neighbors. Within five seconds, Leah decided that if she didn't get one of the heart-shaped silver-foil balloons a young man dressed up as a circus clown was selling at one end of the green, she might just die. Mary, ever the honorary "aunt," promptly bought her one.

Roberta strolled from one booth to the next, examining the wares being offered for sale. Several booths featured wood sculptures, but Roberta saw nothing that came close to the excellent craftsmanship of the cherry-wood giraffe Kyle had carved for Leah several years ago. She recalled his letter about learning the secrets of wood and his remark the previous weekend that he didn't have much opportunity to build furniture anymore since he was deluged with paperwork.

His letters may have hinted at his inner concerns, but Kyle was still an enigma to her. Roberta knew intuitively that he had lost something in the past few years. He'd lost the time to go rowboating, to fuss with his empty lobster trap, to build things of wood. But why? Why had he let these things be lost from his life? The answer to that question was what was missing from his letters. The answer would explain the coldness that sometimes altered his eyes. Until she knew the answer, she'd continue to feel as though she didn't know him very well.

They returned to Mary's house an hour before Kyle was due to pick Roberta up. Mary kept Leah occupied with a storybook while Roberta showered and dressed. She had just fastened the waist button of the cream-colored wraparound dress she'd brought with her when Leah barged into the bedroom to critique her appearance. "You look nice," she decided.

"Thank you," Roberta said, moving to the mirror and putting on a pair of simple gold earrings.

Mary appeared at the doorway. "Now that's what I call an efficient dress," she observed as Roberta turned to greet her.

"Efficient?"

"One button and it's off," Mary teased.

Roberta blushed and shot a quick, meaningful glance at Leah, who, fortunately, was busy staggering around in her mother's high-heeled sandals and hadn't heard Mary's remark. "This dress," Roberta asserted dryly, "is very plain and unsuggestive. I've even worn it to work."

"Oh, come now," Mary clucked. "Here you are, going out on your first date in how many years—"

"I went out on dates in California," Roberta disputed her.

Leah kicked off the sandals and bounced on the bed. "This isn't a date," she claimed with all the pompous certainty of Emily Post. "Mommy knows Kyle. He's a friend. You don't date friends, so it can't be a date."

Roberta chuckled, but Mary seemed indignant. "If you don't date friends, who *do* you date?" she challenged Leah.

Leah faltered. She hadn't thought things through that far, evidently. "I don't know," she finally admitted. "Strangers, I guess."

"See?" Roberta eyed Mary and laughed. "Leah's figured this whole thing out a lot better than you and I." She assessed her reflection in the mirror above the dresser, then appropriated the cut-crystal atomizer she found at hand and sprayed its contents, a light cologne, behind her ears.

"If it isn't a date, how come you're dousing yourself with my perfume?" Mary asked.

Roberta was spared from answering by Leah, who leaped off the bed and shouted, "I just heard someone drive up! I bet it's Kyle!" She tore out of the room.

Roberta frowned reproachfully at Mary. "Please don't say things like that in front of Leah."

"Leah," Mary returned, "obviously knows more about dating than you and I combined. I'm sure there's nothing I can say that could possibly shock her."

"Yes, but . . . well, just don't make such a big deal out of this date, or whatever it is. I mean, it's not really a date; she was right about that. Kyle and I are just going to talk. That's what he said last weekend. He wants to get together and talk."

"What do *you* want?" Mary asked.

"Mommy!" Leah yelled from the parlor. "Kyle's here!"

Once again spared by Leah from having to answer Mary's nosy questions, Roberta cast her friend an impassive smile, grabbed her purse and swept past her and out of the bedroom. She honestly didn't know what she wanted with Kyle—except that she *did* want to talk to him. She wanted to find out why he'd stopped boating and carving and creating. She wanted to find out why his eyes sometimes became icy, why his smile became bitter, and why, at other times, his eyes were heart-meltingly warm and his smile sweet and tender. She wanted to find out whether she was ready to act on her attraction to a man, or whether the man in question was ready for her to act on it. Whether they were friends or something more, or something less.

He was examining Leah's silver balloon when Roberta arrived in the parlor. Dressed in an impeccable slate-gray suit and a conservatively striped necktie, he looked as unlike a beach bum as Roberta could imagine. He straightened up at her entrance, gave her a quick but comprehensive perusal, and smiled slightly. "Hi," he said.

Roberta took his less-than-romantic greeting as a harbinger for the date, and reconciled herself—with a touch of relief—to an evening of friendly talk. She wasn't sure if she was up to genuine dating yet. At least not with Kyle. "Hi," she responded, doing her best to match his casual tone. As she moved toward the door, she issued final baby-sitting instructions to Mary. "Remember, Leah isn't going to stay up half the night running you ragged," she lectured. "She's to be in bed by eight."

"I'm sleeping on the couch, not in bed," Leah contradicted her mother.

"Wherever you're sleeping, the sleeping begins at eight o'clock," Roberta said firmly, then bent and kissed her daughter's forehead. "Be a good girl, okay? Don't take too much advantage of Aunt Mary."

"Ha!" Mary snorted, waving Roberta and Kyle out the door. "You think this little punk is going to take advantage of a Simon Legree like me?"

Roberta heard Leah questioning Mary about the identity of Simon Legree as she and Kyle stepped off the porch. Kyle apparently overheard Leah, too, because he glanced down at Roberta and laughed. His failure to take Roberta's hand or arm as they strolled down the walk to the driveway reinforced her impression of how their dinner would proceed. Roberta could already predict that it would end with one of his affectionate kisses on her cheek, period.

Which was undoubtedly as it should be, she decided. If and when she was going to embark on a romance, Kyle Stratton probably wasn't the man to have it with. Intellectually, Roberta knew that. That she happened to find him hypnotically handsome—particularly now, in his well-tailored suit, with his cheeks newly shaved and his skin exuding a fresh, faintly minty aroma—was unfortunate, but not tragic. She wanted Kyle as a friend, for both Leah and herself, and she wouldn't risk that friendship just because he was exceptionally good-looking.

The car he led her to was a new red Saab. She should have assumed that he wouldn't be taking her out to dinner in his pickup, but she was still surprised to see the glistening car waiting for them. Kyle courteously opened the passenger door for her and helped her into the seat, then moved around to the driver's side and climbed in behind the wheel. He said nothing as he backed out of the driveway and steered away from the beach.

His silence disconcerted Roberta. She glanced at him and found him facing forward, his eyes on the road, his lips flexing as if he were considering the option of speaking. He said nothing.

Her gaze dropped to his hands, which gripped the padded steering wheel more tightly than necessary. It dawned on her that Kyle might be as uneasy and confused about this date as she was. That realization, paradoxically, relaxed her. "Nervous?" she asked, hoping to relax him as well.

He shot her a quick glimpse, then turned his attention back to the road. The corners of his mouth twitched upward. "Maybe a little."

"Good," she said, laughing. "So am I."

He eyed her again, his smile broadening. "Why?"

"Because..." She decided she might as well be honest with him. "Because we've got a pretty weird history, Kyle, and I just don't know what to expect from tonight. Not that I'm the sort of person who has to know going in exactly what's supposed to happen, but in this case—I mean, I don't know whether this is a *date* or just a dinner, or maybe a dinner date." She laughed again, feeling her anxiety dissipate as she gave voice to it. "How about you, Kyle? Why are you nervous?"

He mulled over what she'd said. "Do you always say exactly what you're thinking?" he asked.

She cringed as she considered her verbose answer to his question, then sighed. "Most of the time," she allowed. "It comes from living with Leah, I think. Kids can usually sniff out a lie a mile away. So as a rule I speak my mind, and so does Leah." She tossed him a suspicious look. "Do you always evade questions?"

"I don't evade questions," he objected.

"Then answer mine."

"Why am I nervous?" he repeated thoughtfully. While he considered his answer, he steered onto the paved parking lot of a dockside seafood restaurant. He located a parking place, stopped the car and turned off the engine. Then he twisted in his seat to face Roberta. "I'm nervous," he said slowly, "because you're an extraordinarily beautiful woman."

That wasn't the answer Roberta was expecting, and she took a moment to recover. "Why does that make you nervous?" she asked, then laughed bashfully. "That's not to say I agree with your assessment of me, Kyle. But if we assume, for the sake of argument, that I *am* extraordinarily..." She laughed again and shook her head, unable to apply such a lavish compliment to herself. "Why should the way I look make you nervous?"

His cool gray eyes ran over her face, momentarily pausing at her gently pursed lips, her arched cheekbones, her high brow crowned with lush dark curls. Then his eyes met hers, and his smile became tentative. "I don't know," he admitted. "I've known beautiful women before, but..." He seemed to be having great difficulty expressing himself. Finally he shrugged. "Maybe you expressed it best when you said we've got a pretty weird history, Roberta. You're not just a woman I'm taking to dinner. And looking the way you look right now, I almost wish that you were."

His statement puzzled Roberta, but before she could probe further, he was out of the car, locking his door and then strolling around to her side to help her out. As soon as she was on her feet, he released her hand. They walked side by side to the restaurant, but he made no further move to touch her. His having explained his nervousness clearly hadn't relaxed him the way her explanation had relaxed her.

Kyle provided the maître d' with his name, and after checking his reservation list, the host led them to a cozy table against the far wall, which contained a row of wide picture windows overlooking the water. A waiter appeared and asked if they wanted drinks. Kyle glanced questioningly at Roberta. "I'll have a glass of wine," she said.

He lifted the wine list. "Let's order a bottle," he suggested, skimming its offerings. "How about a Mosel?" The waiter nodded and left the table.

"What's Mosel like?" Roberta asked Kyle.

He stared curiously at her. "It's a dry white wine. I gave you Mosel at my house last week." Roberta nodded; she'd liked that wine. "You're not much of a drinker, are you?" he asked.

"As a matter of fact, I'm not," she admitted. "I stopped drinking completely as soon as I became pregnant. Before that, actually, when I started *trying* to become pregnant. Just in case. Alcohol is supposed to be bad for the fetus, and I didn't want to take any chances. And then after Leah was born, I was usually too tired to be interested in a drink. Liquor makes me sleepy, and when you've got a little kid, the last thing you need is something that makes you sleepy."

Kyle seemed to absorb her every word. She didn't think that what she'd said was all that intriguing. Then she recalled Kyle's fascination with everything she'd told him about Leah last week. He'd hung on her words then, too. Hearing that a mother could learn when her child was mature enough to handle the rejection of a well-intended bouquet of weeds had been a nearly earthshaking revelation to Kyle. Once again, she was forced to recognize that he didn't know much about what it meant to be a parent.

By the time the waiter brought their wine, they'd had a chance to read the menu and decide on dinners. Roberta requested broiled scallops and Kyle a salmon steak. "Are you sure you don't want lobster?'' he asked her, smiling playfully.

"When you get yourself a lobster trap and catch one for me, I'll eat it,'' she promised, handing over her menu. "You really ought to get a trap, Kyle.''

He accepted her advice with a brisk nod. "I really ought to," he agreed, then lifted his crystal goblet in a toast. Roberta clinked her glass to his, planning a toast to Kyle's future as an amateur lobsterman. But before she could verbalize such a toast, he had already sipped and lowered his glass. Reluctantly she sipped her wine as well.

Setting her glass down on the linen-covered table, she again prepared to embark on an inquiry about Kyle's abandonment of his boating and lobstering. But Kyle changed the subject before she could start grilling him. "Tell me about your new job," he urged her. "How is it going so far?''

"It keeps me busy," she answered. "I can't complain. Right now I'm assisting on a couple of projects, but once I've been there for a few more months, I'll start getting my own ad campaigns to design. Small stuff at first, of course, newspaper layouts and the like. But you've got to start somewhere.''

"You were lucky to land a job like that," Kyle commented. "I'll bet the competition for jobs in advertising is deadly, especially for an artist.''

Roberta grinned. "It took more than luck," she confessed. "The man who hired me was an old friend of my husband's.''

Kyle's eyes flashed in surprise. Then they grew soft and hazy again. "Your husband," he echoed uncertainly.

Roberta remembered that he still didn't know anything about Lee. "My *late* husband," she clarified herself. The circumspect way Kyle gazed at her made her wonder whether he had mistaken her comment to mean she was currently married. "Leah's father."

"He died before she was born," Kyle recalled. He studied his wine, as if unsure of his right to question Roberta about Leah's father.

"Go ahead, ask," Roberta invited him.

"How long were you married?"

"About a year and a half."

"I'm sorry," he murmured.

Roberta gave him a bittersweet smile. "Thank you, but there's no need to be. It's been five and a half years now, and I'm doing fine."

"Yes, you are," Kyle observed, leaning back in his chair and appraising her contemplatively. "Maybe I was saying I'm sorry for thinking you weren't...that you were never—"

"I know," Roberta rescued him, then grinned reassuringly. "I realized you must have assumed I was an unwed mother the day Leah was born, but I just didn't have the energy to explain the situation to you. And I didn't want you pitying me. If I'd told you about Lee and you'd gotten weepy and mournful, then *I* would have gotten weepy and mournful, too, and then where would we have been? I needed to be thinking positively to get through the birth."

Apparently that made sense to him. The waiter brought their salads, and Kyle toyed with his for a moment before pointing out, "You could have explained in a letter, though."

"What should I have written? 'Dear Kyle, By the way, even though you never asked, Leah isn't illegitimate.' Wouldn't that have been a little silly?" She tasted a forkful of the salad, swallowed, and added, "Frankly, you didn't seem like the type who'd pass judgment on me one way or the other."

"I'm not," he concurred, then stopped himself. "But I did pass judgment on you," he muttered contritely.

Roberta looked up from her salad, surprised. "Did you?"

"Last week," he said. "When Leah started talking about her father, I wondered, what if you had invented a story, what if you had created a fantasy father for Leah and lied to her? I knew I had no right to condemn you if that's what you had done, but . . . but you *do* seem so honest with Leah that I couldn't accept the thought of your lying to her about something like that. It was wrong of me," he added apologetically. "I'm in no position to judge you, Roberta. Anyway, I should have realized that Leah is too intelligent a child to swallow a lie like that."

"You got it," Roberta confirmed. "I can't pull anything over on her."

He smiled briefly. "You said his name was Lee?"

"Yes. Leah was named after him. That's a Jewish tradition—you honor the dead by naming your children after them. Lee was Jewish, so I decided to name our child after him. I'm not sure whether a girl can be named after a man, but I don't think Lee would mind. He should have explained it to me a little better before he passed away."

"I'm sure he'd be very honored," Kyle declared, then scowled slightly as he digested what Roberta had said. "If children are supposed to be named after the dead, wouldn't it have been kind of morbid for your husband to be explaining about whether you could name his own daughter after him?"

Roberta set down her fork and contemplated the man across the table from her. She felt remarkably comfortable with Kyle right now, and she sensed that his nervousness had also vanished. They were indeed talking, talking about things they'd never mentioned in their letters, things that were important. She felt close to Kyle; she felt that he was the intimate, special friend she'd always thought him to be. So it seemed right for her to share with him the circumstances surrounding her short marriage to Lee and their decision to have a child.

He listened, engrossed, as she described Lee, the scruffy artist in the loft who was, in fact, successful and sought-after, talented and reputable. She described her parents' chagrin, and her mother-in-law's, when she and Lee got married, and their horror at her decision to become pregnant despite Lee's bleak medical prognosis. She described to Kyle the shaky, frightening months she'd endured after Lee's death, and her determination to raise her daughter with all the love she'd once felt for her husband, and with all the love she knew Lee would have felt for his daughter.

"You can see why I was so panicked when I went into labor six weeks early," she concluded. "If something had gone wrong and I'd lost my baby so soon after losing Lee, I don't think I could have survived it."

Kyle smiled tenderly, his admiration for Roberta evident in his luminous eyes. "As I recall, you weren't panicked in the least," he remarked. "You were rational, completely in control. I was the panic-stricken one."

"You?" Roberta scoffed. "No, Kyle, *you* were the rational one. You were the one who insisted it wasn't false labor, and told me to call my doctor, and refused to leave me alone. If it hadn't been for you, I would have fallen apart."

"I guess we were both panic-stricken," he said with a laugh. "And each of us was doing a damned good job of hiding our panic from the other." The waiter arrived with their entrées, and Kyle waited until he was gone before asking, "Why did you move to California to be with your parents? Given their attitude toward your marriage, and your pregnancy—"

"It was a difficult decision," Roberta acknowledged. "But I was honest enough to recognize that I needed some help, and I wasn't so proud that I'd turn it down when it was offered. And then a funny thing happened—my parents saw Leah. Suddenly they decided that Lee couldn't have been so bad, and our decision to have a child was obviously a brilliant one. Leah worked her magic on them, and they fell in love with her and saw everything from a new perspective."

"Leah can do that to people," Kyle murmured cryptically. He cut a piece of his salmon steak and consumed it. "This is delicious. How's yours?"

Roberta tasted a fresh, butter-drenched scallop and nodded her approval. "Very good," she said, though her thoughts remained on Kyle's enigmatic remark. "What magic did Leah work on you?" she asked. "I've been going on and on about my life. Now it's your turn to reveal your deep, dark secrets."

"Deep, dark secrets?" He laughed and shook his head. After eating a bit more of his dinner, he put down his fork and reached for his wine. He took a long, fortifying sip, refilled his glass and Roberta's, and sighed. "The magic Leah worked on me," he finally answered, "is that—" he considered his words carefully "—seeing her born, helping her to be born, was the most important thing I've ever done in my life. I'd never thought about it before that day, Roba, but once Leah was born, once I'd held her in my hands and felt her little heart beating against my fingers..."

He sighed again and took another sip of wine. His gaze grew distant, as if he were reliving the moment of Leah's birth, experiencing all over again the emotions he'd experienced then.

After a long while he continued. "I realized that nothing I'd ever done before could match that in importance. I was a pretty happy-go-lucky guy in those days, Roberta, having a good time, a kid with a useless degree in philosophy and a pair of good hands, rebuilding old furniture and hanging out on the beach.'' He hesitated, his eyes focusing once more on his memory. ''And then, one foggy afternoon I found myself with more responsibility than I'd ever had before, and I—I loved it. I wanted that responsibility. I'd never felt so necessary in my life.'' He raised his glass to drink, then caught Roberta's bemused expression and paused. ''Does that make any sense?''

''Yes,'' Roberta assured him. To her, of course, the arrival of Leah had brought an immense responsibility. But she could see how Kyle might have also felt that responsibility. He'd been a substitute father during the birth. Why shouldn't he momentarily feel a sense of the significance of fatherhood? ''So it was your desire for responsibility that drove you to Boston?'' she guessed.

''In a way,'' he granted. ''I wanted to learn more, expand my horizons, do something real with my life. I worked hard, I learned, I developed more confidence in my talent and more business savvy than I'd ever had before.''

''But you missed Madison,'' Roberta reminded him, lowering her silverware and studying him speculatively. He'd written her all of those things about his life, about his learning from Peter and gradually developing into Peter's equal, forging a partnership with him, and setting up his own workshop not far from the seaside Connecticut town he loved so much.

But although he'd written about those things in his letters, she had suspected that there was something he wasn't writing her. And now she suspected that there was something he wasn't telling her. She had told him everything about herself; she expected the same candor from him. '''Fess up, Kyle,'' she goaded him. ''It was more than just wanting responsibility that sent you to Boston.''

His eyes flickered, and his lips twitched into a reluctant smile. "Oh?" he mumbled noncommittally.

"Come on, Kyle. What was it? A woman?"

His eyes flickered again and he conceded with a laugh. "There was a woman, yes."

Roberta was temporarily stunned by her accurate guess. A woman in Boston? Why not? Kyle was a virile, healthy man. Surely Roberta wasn't the first woman who'd ever found him inordinately attractive. "Ellie," she murmured, the name suddenly materializing from her subconscious.

"Ellie?" He scowled. "Ellie who?"

"The day Leah was born," Roberta refreshed his memory, "you telephoned someone named Ellie and broke a date with her."

"Oh, God, yes," he remembered, rolling his eyes. "Ellie Cashman. We went out just a few times. There was nothing serious there." He chuckled as he reminisced. "She broke up with me the next time I saw her. She told me that anyone who'd prefer to watch something as disgusting as a baby being born instead of taking her out dancing didn't deserve her. I didn't argue the point." He finished his meal, then leaned back in his chair and scrutinized Roberta, his gaze gentle, appreciating her astuteness.

"So?" she prodded him. "What about this woman in Boston?"

His smile faded slightly, and he emptied his wineglass. "We met a couple of months after Leah was born. She lived in Boston, but she was visiting some friends in Madison and we met at a party. She was very bright, nice-looking, interesting. Her name was Ursula. She was a social worker."

"And you fell in love," Roberta supplied for him. She didn't speak jealously, or even mockingly. She was thrilled to think that at long last she was going to get to learn more about her special friend with his many mysteries.

He weighed her supposition, but didn't confirm or deny it. "I felt strongly about her," he admitted. "When she asked me to move in with her, I did. We even discussed marriage a couple of times."

"Kyle," Roberta reproached him amiably. "This was a serious relationship. Why didn't you write to me about it?"

He shrugged. "You never wrote to me about your social life."

"I didn't have one to write about," she pointed out with a laugh. "But I wrote to you about everything important: Leah, my schooling, my free-lance jobs. The most important things in my life. How could you not write to me about the most important things in your life?"

"I did," he defended himself quietly.

"All you ever wrote about was your work, and how much you missed Connecticut," Roberta asserted.

He meditated for a minute, then smiled wryly. "Maybe Ursula wasn't as important as those things." He lapsed into a reflective silence, his eyes drifting past Roberta to the water view beyond the window. "I wanted her to be important. I wanted...I wanted to have a baby with her, Roberta. But every time I broached the subject, she said she wasn't ready to become a mother yet. She was too young, she claimed, or her career was too important, or she had too many other things going on in her life at the moment. Maybe in a year, maybe in a couple of years..."

He exhaled. Slowly his gaze returned to Roberta and settled on her. "So I worked, instead. I devoted myself to work, learning the business, building it up, earning money, taking responsibility for whatever I could take responsibility for. When Peter began to talk about retiring and selling me his share of the business, I decided to move back to Madison, leaving the Boston operation going, but setting up a branch here. We already owned a plant down in North

Carolina, which is a big furniture-making region, so I knew I could handle the long-distance management. So I left Boston and came home."

"What about Ursula?" Roberta asked.

Kyle's gaze moved to the water again. "We'd already broken up by then."

"Because she wouldn't have a baby?"

He turned back to Roberta, his eyes sharper and more focused than before. "Because of you," he said.

"Me?" Flabbergasted, Roberta gaped at him. He nodded for emphasis. She suddenly felt slightly queasy. She'd never knowingly come between a man and a woman before. She didn't understand how she could have broken apart a relationship between a man she scarcely knew and a woman she'd never even heard of. "I—I don't see how that's possible," she managed, laughing weakly. "I was living three thousand miles away, Kyle. All we did was write letters."

"That's right," he agreed, then paused to remember. "One evening, Ursula found a letter I was writing to you. I'd just finished it, and then I got a telephone call, and when I came back to my desk, Ursula was standing there, clutching the letter and fuming."

Roberta shook her head in disbelief. "Fuming? Whatever for? You never wrote anything to me that would have made her fume."

Kyle angled his head slightly, then rubbed his index finger along his jaw. "Oh, yes, I did," he insisted. At Roberta's puzzled frown, he said, "It was a letter about the joy I felt when I worked with wood. Do you remember that letter?"

Roberta nodded. All of Kyle's letters were fresh in her mind, since she'd reread them just the previous night. But

that letter in particular stood out for its heartfelt sentiments and its poetry. "It was a beautiful letter," she said.

"I'd never expressed my feelings that way to Ursula," he
explained. "I tried to once or twice, but she didn't seem all
that interested in my work, so I stopped trying. Instead, I'd
write my feelings down on paper and send them to you." He
took a long breath, then let it out slowly, steadily. "When
Ursula read that letter, she felt betrayed. I was telling another woman things I'd never told her."

"But—but didn't you explain to her who I was?"

"It didn't matter what I told her," he insisted. "She
understood the truth—which was that I wrote to another
woman about things I didn't discuss with her. The circumstances of how you and I met—Roberta, that was irrelevant. All that mattered was that I could confide in you, and
I couldn't confide in Ursula. She recognized that. So..." He
shrugged in conclusion.

Roberta dared to lift her eyes to Kyle's. He seemed not at
all heartbroken, or even disappointed. Perhaps a touch
wistful. His gaze remained on her, trying to make sense of
the tangled emotions that caused her dark eyes to glimmer
and her cheeks to grow pink.

"What's on your mind?" he asked her.

She ran the tip of her tongue over her lips, hoping that
that would allow the words to come more easily. "I don't
like feeling like the Other Woman," she muttered.

He laughed gently. "You aren't the Other Woman, Roberta, so don't feel like one," he told her. "What happened
between Ursula and me was between her and me alone.
Things were already falling apart when she read my letter.
The fact that she would read the letter while I was out of the
room proves that there wasn't enough trust between us. So,
for heaven's sake, don't feel guilty."

Roberta folded her hands primly before her on the table as the waiter cleared their dishes. She didn't quite feel guilty, but... She didn't know what she felt. Kyle had never breathed a hint in his letters that he'd been living with a woman, that he'd wanted a child, that he'd been contemplating marriage. To learn all these things now overwhelmed her.

And yet...what had he said? He'd written what was most important to him, things he'd been unable to discuss with his lover. Roberta tried to recall some of the things she'd written to him—long-winded descriptions of the length of Leah's eyelashes, of the way Leah sometimes smiled in her sleep, of Leah's habit of sneaking up behind Roberta and hugging her knees. She'd written to him about how Leah wouldn't go to bed at night unless the stuffed giraffe Kyle had sent her was sharing the pillow with her, and about how, by the time Leah was three or so, her favorite bedtime story was the exciting story of her birth. "And a stranger borned me?" she'd squeal. "And he put me in a towel? And he thought I was beautiful?"

Roberta had written Kyle these things. She'd never told them to anyone else. She wouldn't have wanted to bore her neighbors and associates by describing Leah's every gesture, her every cute mispronunciation, her every bit of adorable mischief. But she'd written them to Kyle, maybe because he never seemed to mind learning such details about Leah, or maybe...maybe because Roberta could express feelings to Kyle that she couldn't express to anyone else.

The waiter returned to their table and asked if they wanted dessert. Roberta shook her head, and Kyle sent him away. Her gaze met Kyle's across the table, and she smiled meekly. "What are *you* thinking?" she volleyed back his question.

He studied her for several moments, his eyes unwaveringly on her. "I'm thinking," he whispered, "that I want to take you home with me tonight."

His statement didn't exactly astound her. She wasn't sure what lay behind it, though. He'd told her before they'd entered the restaurant that he found her beautiful and that that made him nervous. But he didn't seem at all nervous now. She wanted to think that his professed desire wasn't simply a matter of his finding her beautiful but, rather, was a natural outgrowth of their dinner conversation, their getting to know each other, their renewal of trust in each other.

She said nothing as Kyle settled the bill and helped her out of her chair. He touched her elbow lightly, guiding her among the tables to the door and out of the restaurant. The evening had grown foggy—not as foggy as the day they'd met, but the air was thick with a damp, fragrant mist.

Kyle led her to his car and turned her to him. He peered down at her upturned face, her eyes wide and dark, her lips slightly parted, her soft brown curls floating about her face as a cool breeze mussed them. He cupped his large hand over her cheek, then brushed her hair back from it. "Feel free to say no," he invited her.

It might be wiser to say no, Roberta mused. *It might be safer.* But she could no longer ignore her strong attraction to Kyle. And she couldn't deny that she trusted him.

She took a deep breath, slid her hand to his jaw and guided his mouth to hers.

Chapter Seven

His lips touched hers shyly, barely moving. Just a light whisper of a kiss, and then he pulled back.

Roberta averted her eyes. Maybe this was a bad idea. After their "weird history," it was probably ridiculous to think that they could become lovers, no matter how extensive and personal their correspondence, no matter what they'd talked about during dinner.

A cold disappointment settled over her, but she resolutely forced a smile. "Kind of like kissing your sister, huh?" she mumbled.

Kyle almost laughed out loud. Nothing could be further from the truth. He had held back when he'd kissed her only because, until the moment he'd felt her soft, full lips beneath his, he hadn't believed that this was really going to happen. He hadn't believed that Roberta, a woman unlike any other he'd ever known, unlike any he'd ever wanted before, could desire him as much as he desired her.

She did. He'd felt the truth of her desire the moment their mouths had come together. Roberta wanted him, too.

He slipped his thumb beneath her chin and lifted her face back to his. The slight roughness of his callused finger on the satiny skin beneath her jaw was unexpectedly arousing. So was the profound gentleness of his eyes as they absorbed her dejected expression. "Believe me, Roberta," he murmured, "it was nothing like kissing my sister."

His hand glided to her throat, then around to the nape of her neck as he drew her to him for another kiss. This time there was nothing hesitant in his actions, nothing restrained. His lips moved willfully against hers, and then his tongue, probing her teeth, demanded entry. His understated aggressiveness caused a dark thrill to ripple through her, and her mouth readily opened to him.

When his tongue found hers he groaned softly. His fingers furled in her hair, holding her head steady as his kiss deepened. His other hand wandered over the arch of her cheek to her ear, to her neck, then down along her dress's modest neckline, which shaped a V beneath her collarbone. His fingers brushed her warm skin and she sighed.

She'd been wrong to entertain even an instant of doubt, she realized as her arms coiled around Kyle's broad shoulders. He was no longer her savior, the knight in shining armor who had emerged from the mist to rescue her. She was no longer the all-knowing Earth Mother. Right now they were nothing but a man and a woman, two people who shared far more than just one intense afternoon five years ago. What they were sharing at this moment had but one thing in common with what they'd shared before, and that was that it blossomed from trust. Roberta trusted Kyle as much now as she had then.

Slowly, reluctantly, he ended the kiss. He drew back and viewed her flushed face as she tried to catch her breath. His eyes glowed, and his lips shaped a tenuous smile.

He wanted to tell her everything he hadn't already told her about himself. He wanted to tell her how much he admired her, how much he revered her, how much the mere sight of her excited him. But she probably already knew those things. He didn't have to write them down and mail them to her. And he wouldn't have been able to speak them even if he'd tried.

It didn't matter. She already knew.

He opened Roberta's door for her. Once she was in the car, he kissed her cheek. It wasn't like the kisses he'd given her before, those polite, vague kisses of the sort a gentleman gave to a lady. Even brushing his lips lightly against her cheek, he was a man kissing a woman. Roberta could tell the difference.

Moving around the car to the driver's side, he loosened his tie. Neither spoke during the drive to his house, but he covered her left hand with his right, letting go of it only when he had to shift gears and then hastily recapturing it again.

Feeling the leather-hard surface of his palm against her smooth knuckles, she thought about the letter he'd mentioned during dinner, the letter that had brought about the end of his relationship with his lover in Boston. Remembering his beautiful description of how he felt when he plied his craft, she tried to picture him carving a piece of wood, sanding it, staining it, making it his. She discerned in the sureness of his grip that his were hands that could master a woman's body as well as they mastered wood, that they could unlock a woman's secrets, bring out the whorls of her soul, make her his. She'd never before realized how erotic his letter had been.

He parked the car alongside his pickup in the double garage attached to his house. Then he ushered Roberta through the mudroom to the kitchen. He halted at the entry to the dining room to kiss her again.

Their lips came together, and then their tongues, no longer reveling in the new discovery of each other but, rather, meeting as old friends, intimate friends. Kyle's arms ringed Roberta's waist, and hers his neck. Her nostrils filled with his clean, minty scent, and her fingers explored the silky dark blond hair that curled in soft waves over his collar.

Breaking for air, Kyle leaned back against her hands and gazed down at her. Again she saw the passionate glow in his eyes and the almost tentative cast to his smile. "Nervous?" she asked him.

His hands slid to the sides of her waist, his fingers arching along her ribs. His smile expanded. "Maybe a little," he said, echoing the answer he'd given her when she'd asked him the same question earlier that evening. "How about you?"

She nodded meekly, her expression as wistful as his. "We could be risking a very special friendship, you know."

His smile faded, but his eyes remained riveted to hers. His hands rose up her sides to her shoulders, then down her arms to her wrists. He clasped her hands tightly, lifting them to his lips and kissing each in turn. "We could be making a very special friendship even more special," he pointed out.

Bolstered by his faith that their friendship would survive their lovemaking and perhaps even be enhanced by it, Roberta stilled her apprehension and let him lead her through the house to his bedroom, which stood at the end of a short hall beyond the living room. It was a large, airy room featuring a sliding glass door to a small, private deck off the side of the house. The wide platform bed boasted a highly polished oak base, which matched the sleek modern oak dressers and night tables. The corner near the door to the deck was occupied by a bizarre-looking chair composed of slats of leather-padded wood. "What is that?" Roberta asked as Kyle removed his jacket and tossed it onto the chair.

"It's a Stratton chair," he told her as she approached it. "In fact, that particular chair is the prototype. The Stratton chair is one of my big sellers. The slats move independently, so they adapt to the shape of your back, even if you move. But they offer more support than regular upholstery.'' He took her arm and tugged her away from the chair. ''If you sit in it, you'll never want to stand again.''

''It's that comfortable?'' she asked.

Kyle nodded in confirmation, his eyes sparkling with humor. ''And quite frankly, Roberta, the last place I want you right now is sitting in a chair.''

''Oh?'' She grinned. ''Exactly where do you want me?''

Her playful tone inspired him to grab her by her waist and heave her into the air. Ignoring her shrieks of protest, he marched with her to the side of the bed and then lowered her to her feet. ''Exactly here is where I want you,'' he declared.

''You could have just pointed out the spot,'' she reproached him, still laughing.

''I prefer holding you,'' he defended himself, his voice suddenly hushed. He skimmed his hands across the front of her dress, letting them come to rest at her waist. ''You're so...so thin, Roberta,'' he commented, running his thumbs along the narrow line of her waist.

''Do you think I'm too thin?'' she asked.

''No,'' he hastened to assure her. ''No, you have a lovely figure. It's just that...'' He shook his head and laughed quietly. ''The way you looked the last time I saw you—''

''The last time you saw me,'' Roberta reminded him, ''I was wearing a bathing suit and weighing exactly what I weigh now.''

''Mm,'' he grunted in recollection, his smile gone and his gaze moving slowly down her slender body. ''That was a shock, too. I meant the way you looked the time before that. I guess I still haven't completely shaken my mental picture of you, when you were so...so round and full.''

"Round and full?" she scoffed, amused by his euphemisms. "I was fat and bulky. I looked like—"

"Neither a cow nor a walrus," he silenced her. His fingers located the button holding her dress closed, and he unfastened it. The dress fell open, and he easily found the inner button holding the other side of the dress in place. He opened it and slid the dress down her arms and off. "A woman," he whispered, running his fingertips lightly over the naked expanse of skin between her bra and her panties.

She didn't know whether he meant she looked like a woman then or now. Perhaps both, she mused hazily as every nerve ending in her body was jolted awake by his gentle touch. The woman she'd been then, whether she'd been full and round or fat and bulky, no longer mattered. All that mattered was the woman she was now, the woman responding to Kyle, to his fingers meandering across her flesh, patiently learning the secrets locked inside her body.

His hand rose to her breast, arching over the soft swell and massaging it through the thin fabric of her brassiere. "Kyle," she whispered shakily, feeling sharp twinges of sensation arise in her breast and shoot down through her. His other hand covered her other breast and she moaned.

Her eyes closed as she let her spirit sink into the sublime cushion of sensation enveloping her. Kyle's lips grazed her brow, her temple, her cheek, her ear. His warm breath gusted over her throat and she moaned again. "Kyle."

He took her hands and placed them on his chest. Opening her eyes, she sucked in an uneven breath and undid the buttons of his shirt. The chest she uncovered was lean, sheathed in smooth muscle and, as she'd glimpsed on the beach last week, adorned by a tapering mat of pale golden hair. As her fingers combed through the soft tendrils, he shook his shirt from his arms and tossed it onto the chair.

He watched her as she stroked his torso, delighting in the texture of his skin and hair, in the subtle, reflexive movements of his muscles. When her hands arrived at his waist he shuddered slightly. "You're very sexy," he noted hoarsely, sounding almost surprised.

She glanced up at him. "Under the circumstances, I'd like to think I would be," she teased, though her voice was thick and tremulous.

He seemed on the verge of saying something, but kissed her instead. His hands moved to her back and unfastened her bra, then stripped off her panties. He made quick work of his trousers, and as soon as he was fully undressed, he urged her onto the bed, stretching out beside her.

His hands conquered her body with tender caresses, traveling with an almost frustrating leisureliness from the hollows along her shoulders to the valley between her breasts, from their pale flesh to their swollen red tips, then down to her flat abdomen, the small peaks of her hipbones, her smooth, supple thighs. He was relentless in his determination to learn every inch of her, every nerve and cell of her body, to unlock her every secret and master it.

He did unlock her secrets. She felt the secret coil of her femininity unwinding, relaxing, flowering open and outward, spreading its magic through her, rising to her surface like whorls and knots, eddies of life and feeling. She tried to match Kyle's lovemaking with her hands on his body, but she found it progressively harder to function when her own body fell deeper and deeper into his power.

She sighed his name, intending to apologize for lying so passively beside him, for letting the dazzling sensations he elicited sap her of the ability to reciprocate. Yet without even being conscious of it she *was* reciprocating, her legs moving seductively against his, her thigh rubbing his aroused flesh, her lips and teeth nipping at his shoulder as his chest bore down on her. She wasn't actually aware of the effect her breasts had on him when they pressed up into him, or her hand when it came to rest on the hard curve of his buttocks, or her breath floating into his hair, whispering his name again and again. Her motions were instinctive, unreasoned, yet undeniably sensual.

She heard his erratic breathing as his hips drove against hers. "Roberta," he groaned, drawing back, peeling her hand from his upper thigh. His eyes met hers, and she saw the blissful strain in his face. "God..." He fought for breath. "You're making me crazy. Don't make me lose myself."

She opened her mouth to object, to argue that she wasn't deliberately trying to make him crazy, that quite the contrary, she was afraid she wasn't doing enough to make him crazy. But his hand suddenly slid between her thighs, and the only sound to emerge from her was a plaintive cry. Kyle's fingers achieved their ultimate mastery of her, her every secret revealed to him in the choked, ecstatic sobs rising from her lips, the nearly desperate tensing of her muscles, the rhythm of her body rising against him, and then sinking back to the mattress, rising and sinking. "Kyle," she gasped, reaching for him, imploring him. "Oh, Kyle..."

One of her hands arched over the back of his head, guiding him to her for another kiss. His body followed onto her, his legs forcing hers apart, his flesh losing itself to the crazed longing Roberta had unknowingly freed within him.

She heard herself speak his name, again and again, a deep, throaty song of love as he moved powerfully inside her. She thought vaguely about the fact that Kyle knew her body in a way no other man ever had. His first exposure to her body had occurred five long years ago, but she felt so right with him now, so natural, that she couldn't help wondering whether he had learned all her secrets that day and remembered every one, saving the memory for this moment. His pace was hers, his energy energized her, his each thrust compelled a more profound response from her. He slid one hand beneath her hip and pressed her closer to himself, demanding more of her, giving her more of himself until she, too, was lost, lost in his embrace, in his love, in the heavenly sensations he had awakened in her.

The release came suddenly, stealing her breath, her strength, everything but her ability to savor the luscious pulses in her womb, in her soul, resonating through her flesh. His name fell from her lips one last time in a breathless cry, weary but exultant. Her ragged moan incited him, and with a final, wrenching thrust he surrendered to his own climax, as fierce and subsuming as hers.

He remained on top of her, unwilling to move from her even after his body slackened. His lips browsed languorously through the soft round curls of her hair, then ranged across her face, finally meeting and merging with her mouth. Her hands slowly relaxed in his hair, and only then did she realize how tightly fisted they had been. They floated through the soft gold-tinged locks to his back, taking comfort in its strong arch, and then to his waist.

He propped himself up on his arms and gazed down at her. "Five years ago," he whispered, "I never would have believed that this would happen to us."

"I know," Roberta concurred with a sweet, satisfied smile.

He traced the delicate curve of her lower lip with his index finger, as if he were in fact carving her smile instead of simply viewing it. "Right now," he continued, his voice still muted, "I can't believe that this *wouldn't* have happened."

She nodded. It seemed inevitable to her that she and Kyle should be lying in each other's arms tonight, defining their intimacy in a new way. For they'd been intimate from the moment they'd met. It astounded Roberta to think that what appeared so obvious to her and Kyle now would have seemed unbelievable five years ago.

"Spend the night with me," Kyle requested, his eyes still on hers, his hands brushing the tumble of dark curls back from her face. When she didn't respond instantly, he added, "Please."

She couldn't have left his bed even if she'd wanted to. She couldn't imagine wanting to. She belonged with Kyle tonight. "I'll stay," she agreed.

Her promise gave him the fortitude to roll off her; evidently he trusted her not to slip away from him if he loosened his hold on her. Still, he didn't release her completely. He remained on his side, one arm tucked beneath her head and his other hand tracing ethereal patterns over her tingling skin.

"I'll have to call Mary," Roberta remarked, her brain struggling for lucidity. "I don't want her worrying about me when I don't return to the cottage."

Kyle nodded. "There's the phone," he said, gesturing toward the telephone on the night table beside Roberta.

She reached for the receiver, then bit her lip. "I'll—I'll have to tell Leah, too," she muttered, pulling herself to sit and trying to figure out how to explain her night with Kyle to her daughter.

Kyle sat up, too, studying Roberta's mild scowl. "Is it going to cause trouble?" he asked tactfully.

Roberta noticed his worried expression and smiled unevenly. "I hope not."

"Will she hate me?"

Her smile gave way to a low laugh. "Oh, Kyle, she's so wild about you, I don't think you could do anything to make her hate you." Her laughter waned. "But it *is* kind of an awkward situation. I hope she can handle it, that's all."

"How has she handled it in the past?" he asked.

"It hasn't cropped up in the past," Roberta answered laconically.

Kyle considered her statement and interpreted it the only way it made sense to him. "You mean . . . you invite men to your home, instead of spending the night away from Leah?"

She grinned crookedly. "That hasn't cropped up, either," she said.

Kyle's bewildered frown intensified. "Roberta, Leah's five years old."

"I know how old she is," Roberta retorted, beginning to grow uncomfortable with the conversation.

"You're telling me you haven't been with a man in five years?" His scowl was replaced by an incredulous laugh. "I don't believe it."

"Do you think I'm lying?" Roberta snapped indignantly.

Seeing how hurt she looked, he stopped laughing. "Of course I don't," he assured her. His gaze ran the length of her body, then rose to her face again. "It's just that..." He sighed, trying to come to terms with what she'd just told him. "Roberta, you're so beautiful, so...so womanly. What I can't believe is how someone like you could keep men away from you for so many years."

"I've won a few wrestling matches," she informed him dryly.

He scrutinized her, his gray eyes intense, his brow creased. "Why? Why have you been avoiding men all this time?"

Unable to meet his piercing stare, she lowered her gaze to the wrinkled beige bed sheet beneath her. "I haven't been avoiding them. I've been on a few dates." She fussed with a crease in the linen, smoothing it out with her fingertips. "I was in mourning at first, Kyle. For a few years after Lee died, I just couldn't deal with other men romantically. I wasn't emotionally ready for it. I missed Lee too much.''

Kyle nodded sympathetically.

"And then," she continued, "well, it just seemed that I had so little time and energy. I was taking courses, working, trying to keep the apartment tolerably clean. What little time I had left I wanted to spend with Leah, not with some strange man, asking him what his sign was and whether he thought the Chargers had a shot at the Super Bowl this year, and then traipsing off to his place for a night of fun. I'm not abnormal, Kyle, and I'm not a nun. But getting involved with men just wasn't important to me.''

"Is it now?" he asked softly.

She forced herself to look at him. His face was open, his concern fully exposed in his eyes, in the line of his mouth, the angle of his jaw. Getting involved with *men* had never been important to her, she realized. But one man was important. And she'd been involved with him, in her own peculiar way, for five years.

He awaited her answer. His candor compelled the same from her. "Yes," she said. "It is."

His lips softened into a grateful smile, and he kissed her mouth lightly. "You'd better make your call."

She reached for the phone, then stopped and gave him a probing stare. "Does it bother you, what I just told you?" she asked. "That you're the first man I've been with since Lee?"

His eyes seemed to dive into hers, to reach for her mind, her soul. He eased her face to his and kissed her mouth again, a longer, deeper kiss. Slowly he released her and drew back. "No," he answered. "Not at all."

Nudging Roberta toward the phone, he relaxed across her half of the bed and drew her down onto him so that his chest formed a backrest for her. She dialed Mary's number, and while it rang, she glanced at the alarm clock beside the phone. A few minutes past ten o'clock. She wouldn't have to explain anything to Leah until tomorrow, she realized.

"Mary? It's Roberta," she greeted her friend when the phone was answered on the other end.

"Roberta? What happened?" Mary asked. "Is something wrong?"

"No," Roberta calmed her. "Nothing's wrong. I'm at Kyle's house right now." She swallowed, then asked, "Leah isn't awake, is she?"

"Of course not," Mary sniffed, feigning offense. "You told me to have her in bed by eight. Are you questioning my abilities as a baby-sitter?"

Roberta chuckled. "Admit it—you were probably sharing an ice-cream sundae with her no less than an hour ago."

Mary conceded. "An hour and a half ago," she confessed. "But I had her in bed by eight. She ate the ice cream in bed."

Leave it to her closest friends to spoil her daughter for her, Roberta thought with a resigned sigh. "If you want to ruin your furniture that way, Mary—"

"The hell with my furniture," Mary cut her off. "You didn't call just to check up on me and your daughter, did you?"

"No, Mary." Roberta swallowed again, then bravely announced, "I won't be coming home tonight, and I didn't want you to worry. I'll be spending the night at Kyle's house."

Mary didn't respond immediately. Roberta offered a silent prayer that her friend wouldn't make any wisecracks about Roberta's "efficient" dress. Blessedly, all Mary said was, "What time should we expect you tomorrow?"

"I'll be there by noon," Roberta predicted.

Kyle's hand drifted to the small of her back and massaged it. She recalled the back rubs he had given her when she'd been in labor, and their ability to ease her tension. Perhaps he was able to discern how tense she was now. He ran his fingers in penetrating circles over the taut flesh at the base of her spine. Miraculously her tension began to dissipate.

She twisted her head so he could see her grateful smile, then returned her attention to her telephone conversation. "When Leah wakes up tomorrow," she advised Mary, "tell her that I'm fine, and that I'll see her at noon if not earlier, and that if she has any questions, she should save them and ask me when I get back. I promise I'll try to answer them as well as I can. Will you tell her that?"

"Of course," Mary promised. "Uh—what should I tell her if she starts asking *me* all those questions?"

"Tell her..." Roberta closed her eyes for a moment, concentrating on the soothing pressure of Kyle's hand against her lower back. His massage seemed to clear her mind. "Tell her that I'm with Kyle, and that I love her very much. I don't think you need to say anything more than that, Mary."

"Okay," Mary agreed. "I'll make her pancakes for breakfast. That should keep her distracted. Meantime..." Once again Roberta prayed for Mary not to say anything crude or teasing. She was gratified to hear Mary sign off, "Have a fine evening, Roberta."

"I will. Good night, Mary, and thanks."

"No problem. Don't forget, my baby-sitting rates double after midnight," Mary said before hanging up.

Roberta dropped the receiver into the cradle and turned to Kyle. He studied her face. "Are you okay?" he asked.

Roberta shrugged. "I suppose this was bound to happen sooner or later. Just one more minor misery of being a mother."

"One more?" he asked. "How many minor miseries are there?"

"Who can count that high?" she said with a breezy chuckle. "Isn't there a song that goes something like, '*M* is for the misery I cause her...'?"

Kyle assessed her carefully, trying to determine how serious she was. "It isn't really misery, is it?"

Roberta laughed at his unnecessary frown. "I hate to break the news to you, Kyle, but motherhood does have its drawbacks."

"What drawbacks?"

"We could kill the whole night with this," she muttered with mock disgruntlement. But Kyle seemed so earnest that she decided he deserved some sort of answer. She settled back into the pillow and smiled. "One drawback, obviously, is that you have to justify your social life to a five-year-old busybody."

"I only heard half that phone conversation," Kyle admitted, "but it didn't sound so miserable to me."

"Mary isn't my daughter," Roberta reminded him. "She isn't going to ask me a whole lot of awkward questions. If I know Leah, she isn't going to let me off so lightly."

"Tell her you love her," Kyle suggested, repeating Roberta's instructions to Mary. "Tell her you were with me and you love her very much. She's young. That might be enough for her."

Roberta snorted in disbelief.

"All right," Kyle allowed. "Maybe tomorrow will be a little rough. Nothing you can't handle, though." He twirled his index finger through a ringlet of hair near her temple. "What other miseries are there?"

"Do you really want to know?" Roberta asked. At his solemn nod, she gave the topic some thought and then answered Kyle soberly. "She sometimes gets into a snit when she doesn't get her way. She'll pout and slam herself into her room and scream through the door that she hates my guts and hopes I die a horrible death just because I won't buy her a set of pencils with her name stamped on them in gold."

"She doesn't mean that," Kyle swiftly defended Leah.

"Of course she doesn't, but it isn't much fun to go through. She can run me ragged, Kyle. She's got so much energy, and I'm too old to keep up with her."

"Too old?" He burst out laughing.

"Look at me, Kyle," Roberta demanded, her smile indicating that it was her sense of humor alone that made all the "miseries" she was enumerating bearable. "Motherhood has aged me. Look at my face. Don't I look old beyond my years?"

"I don't know what your years are," he pointed out.

"I'm thirty. I think I look at least thirty-five. Maybe forty."

"No," he disputed her. His fingers ran over the faint crease extending from the outer corner of her eye, and then the even fainter parallel lines running up from the bridge of her nose, frown lines that used to vanish completely the minute Roberta stopped frowning, but had recently begun to linger like barely visible scars. "You look older than you looked five years ago, sure, but . . . but you looked like a little girl then. Now you look like a woman."

Roberta rolled her eyes and laughed. "You have such a nice way of putting things, Kyle. I used to look round and full. Now I look like a woman. By all means, keep it up. You could give me an incredibly swelled head."

Kyle joined her laughter, but he remained adamant in his assessment of her. "You look more mature now, Roberta, more experienced—which you are. I'm five years older, too," he reminded her.

"Yes, Kyle, but in our society men improve with age. Their faces develop 'character.' Our faces develop wrinkles."

"Character," he appropriated the term. "That's what's happened to your face. It's got character now." He bowed down to kiss the tiny creases between her eyebrows. "You're very beautiful, Roberta. I don't see how you can call these changes drawbacks."

"Okay. Maybe crow's-feet turn you on," she conceded good-naturedly. "From the neck up, motherhood has aged me, and from the neck down it's stretched me."

"Stretched you?" Kyle swept her lithe, slender body with his gaze. "Where?"

She pointed to the pale ripples in her skin just forward of her hipbones. "Stretch marks, Kyle. I've got a terminal case of them, I'm afraid. The one thing that makes me glad I didn't carry Leah to full term is that the stretch marks would have been even worse if I had."

He slid down the bed to examine them more closely. "These?" he asked, squinting at one. "These microscopic lines?"

"They're not microscopic, Kyle," she argued with an impatient laugh. "Don't flatter me. Be honest, for heaven's sake."

"All right," he relented. "They're not microscopic. But they're not so terrible, either. I kind of like them," he added, bending to kiss the affected skin on each end of her pelvis. "They remind me of the day we met. Yes, I definitely like them."

Roberta smiled. She couldn't imagine having this conversation with any other man in the world. But with Kyle she could analyze her crow's-feet and her stretch marks. No man knew her body as he did; no man understood it more completely. She wanted him to know everything about her body, even the flaws. When he worked with wood, he could find beauty in the flaws and create beauty from them. That was how she wanted him to see her.

His lips were still on her abdomen, having abandoned her stretch marks for her navel. She reached for his head, raking her fingers through his hair, and he kissed a route to her breast. His mouth closed over the nipple and he sucked.

She issued a shaky moan as the fluid heat of yearning that had barely subsided from their lovemaking welled up again and coursed through her. "Kyle," she whispered, sliding her legs along his, delighting in his revived arousal.

He lifted his head from her breast and rested it in the cradle of her elbow. "Did you breast-feed Leah?" he asked.

The question startled her. She enjoyed talking about Leah, but not when she was on the verge of being swept away by physical desire, when her emotions were geared to the rapturous sensations Kyle had kindled inside her with his lips and tongue, when—as Mary would put it—Roberta's needs were taking precedence.

Her eyes came into focus on Kyle, and he looked so guileless that she forgave him his bad timing. "Yes," she said, regaining control of her breath, smothering the tremor in her voice. "I breast-fed her."

He touched her breast with his index finger, drawing a circle around it, then centering on the erect, sensitive nipple. "What was it like?" he asked, intrigued. "What did breast-feeding feel like?"

"What you're doing right now feels much better," Roberta murmured, cupping her hand over his and holding it against her. Her hips surged involuntarily closer to his, and he slung his leg over hers, wedging his thigh between her legs. She groaned with pleasure.

"But what did it feel like?" he repeated insistently. "Please, Roberta, tell me. These are things I can never know—the sensation of feeding a baby at your own breast, from your own body; you've got to describe it to me." Her incredulous laugh only made him more adamant. "The idea of a nursing mother," he rhapsodized, "the picture of it— don't laugh at me, Roberta. It's like something sacred, something so magnificent. How can you laugh about it?"

"Oh, Kyle," Roberta cut him off with an uncontrollable guffaw. "Kyle, I hate to disillusion you, but there's nothing all that sacred and magnificent about it. Your breasts balloon out, and they're hot and heavy, and sometimes they leak. Your baby uses you as a teething toy, and after a while all your blouses smell like sour milk. I did it because it was convenient and economical, and because I thought it would be healthy for Leah, but there certainly wasn't anything *sacred* about it."

Her blunt statement clearly disturbed him. His brows dipped in a frown, and his hand moved pensively over her skin, slipping out from beneath hers as if he wanted to rethink his opinion of her breast. It occurred to Roberta that she *had* disillusioned him, that he'd clung to a notion of breast-feeding based less on reality than on some groundless romantic concept he'd invented.

She felt the need to apologize to him for having spoiled his little fantasy. "I don't regret having done it," she said. "It was healthy for both Leah and me. But, Kyle, you've got to understand, motherhood isn't quite as pretty and charming as you imagine it to be."

He stared at her, deep in thought. Roberta sensed bewilderment in his attitude and maybe even disapproval. The possibility that he might reject her for stating the facts about her experience with motherhood sliced through her, chilling her. But she wouldn't retract what she'd said. She owed

Kyle her honesty, even if what she said struck him the wrong way.

When his silence continued, she prodded him. "Spit it out, Kyle. You think I'm a rotten mother? You think I don't deserve Leah? What?"

He flexed his mouth, contemplating his words. Then his eyes grew gentler, and his hand stroked consolingly down her arm. When he reached her hand, he wove his fingers through hers and brought them to his lips for a kiss. "I think I have a lot to learn," he said slowly.

She squeezed his hand. "Don't misunderstand me, Kyle. Leah is fantastic. I adore her. In many ways she's the best thing that's ever happened to me. But I don't want to lie to you. Being a mother can be frustrating, irritating and sometimes nerve-racking. I wouldn't give up all the good parts just to rid myself of the bad, but I'm honest enough to admit that sometimes the bad parts can get pretty bad."

He nodded. "I don't want you to lie to me," he claimed. "I want to know the truth about it. I guess . . . I guess it just surprises me to hear you talk this way, after reading five years of letters that did nothing but sing Leah's praises."

Roberta chuckled. "One thing about motherhood: when your child does something wonderful, you remember it forever. When she does something terrible, you do your best to forget it as quickly as you can. So when I used to sit down to write to you, and I'd think about everything Leah had done since the last time I wrote, all I could remember was the wonderful stuff."

"That sounds like a very wise strategy," Kyle observed.

"And, let's face it, Leah *is* a wonderful child, an occasional snit notwithstanding," Roberta defended her daughter.

"She's a wonderful child," Kyle seconded. He leaned over and kissed the tip of Roberta's nose. "And she has a wonderful mother."

"I won't argue that point," Roberta concurred with a smile.

Then Kyle's mouth came down on hers, hungry and potent, and there was no more need for discussion.

HE WATCHED HER SLEEP.

Her dark, disheveled hair contrasted vividly with the beige pillowcase upon which she rested her head. Her face was a picture of tranquillity in repose. The top sheet draped gently over her body, dipping at her waist, scaling the feminine rise of her hips, shrouding her long, well-shaped legs. One arm extended over the top of the sheet, bent slightly at the elbow, her hand a motionless study of beauty where it lay between her body and Kyle's on the bed.

It had never been like this before.

Everything about Roberta was special, but if he had to rate all those special things, making love with her would soar to the top of the list. He'd imagined, he'd dreamed, but the reality of it surpassed even his overblown fantasies. He'd never known such satisfaction with another woman. As far as he could tell, he'd never satisfied another woman in quite the same way he'd satisfied Roberta.

Closing his eyes, he willed the memory of her voice to echo inside his mind. It didn't matter to Kyle that she hadn't known a man in five years. It wouldn't have mattered to him if she'd known a thousand men. Only one sound had emerged from her when their bodies had joined, only one word. She had expressed her astounding responsiveness to him with one thought, one utterance: *Kyle*. Sometimes a whisper, sometimes a plea, a prayer, a sob, a jubilant song. *Kyle*.

Hearing the rustle of the sheet as she stirred, he opened his eyes. She had barely moved, only shifted her head a millimeter closer to his and slid her hand upward so that her knuckles brushed against the silky tendrils decorating his chest. He covered her hand with his and smiled.

She really was perfect, he mused. As if there were such a thing as perfection. He'd read enough philosophy to find himself at times wondering whether there actually could be such a thing as existence, let alone perfection. But the woman lying beside him, breathing the night air with him, unconsciously molding her hand to the contours of his palm and filling him with an exhilarating sense of his own aliveness—she was as close to perfect as it was possible to be.

Not that he hadn't been rattled by her disparaging remarks about motherhood. But he dismissed her comments about breast-feeding and about the exasperation of raising a child as a standard, meaningless litany.

The only other mother Kyle knew intimately was his own. He couldn't remember how many times, when he and his sister were growing up, their generous, bighearted mother would call her beloved children "absolute pains in the neck," or bemoan her fate in having to launder their grimy jeans, or rant mercilessly when, as teenagers, they arrived home after curfew. He couldn't remember how many times his mother had slumped on a kitchen chair, rested her head heavily in her hands and moaned, "If I had it to do all over again, I swear I'd never have had kids. Never!" Kyle knew that she didn't mean such sentiments—or that she meant them only at that one instant when she was faced with the impossible chore of restoring her son's greasy, grass-stained dungarees to cleanliness, or at that particular moment when, after tiring of waiting up for him, she swung open the back door and found him on the porch groaning and clutching his stomach as his seventeen-year-old body rebelled at the quantity of beer he'd consumed. "God help me, if I had my life to live all over again, Kyle, you wouldn't be a part of it," she'd wail.

Yet she loved her children fiercely, and her children loved her. Mothers sometimes said such things, but they didn't mean them.

Roberta hadn't meant what she'd said, either. She hadn't honestly meant that breast-feeding was equated in her brain with blouses that smelled funny, and that she'd nursed Leah only for health reasons. Kyle knew that Roberta had breast-fed her daughter because breast-feeding would allow her to unite with Leah as intimately as possible, would allow her to give of herself, give of her own strength and substance to nourish the precious part of her that was her child. It wasn't for health reasons but for spiritual reasons, and smelling of sour milk had nothing to do with it.

She shifted again, rolling from her side onto her back. The top sheet settled around her, reshaping itself along her body, simultaneously revealing and concealing. He'd never before realized how marvelous a creation a woman's body was. He'd appreciated women's bodies before, of course, and enjoyed them and taken pleasure in returning the enjoyment. But Roberta's body meant so much more. It was a body that could nurture him as well as it had nurtured her child. The lines and wrinkles that marked it were things of unspeakable beauty to him. Her immeasurable capacity for giving was matched by her eagerness to receive, her joy at accepting whatever Kyle could give her.

He moved closer to her, as close as he could without disturbing her sleep, and shut his eyes again. Tonight he felt as if he'd shared in another miracle with Roberta, a miracle much different than the last one they'd shared, but no less vital.

He wasn't going to let this miracle slip away, as the last one had, before he understood it.

Chapter Eight

"I think we ought to get married," said Kyle.

His statement should have stunned Roberta, but for some reason it didn't. She serenely lowered her coffee mug to the dining room table and let her gaze wander from Kyle to the sun-filled panes of glass overlooking the deck and the backyard. A thin layer of white mist hovered above the dewy lawn, blurring the woods beyond it and giving the yard a surreal appearance.

The notion of marrying Kyle neither surprised nor disturbed her. In fact, it had a certain appeal. She felt remarkably comfortable as she greeted the morning in his modern dining room, wrapped cozily in his royal-blue bathrobe, with its shoulder seams drooping down her arms and its sleeves cuffed three times to free her hands. She felt at home sipping coffee from one of his oversize ceramic mugs, her bare feet propped up on an adjacent dining chair. She felt natural waking up with him, starting her day with him.

Her gaze followed him as he rose from the table and moved around the counter to the kitchen. He had on a pair of gray sweatpants and nothing else. She admired the lean male shape of his chest, and the way the soft curls covering it caught the sunlight and shimmered like gold. A glowing warmth filtered through her flesh as she mentally relived the sensation of his chest crushing down on her breasts, his strong, muscular arms enveloping her body, his work-roughened hands running across her smooth, sun-bronzed skin, transporting her with his touch, with his possession. To marry Kyle would mean to experience such sublime lovemaking on a regular basis. She certainly had no objection to that.

He carried the coffeepot into the dining room to refill their mugs, then returned it to its hot plate in the kitchen. When Roberta remained silent, he resumed his seat facing her and inhaled deeply. "Any comments?" he asked.

She smiled and traced the rim of her mug with her index finger. "You've got to admit we have a strange relationship, Kyle," she commented.

He tapped his fingertips together, studying her intently, trying to gauge her reaction to his proposal. "We have an unusual relationship," he allowed, choosing a more pleasant word to describe it. "But I think that could work in favor of a marriage. We've shared some significant things, Roberta. Leah is so very special to me. I could be a father to her. Not that I want to replace her real father, nothing like that. It's important that you keep his memory alive for her, as you have all along. But I could be a second father to her, or a stepfather, a man in her life. I think she needs that. Children should have two parents whenever it's possible."

Roberta leaned back in her chair, her eyes locked on to Kyle's. He looked solemn and sincere. She recalled the conversation she'd had with Mary about how Leah needed a father figure in her life. "You could be a father figure for Leah even if we didn't get married," Roberta observed.

"It would be more sensible if we did," he argued. "I want to be a full part of her life, not just someone she visits every now and then. She likes me, Roberta, and I like her."

Roberta chuckled softly. "Maybe you ought to marry *her*, then," she suggested.

He scowled, but recovered when he realized from Roberta's amused expression that she was only teasing him. "I'm going on at length about Leah because I'm aware that stepparents and stepchildren can have their difficulties. But I can't imagine Leah and me having any difficulties like that. It seems to me that if you and I got married, it would benefit Leah. And me." He thought for a moment, then added, "And you. I hope." He shook his head and snorted at his ineptitude. "I'm doing a lousy job of this, aren't I?"

"Keep going," Roberta invited him, still amused. "You're bound to improve."

His eyes met hers and he permitted himself a begrudging smile. "You really want me to keep going?" he asked hopefully.

"I'm all ears," Roberta assured him.

He drew in a deep breath and mulled over his thoughts, attempting to organize them before he started rambling again. "Okay," he said with certainty. "I've been thinking a great deal about this—"

"We only just got together a week ago," Roberta broke in. "When on earth have you had the chance to think a great deal about this?"

"Last night," he replied.

Roberta eyed him sharply, and then her lips spread in a sly grin. "My memory of last night," she said, "was that we were both much too busy to be doing a whole lot of thinking."

Kyle grinned briefly, then became solemn again. "After you fell asleep, Roberta, I lay awake for a long time, thinking this whole thing through. It feels right to me," he said frankly. "It makes sense. I care for you a lot, Roberta. You've always been special to me. We've always been friends. After last night—well, I think it's clear that we can be more than friends."

Her smile was enigmatic but steady. He wished she would speak, but she only continued to smile.

At least she wasn't grimacing, he consoled himself, taking heart in her glowing expression. "How am I doing?" he asked. "Would it help if I got on my knees?"

"I don't know." Her gaze flitted to the window and back to him. "Maybe a bouquet of dandelions might soften me up," she suggested impishly.

"Roberta, I'm being serious."

"I know, Kyle, I know." She raised her mug to her lips and drank, using her coffee to prevent herself from impulsively accepting his marriage proposal. Her immediate reaction was that marrying Kyle was a splendid idea. He was as special to her as she was to him. In addition, as he'd pointed out, the glorious night they'd spent in each other's arms proved that she didn't have to worry about their physical compatibility. Obviously they could be lovers as well as friends.

The fact that Kyle had approached the subject of their getting married in a distinctly unromantic way didn't bother her. When Lee had asked her to marry him, he'd been just as rational, just as pragmatic. Roberta stared outside at the gradually evaporating mist and remembered the afternoon Lee had proposed to her.

They had been riding downtown on a transit bus, returning to their SoHo home after a visit with Lee's doctor, who had analyzed the multitude of test results he'd received on Lee's condition and had presented Lee and Roberta with his grim prognosis. During the trip home, they'd been subdued, but both of them had remained dry-eyed and kept a stiff upper lip.

"We've got to be sensible here," Lee had announced. "If we get married, you'll be in much better shape if I should die. We can put the loft in joint ownership to save you from having to pay inheritance taxes on it. And you'll automatically be covered by my insurance. It seems like a smart move."

"Of course, nothing's going to happen to you," Roberta had claimed.

Lee had shot her a wry smile. "Of course," he'd concurred. "Meantime, let's get married."

If Kyle had dropped onto one knee before Roberta now, and had kissed her hand and quoted something suitably sentimental from a Shakespeare sonnet, she would have been less inclined to accept his proposal. The fact that he approached the subject so rationally appealed to her.

Yet, as unromantic as Kyle was, she knew that in at least one area he was excessively romantic. A few of the things he'd said the previous night had indicated that to her "Kyle," she murmured gently, "do you really know what you'd be getting yourself into if you married me?"

"I haven't got a crystal ball," he said. "But I'd like to think I'd be getting myself into a permanent relationship with a woman who means a lot to me—"

"And her little girl," Roberta reminded him.

"Of course. That's one of the best parts."

She smiled indulgently. "You really have no idea what being a parent is like," she reminded him.

He considered her mild accusation and nodded slightly, but it didn't discourage him. "I'm not a moron," he defended himself. "I could learn."

"I'm sure you could," she granted. "But don't you think it would make more sense if you learned *before* you got stuck in something permanent?"

He mulled over her point. "You think I'm not going to enjoy being a stepfather to Leah?"

"I don't know whether you'd enjoy it or not," said Roberta. "What I do know is that you have some unrealistic concepts of what it's all about."

"What unrealistic concepts?" he challenged her.

"You thought breast-feeding was sacred," she reminded him.

Kyle refused to surrender. "I still do," he asserted. "I don't care what your blouses smelled like, Roberta. To me, the whole miracle of it—the way mothers sustain infants, before birth and then after it, the way the mother's body nurtures the baby's—and yes," he alerted her before she could interrupt, "I think childbirth is sacred, too."

Roberta was touched by his lovely view of maternity. But while she might subscribe to such a view in theory, she knew it didn't reflect the day-in-day-out reality of child rearing. She loved Leah; she loved her little girl with a devotion—a passion—that couldn't be measured. But that didn't negate the fact that sometimes she found Leah to be a first-class pest.

Kyle didn't understand that; he lacked the experience to understand that a mother could be nearly insanely dedicated to her child and could believe that, yes, the child's birth and life were something bordering on sacred, and yet could see the situation objectively and admit that her "sacred" little child could transform into a devil at times. And while the thought of marrying Kyle, living with him, sharing the burdens and joys of parenthood with him thrilled Roberta, she simply couldn't allow him to commit himself to becoming a stepfather when he was so totally unfamiliar with everything that the position would entail. Roberta loved him too much to hold him to a promise made in ignorance.

Something froze inside her at that realization, momentarily halting her heartbeat, stifling her breath, causing her entire body to become utterly still. She blinked, as if that could clarify her thoughts, her feelings. Perhaps it did, because once her nervous system stirred to life again she was even more certain of herself.

She loved Kyle.

It wasn't merely because of the night they'd spent together that she loved him, although last night might have brought the truth home to her. As she thought about it, she comprehended that her love for Kyle had in fact been a gradual development, beginning with the enormous faith she'd had in him the first day they'd met, the unshakable faith she'd possessed in order to trust him with her own life and her daughter's. It had grown over the years, from the first stilted letters they'd exchanged to the longer and more free-flowing ones. She remembered how much she'd looked forward to Kyle's letters, how pleased she'd been whenever one arrived, how she'd read each one again and again before adding it to the stack and tying the string around it.

She hadn't been saving his letters for Leah's sake, she admitted to herself now. She'd been saving them as any woman would save letters from a man she loved.

But it wasn't love that made Roberta want to say yes to Kyle's offer of marriage. It was desire, and a longing for comfort and companionship. Her love, oddly enough, was what compelled her to hold back, to protect him from his own ignorance by refusing to marry him.

That, plus the recognition that not once in his long-winded proposal had he mentioned that he loved her.

She felt something tighten in her throat. For all the sweet things Kyle had said about her, for all his expressions of affection for her and confidence in their friendship, he hadn't spoken the word "love." He'd never even hinted that love had anything to do with his feelings for Roberta.

She swallowed down her disappointment and managed a smile. "Are—are you lonely?" she asked Kyle.

Her question jolted him. He sat up straighter. "What gives you that idea?" he returned.

"Actually, it was Leah's idea, not mine," Roberta told him. "Yesterday when we were on the train, she suddenly declared that she thought you should get a dog because you must be lonely living all by yourself."

"I'd rather live with you and Leah than with a dog," Kyle remarked. "But no, I'm not particularly lonely." He lifted his mug, then lowered it again without sipping. His eyes remained on Roberta, glinting with curiosity. "Why do you ask?"

She lowered her gaze to her own mug. "I want to know what you're looking for in this marriage you're proposing. If you're lonely and you're looking for company—"

"Roberta, I was lonelier living with a woman a few years ago than I am living alone now. I don't mind living alone. I'm not looking for company—not in a general sense. It's *you* I want to marry."

"Then what are you looking for?" she pressed him.

He didn't answer immediately. Had he expected Roberta simply and happily to say yes, without analyzing his motives and feelings? He should have known better. She was an intelligent woman, too wise to leap into a marriage impulsively. He respected her for her rationality.

Her question deserved the careful thought he gave it. "I'm looking for a chance to build something meaningful with you and Leah," he finally answered.

He lifted his mug again, changed his mind and set it down with a thud. His respect receded, replaced by a heavy sense of dread. "Tell me, Roberta," he implored her quietly. "Am

I completely off base here? Do you find the idea of our marrying laughable? Do you wish I'd shut up and leave you alone? Give me a clue as to what you're thinking.''

She reached across the table and took his hand. Her tender smile offered him a glimmer of hope. ''I'm not going to say no,'' she told him, her voice muted but her eyes resolutely on his. ''I'm not going to say no, Kyle, but...I want to wait before saying yes. All right?''

Her statement mollified him somewhat. He rotated his hand until his palm faced hers, then twined his fingers through hers and squeezed them. ''Fair enough,'' he conceded. He studied her oval fingernails, then kissed her thumb and sighed. ''Can you give me a clue about what you're waiting for?'' he asked, lifting his eyes to hers once more.

She laughed at his impatience. ''Maybe we've known each other a long time, Kyle. But when it comes to daily living, we still have a lot to learn about each other. Marriage isn't just a legal relationship, you know. It's also a matter of where you squeeze the toothpaste tube and whether you steal the entire blanket in the winter and how you organize the silverware drawer. And then when we throw Leah into the bargain, we increase our chances for disagreement by a thousand percent.''

He accepted her sensible observation, though he obviously didn't agree with it. ''I think we're both mature enough to handle those sorts of disagreements without destroying our relationship,'' he insisted. ''I'm an optimist.''

''And I'm a realist,'' Roberta countered. ''All I'm saying is that I don't want you to enter into anything with me unprepared. I want you to go into it with your eyes open.''

''Then by all means, open my eyes,'' Kyle invited her.

She nodded, accepting his challenge. ''Why don't you come to New York next weekend and spend some time with us? It might be a good idea to let Leah see us together—in the same house, in the same room. She's very fond of you, Kyle, but I don't know how she's going to feel about you and me together.''

"Fine," he agreed. "I'll come to New York."

"And I'm not going to discuss with her the possibility of our getting married," Roberta added. "I think we ought to take this thing one step at a time and see how it goes. We don't win points for speed, you know."

"All right," he acquiesced. He lifted her hand to his face and rubbed her knuckles gently along the scratchy surface of his jaw. "I know this is right, Roberta," he whispered before grazing her inner wrist with his lips. "You and I have something going. And Leah's a big part of it. I just want to make it legal. For Leah's sake, especially." He spread her fingers flat and touched his lips to her palm.

His words carried logic, but that logic was superseded by the much more persuasive case his kiss made in support of marriage. The pressure of his mouth against her hand set loose a tide of desire inside her, and her thighs clenched in a distant but definite response. "What time is it?" she mumbled shakily.

"Hm?" He glanced at a wall clock in the kitchen. "Quarter to ten."

"I told Mary I'd be back at her cottage by noon," Roberta reminded Kyle, her eyes radiating her yearning, her cheeks rosy with excitement.

He easily comprehended what she was saying. Smiling, he released her hand and stood up, then strode around the table to help her to her feet. Leaving the coffee mugs on the table, he hoisted her high into his arms and carried her to his bedroom. "By the way," he whispered as her mouth buried itself in the hot crook of his neck, "I squeeze the toothpaste tube at the bottom. How about you?"

"The middle," she murmured airily. "That could mean big trouble."

"I think we'll survive it," Kyle predicted before tumbling with her onto the bed.

"AUNT MARY MADE ME PANCAKES for breakfast," Leah said by way of greeting as Roberta and Kyle entered the breeze-filled summer cottage. "She made them in different shapes, too, only they all looked the same. She said one was supposed to be the sun and another was supposed to be a ball and another was supposed to be a stereo record. They all looked exactly the same to me."

Roberta glimpsed Mary, who shrugged. "So they were all round," she said in her own defense. "Shoot me."

"They were good," Leah consoled her. "But my mommy can make pancakes that look like rabbits."

"Your mother's an artist," Mary reminded her.

"And the artist is going to change into some jeans," Roberta announced, heading for the bedroom. "I'll be out in ten minutes."

"Good," Mary called after her. "I'm about to make some lunch. I don't know about you guys, but we had breakfast at eight. A certain small but noisy person around here doesn't know what it means to sleep late on weekends."

Chuckling, Roberta shut herself inside the bedroom and unbuttoned her dress. She didn't want to leave Kyle alone with Leah any longer than necessary, given that Leah might begin to spout pointed questions about what he'd been doing with her mother all night. But Roberta also didn't want to spend the rest of the day in her elegant cream-colored dress. She removed it and hastily arranged it on its hanger, then slipped on a cotton T-shirt and a reasonably new pair of blue jeans. She ran her brush once or twice through her hair, then tossed the brush onto the dresser and bounded into the parlor.

She found Kyle and Leah on the floor, examining Leah's silver balloon. It had deflated overnight, and Kyle was inspecting the limp silver plastic for a leak. "It could just be that the knot wasn't tied tight enough," he said encouragingly. "If that's the problem, we'll be able to blow it up again."

"I hope so," Leah said. "It's a neat balloon." She peered up at Roberta. "It was okay when I went to bed, but this morning when I got up it was all soft and yucky. Kyle's going to fix it for me. How come you stayed at Kyle's house last night, Mommy?"

Ten minutes to the second, Roberta muttered beneath her breath as she checked her wristwatch. Back at the cottage all of ten minutes, and the troublesome questions had begun.

She lowered herself onto one of the upholstered wicker chairs and fortified herself with a deep breath. "I stayed at Kyle's house," she answered in an uninflected voice, "because we wanted to spend some time together."

"But you had dinner together," Leah pointed out.

"We wanted to spend more time together than just dinner."

Leah considered this. "Where did you sleep?" she asked.

Roberta was temporarily rescued by Mary, who appeared in the kitchen doorway and asked if tuna fish salad was acceptable to everyone. With a brisk invitation to Kyle to stay for lunch, she vanished from the doorway.

Leah stubbornly repeated her unwelcome question. "Where did you sleep at Kyle's house, Mommy?"

Kyle glanced up from the balloon. His eyes met Roberta's. Their sweet, soft gray reflected a blend of concern and tolerant humor. Roberta clung to their humorous glint as proof that he might be able to adapt to life with a curious, occasionally irksome five-year-old.

But she had a more immediate worry than whether Kyle could adapt to life with Leah. The little girl was staring inquisitively at her mother, waiting for an answer. "I slept in Kyle's room," Roberta answered honestly. She simply couldn't lie to Leah, not with Kyle planning to visit New York next week and stay with Roberta in her room.

She held her breath, awaiting Leah's next question. Leah turned on Kyle and asked, "Is your room big?"

He shot a quick glance at Roberta, then turned back to Leah. "Yes, it's big," he answered. "If you'd like, the next time you visit my house I'll show it to you."

"Can I sleep there, too?" Leah asked.

Kyle shifted uneasily, but Roberta laughed. This was good for him, she decided. Baptism by fire.

He appeared annoyed by Roberta's laughter, and his brow dipped in a frown. Taking pity on him in his obvious discomfort, she bailed him out by saying, "No, Leah. Kyle's room is for grown-ups, not children. Maybe he'd let you take a nap there during the afternoon, but that's all."

"I'm too big for naps," Leah protested indignantly.

Mary reappeared at the kitchen doorway, announcing that lunch was ready. Leah scampered into the kitchen, complaining dramatically about her state of near starvation. Alone in the parlor, Kyle and Roberta exchanged a private glance. "Life with Leah, round one," Roberta whispered.

"I'm bloody but unbowed," he whispered back. "Ready for round two."

As it turned out, Leah had no more awkward questions for Roberta and Kyle that afternoon. She was too preoccupied by more immediate matters: to wit, how one's food was shaped. She spent much of her lunch hour arranging her tuna into different shapes on her plate, demonstrating for Mary how one could create rabbits, teddy bears and automobiles from tuna fish.

After lunch, she insisted that they all take a walk to the beach. On the sand she found the empty white shell of a crab, and the rest of the universe, including the sleeping arrangements her mother and Kyle might have made for themselves the previous night, paled in comparison to such a thrilling discovery. Roberta's announcement that they'd have to return to the cottage and pack up, since they had a train to catch, provoked a minor protest from Leah, but she was so excited by the news that Kyle would be visiting New York City the following weekend that she forgave her mother for making her leave the beach.

KYLE'S UPCOMING VISIT fueled Leah through the week. Anyone unfortunate enough to approach within several feet of Leah heard about it: Natalie the baby-sitter, Mr. Addison in the loft below theirs, the waitress at the corner coffee shop, where Roberta took Leah for dinner one night when she was too tired to cook. "Guess what?" Leah bellowed at the harried waitress. "The man who helped me be born is spending this weekend with us. Isn't that great? He helped me be born and he gave me a dollhouse." Roberta left the waitress a huge tip just for putting up with Leah.

Yet she couldn't deny her pleasure at Leah's enthusiasm over Kyle's visit. The little girl was obviously enormously taken with him. Perhaps she'd be less demanding when she was with him, less draining. Perhaps she'd be on such good behavior that Kyle would receive a false impression of what life with Leah was really like—on the other hand, maybe Leah's love for Kyle would cause a permanent improvement in her behavior.

Roberta wondered whether she'd been exaggerating in her mind the difficulties she expected Kyle to confront in converting from a carefree bachelor to a father. It was always possible that he'd view the difficulties simply as exciting challenges and tackle them with aplomb. During their dinner at the restaurant, and in his letters as well, he'd said he wanted more responsibility. Maybe the very things Roberta feared for him were precisely the things he was looking for in his life.

Maybe, she admitted to herself Thursday night after tucking Leah in and returning to the living room to straighten it out a bit before he arrived the following evening, maybe she was deliberately magnifying the potential problems in her mind. She loved Kyle, and she wanted to marry him. But she couldn't shake her niggling doubt about his reasons for marrying her. He cared for her; he wanted to create a meaningful family with her and Leah; he knew that he and Roberta would have a satisfying sex life. He considered Roberta a close friend. Those were all important aspects of a loving relationship, and as true a description of Roberta's feelings for Kyle as of his feelings for her.

But . . . but where was the love itself?

She ought to be practical, she chided herself as she dusted the coffee table and plumped the cushions of the sofa. Kyle cared for her, and she loved him. Plenty of marriages were based on less stable foundations than that. Roberta could offer Kyle certain things that his life currently lacked. And Kyle, in turn, could offer her certain things that her life lacked: a man, a father figure for Leah, an equal for Roberta to talk to, an adult to share with her the decisions and the responsibilities. Kyle wanted more responsibility, and Roberta had had almost too much responsibility for five long years. A marriage might be a sensible solution to the shortcomings in both of their lives right now.

Sensible. Practical. What was wrong with that? Roberta's first marriage had arisen out of practicality.

But there had also been plenty of love between her and Lee, freely expressed and happily acknowledged. Roberta and Lee may have been married by law, but the essence of their relationship had transcended the piece of paper a city clerk had signed for them one spring day. The love had come first; the love had been the most important part of it. Even if Roberta hadn't married Lee, she would have felt like his widow when he passed away.

With Kyle, however... She loved him, but she just wasn't sure whether he loved her.

It would be good to have him visiting her in her home, she decided. They needed more time together, in more ordinary surroundings than the picturesque, dreamlike world of Madison, with its ocean aroma and its foggy air giving everything a soft-focus prettiness that distorted the truth. In New York, Roberta suspected, she'd get a much clearer picture of Kyle's feelings for her.

Her hope that things would clarify themselves was enough to make her anticipate his arrival with a cheerfulness bordering on elation. He called her during the week to tell her he'd be at her apartment by six o'clock Friday evening; he'd leave work early and drive down from Connecticut. He couldn't wait to see her, he told her, and then he insisted that she put Leah on the telephone. After Leah said goodbye to him, she reported to her mother that Kyle had said he couldn't wait to see her, either.

Roberta checked her watch frequently during the day Friday, knowing that she'd have to leave her office exactly at five in order to get home in enough time to clean the apartment after Leah and Natalie's daily destruction of it. But her boss thwarted her. Her latest assignment, as part of a team designing a four-color magazine layout for a department store chain, represented a big step up for Roberta, so when she was summoned down to the conference room at four o'clock to discuss the project, she couldn't very well refuse to show up. She listened with half her mind to the discussion of the layout, while the other half of her mind measured the ticking of the minutes. The client wanted a clean, high-tech look, one of her colleagues argued. Another disputed him by declaring that the store simply didn't have a high-tech reputation, so what was the point in presenting their down-home fashions against a stark white-tiled background?

The bickering went on and on, and Roberta grew progressively more restless. Her sole contribution to the layout was going to be in the lettering and arrangement of the ad's text; she didn't care whether the lettering was set against white tiles or turquoise peacock feathers.

She remained at the tedious meeting until five-thirty, then excused herself with a promise to work out her lettering concepts over the weekend, one design suitable for a high-tech spread and several others in different styles for comparison. "I'll have plenty of stuff to show on Monday," she promised. "But I really can't stay another minute today. I'm sorry."

Her boss gave her a forgiving nod as she swept out of the room. As soon as the door closed behind her, she muttered a curse at the late hour and another, more flamboyant curse at the realization that she'd have to bring work home with her. This was not shaping up to be the ideal weekend she'd planned with Kyle.

But then, she consoled herself, maybe it was just as well that he see what her life was truly like. Tonight wouldn't be the first time she'd had to bring work home with her. This sort of thing happened all the time, and if Kyle wanted to marry her, he might as well learn the truth of it.

She stuffed the items she'd need—paper, pasteboard, ink and pens, stencils—into her oversize portfolio, zipped it shut, grabbed her purse and raced to the elevator. Since most of the people who worked in the building had already left for the weekend, the elevator arrived quickly, and Roberta didn't have to elbow her way through a crowd in the ground-floor lobby to get to the door and outside. Luckily, she didn't have too long to wait for her subway train downtown. She arrived, breathless and slightly discombobulated, at the loft five minutes before six o'clock.

"Hey, Mrs. Frankel," Natalie greeted her, lifting her shapeless cloth sack of a purse from the sofa, "I'm glad you're home. I've got to run. I've got a date tonight."

"So do we," Leah boasted, bounding in from the kitchen. "Kyle's coming. Did I tell you that, Natalie?"

"Two thousand times today," the baby-sitter groaned good-naturedly.

Roberta briefly scanned the living room. Leah's dollhouse was lying on its side, all of the delicate furnishings scattered across the room. A pile of crayons lay on the carpet in one corner, and at least half of Leah's library of storybooks was strewn across the hardwood floor of the hall. Gritting her teeth, Roberta hastened to the kitchen and tossed her portfolio onto the breakfast table. While rummaging in her purse for her checkbook, she spotted a casserole dish filled with caked-on macaroni-and-cheese in the sink. "What in the world is this?" she asked Natalie, who was loitering in the doorway, anxiously awaiting her payment.

"Oh, that was Leah's idea," the teenager explained. "She wanted macaroni-and-cheese for lunch."

"Natalie, it's late August. It was ninety-eight degrees out at lunchtime today. How can anyone stomach macaroni-and-cheese when it's ninety-eight degrees out?"

"It turns out Leah couldn't," Natalie commented with a shrug. "That's why it's sitting in the sink."

Roberta eyed the gooey mess and cringed. She needed that casserole dish for the beef-and-broccoli stew she was planning to cook for dinner. But she didn't have time to clean the pot now. Biting back the urge to scold Natalie for being so haphazard about things, she scribbled out a check and waved the baby-sitter off. Only one and a half weeks more, Roberta reminded herself, and then Leah would be in school full-time, and Natalie would no longer be on the payroll.

After locking the door behind Natalie, Roberta marched into the living room and located Leah helpfully wiping potato chip crumbs from the coffee table onto the floor. "Forget the dusting for now," Roberta ordered her. "I want you to pick up your crayons and put them in their box. And then I want you to bring your books to your room. This place is a mess."

"Well, we were playing, Mommy," Leah defended herself.

"You couldn't possibly be playing with every single one of your toys at the same time," Roberta reprimanded her. "Kyle is due here any minute, and the apartment looks like a Dada nightmare. I've got to scrub the casserole dish so I can get dinner started. You clean up in here. Macaroni-and-cheese," she added beneath her breath, pivoting on her heel and heading back to the kitchen.

Yanking off her blazer and trying to calculate how much she could hope to accomplish before Kyle showed up, she didn't see the slippery tube of macaroni lying in ambush for her on the linoleum floor. She went into a skid and landed on her knees. One of them merely hit the floor, and the other came down hard on the exquisite miniature drop-leaf table Kyle had given Leah for her dollhouse. The leaf snapped off under Roberta's weight, tearing her stocking and scratching the skin beneath it.

"Damn!" she gasped, easing into a sitting position to inspect the damage to her leg. "Damn it, Leah, why must you leave booby traps all over the house for me?"

Leah materialized beside her, her face registering appropriate contrition when she saw the small line of blood forming at the base of Roberta's kneecap and matting into the nylon of her stocking. Then she spotted the broken dollhouse table and began to wail. "You broke it, Mommy! You broke it!"

"*You* broke it," Roberta retorted furiously. "Why did you leave it on the kitchen floor? People walk on floors. If you didn't leave this place in such a mess—"

"It's broken!" Leah sobbed, grabbing the splintered pieces of the table.

Roberta noticed their sharp edges and snatched the pieces from her daughter. "Don't touch it," she commanded. "You'll cut yourself." She kicked off her shoes and staggered to her feet. Her injured knee ached, and a thick run striped her stocking up her thigh. "How many times have I told you not to leave things on the floor?" she asked Leah rhetorically. "Now you know why. Go finish cleaning up your toys in the living room. I've got to get this casserole dish cleaned."

"I don't want to clean up," Leah howled. "You broke my favoritest piece, and I'll never ever forgive you!"

Before Roberta could let loose with a howl of her own, she heard the doorbell ring.

Chapter Nine

It had been one of the best weeks of his life.

Everything seemed so clear to him now, so appropriate. He and Roberta were right for each other—he knew it, and if she didn't already know it, she would soon.

They were more than right for each other; they were *good* for each other. He could give Roberta what she needed: a father for her daughter and a man for herself. Not that Kyle was a sexist, not that he wasn't impressed by what a strong, independent woman like Roberta could do on her own. More than impressed, actually. He was envious of her ability to make sense of her life in a way he'd been unable to.

Unable, that is, until she reentered his life and made sense of it for him.

He didn't mind her having said maybe instead of yes to his proposal. The more he thought about marrying her, the more confident he felt that she'd say yes eventually. She'd claimed that she was a realist. Realistically looking at the situation, she'd have to acknowledge how sensible a marriage would be for them.

This weekend he'd prove to her that it was more than sensible. He'd prove that he wasn't a total idiot when it came to handling Leah, that Roberta didn't have to behave as though Kyle were too naive to deal with a lovable young child. Hadn't he made a fine birthday celebration for Leah? Hadn't he taken her out in a rowboat? Hadn't they developed an instant rapport, talking and playing with each other as if they'd been together forever? Kyle was crazy about Leah. What more could Roberta ask for?

She'd eventually have faith in his ability to be a father for Leah, he believed. She'd see for herself that he was emotionally ready for the job of parenting. She'd painted a negative picture of life with Leah to test Kyle, to determine if he was serious about marriage. He was. Perhaps Roberta would relax now and admit that Leah was as much of a joy as Kyle knew her to be.

In the meantime, Roberta was already influencing him for the better. Her astute observations about his dissatisfaction concerning his career—and her decision to speak her mind, forgoing tact and courtesy—made him realize that it was long past time for a change in his life. The Saturday he'd spent with his crew working over the late shipment of mahogany had been wonderful. He'd never gotten around to telling Roberta how much he'd enjoyed the strenuous labor of it, the sheer physicality of lining the wood up and sawing it to size, measuring and scoring—touching it, holding it, savoring its heft and hardness.

Thanks to Roberta, Kyle was now able to acknowledge that the pleasure he'd experienced Saturday at the workshop didn't have to be a rarity.

On Monday he'd invited Bob Neilson to lunch. Bob was one of his older employees, but in many ways Kyle related to him much as Kyle's mentor Peter had once related to Kyle himself. Bob had a lot of experience in restoration work, but he was interested in learning other aspects of furniture design and assembly, and Kyle was happy to teach him what he knew. What was more, because of Bob's seniority and patience, the other members of the crew all looked up to him.

"Let's not pussyfoot around," Kyle said as they settled at a scratched table in the rear of a neighborhood pizza parlor and attacked their meatball heroes. "I'm looking for someone to take over a little bit of my paperwork, and I think you'd fill the bill."

"Paperwork?" Bob asked. "What do you mean?"

"I mean, I'm tired of watching you guys execute my designs," Kyle explained. "Designing's only half the fun. I want to be able to spend a little more time in the shop. In order for me to do that, someone's got to take over some of the desk work. You've got the brains for it, Bob. It's a good opportunity for you to learn something new about the business."

Bob twirled the straw around in his paper cup of soda. "Kyle, you keep teaching me stuff, I might be tempted to take whatever I've learned from you, set myself up in my own outfit and go into competition with you."

"It's a risk I'm willing to take," Kyle assured him. "I think I can come up with incentives for you to stay." He bit into his sandwich, chewed and swallowed. "I don't expect an answer this minute, Bob, but it's something to think about. I need more time on the floor and I trust you to cover for me. You're good at detail work, and when you get mad, people quake with fear, which means you'd be great at dealing with our suppliers on the phone. Just think about it for a few days and let me know if you're interested."

"I'm interested," Bob said quickly. "How do you think the gang'll take to the idea of the Big Man standing alongside them in the shop?"

Kyle laughed. "If they don't love it, I'll fire them. Ergo, they'll love it." He took a long quaff of his iced tea and lowered the glass. "Face it, Bob, I'm better with the wood than anyone else in the shop."

"With the exception of yours truly," Bob shot back.

Kyle snorted in mock indignation. "If 'yours truly' were so damned good on the floor, I wouldn't be dragging you into the office to fill out invoices and track down missing shipments. You want me to teach you something about management, Bob? Lesson one: modesty is the best policy. Lesson two: never forget who's boss."

"Oh, yes, sir!" Bob played along, bowing his head deferentially. "Yes, sir, Lord Stratton, sir. Your humble servant is surely only the second-best carpenter who ever walked the earth, sir."

Kyle crumpled his napkin and threw it at Bob's nose. They both laughed.

On Friday, after having spent several hours during the week observing Kyle's office techniques and his manner of doing business, Bob covered in the office for Kyle while the "Big Man" spent a couple of hours assisting in the assembly of a breakfront frame for the Tucson dining room order. Kyle left work early, feeling cheerful and chipper, rejuvenated by his exertion. He sped home, showered and changed his clothing, tossed a few items into his overnight bag, and climbed into the truck for his drive to New York City. He briefly considered driving down in his Saab, which was air-conditioned and more comfortable, but he decided that the truck would offer a less enticing target to Lower Manhattan's car thieves and street punks than his new Saab would.

He located Roberta's converted loft building without much difficulty, and even found a parking space on the block. One of the best weeks of his life was about to be surpassed by one of the best weekends, he thought as he locked up and strode down the sidewalk to her building's front

door. His anticipation increased as he rode the elevator upstairs, as he rang her bell, as the door swung open.

He didn't have a chance to say hello. He'd barely opened
his mouth to speak when Leah was upon him, blubbering
about her broken dollhouse table. "Mommy broke it, Kyle!
She ruined it! The one with the sides that went up and down.
It was the best thing in the whole dollhouse. Can you make
me another one?"

"I don't see why not," he began. Roberta caught his eye
and shook her head slightly. Confused about why she
wouldn't want him to make Leah another miniature drop-
leaf table, but in no position to question her, he turned back
to Leah, who was glowering furiously at her mother. "We'll
discuss it later," he sagely suggested, stepping inside the
apartment with his overnight bag and shutting the door behind him. He raised his eyes to Roberta.

"How did you get upstairs?" she asked. "I thought you'd
be signaling us on the intercom, so we'd have at least ten
seconds to compose ourselves."

"One of your neighbors held the downstairs door open
for me," Kyle answered. "I guess that's not too safe."

"Well." She shrugged. "Welcome. Come on in and join
the fray." She managed a feeble smile as she limped toward
the kitchen to pick up her portfolio and shoes. "I just got
home a few minutes ago, and the place is a mess—although
I suppose you can see that for yourself. Why don't you make
yourself comfortable while I go change my clothes? Then I'll
do something about dinner."

He followed her as far as the kitchen doorway, watching
as she scooped her shoes up from the floor. "What happened to your knee?" he asked.

"The dollhouse furniture happened to my knee," she replied, waving at the breakfast table where the broken pieces
lay. "It isn't much of a scratch," she reassured him as she

folded up the hem of her skirt to keep it from getting stained by the blood. "What ticks me off is that I destroyed a pair of hose." She kissed Kyle's cheek and smiled lamely. "Things'll calm down in a little while," she promised him. "You timed your arrival a bit poorly, but I'm glad you're here."

Kyle gazed down at her, his lips shaping an enigmatic smile. "Go wash that cut," he ordered her.

"I put some bottles of beer in the fridge to chill for you, so help yourself if you want one," she called over her shoulder. "Leah, you finish putting those crayons in the box." Leah pouted and turned her back on her mother.

Sighing, Roberta picked her way through the mess of books on the hall floor, tossed her portfolio onto her worktable in the study and shut herself inside the bathroom. She peeled off her panty hose and threw them in the garbage basket, then scrubbed her knee and stuck an adhesive strip over the scratch. For good measure, she tossed a handful of water onto her face to cool herself off. After drying her cheeks, she headed to her bedroom, undressed, and slipped on a pair of snug-fitting jeans and a loosely knit short-sleeved jersey. She brushed out her hair, took a deep breath, and commanded herself to be charming for Kyle.

When she emerged from her bedroom, she found Leah's books gone from the hallway, and as she entered the living room, she noticed that the crayons had been picked up. Leah was somberly organizing her dollhouse furniture in the now upright dollhouse. Kyle sat at the table in the dining area, several sheets of newspaper spread before him and a bottle of Elmer's Glue-All at his elbow. He manipulated the pieces of the broken dollhouse table, trying to align them before applying the glue.

The serenity of the scene heartened Roberta. Her gaze traveled from Leah, whose pinched expression indicated that

she was still angry and upset, back to Kyle again. The way
he hunched over the tiny pieces of wood caused the pale blue
cotton of his shirt to stretch smoothly across his broad back.
His hands, though large and hard, worked deftly with the
toy pieces, matching their broken edges with skillful preci-
sion. Yes, Roberta mused silently, she was definitely glad he
was here.

She continued to the kitchen, dumped the uneaten macaroni-and-cheese from the pot, and filled the utensil with
soapy water to soak. Then she gathered the ingredients for
her stew and organized them on the counter beside the stove.
She was cutting onions when Kyle sidled up behind her and
gave her shoulder a gentle squeeze. "How's the knee?" he
asked.

"I'll live," she replied. "I've given myself worse cuts
shaving my legs."

"Then why are you crying?"

"The onions," she explained, sniffling and sweeping her
damp eyes with the back of her hand. "I'm sorry, Kyle, but
it's going to be some time before dinner's ready." She set
down her knife and moved to the sink to scour the pot. "If
you're starving, there should be some potato chips in that
cabinet by the broom closet." Under her breath, she added,
"If Natalie and Leah didn't devour them all today."

"I'm not starving," said Kyle. He leaned against the
counter and watched her scrape the crusted cheese and
noodles from the pot with a sudsy scouring pad. "Is this a
typical Friday night at the Frankel house?"

She eyed him and grinned through her onion-induced
tears. "We have our ups and downs," she admitted. "But
tonight isn't exactly typical. I got held up at work and came
home late, which happens only about thirty percent of the
time. And you're here, which, of course, is a change of pace
for us. Oh," she remembered, tossing down the scouring

pad, "it gets worse, Kyle. I had to bring some work home with me. I don't know when I'll get to it, but it's got to be done this weekend."

He digested this news, then shrugged. "If it's got to be done, then you'll do it," he said. "We'll figure something out." Roberta nodded and turned her attention back to the pot in the sink. Kyle stepped behind her and dug his thumbs into her lower back. "You seem a little tense," he observed, rotating his fingers and massaging the tautness from the muscles surrounding her spine. "Does this feel good?"

How did he know how much she needed the magic of one of his back rubs? The man was clairvoyant, she decided, moaning happily as his thumbs dug into the small of her back. "Does it feel good?" she echoed, leaning back into his hands. "Do birds fly? Kyle, even if I don't marry you, I may just hire you full-time as a masseur." She rinsed out the pot and shook off the excess water. Her lips curved in a nostalgic smile. "Remember the day Leah was born?" she asked. "You rubbed my back then, too."

"I remember."

"It felt so good." She sighed, savoring the massage for one more moment before she broke from Kyle and shifted her dinner preparations into high gear. He considerately kept out of her way, taking a seat at the breakfast table while Roberta filled the pot with meat, broccoli, onions and a sauce of her own invention. Once that was heating on the stove, she measured some rice into a smaller pot and set it to boil.

She was pulling vegetables for a salad from the crisper drawer of the refrigerator when Kyle broke the silence. "Why don't you want me to make a new table for Leah's dollhouse?"

Roberta sighed again, this time not from pleasure but from annoyance. "I'm constantly telling Leah not to leave her toys all over the floor. I tell her that if she leaves them on the floor, they're going to get broken. But she doesn't pay any attention to me. So what happens? She leaves the little table on the floor and it gets broken. I don't think she should be rewarded with a brand-new table for being careless and thoughtless. She has to learn that her actions have consequences. Maybe the next time her things are scattered on the floor, she'll remember the broken table and pick up after herself."

Kyle accepted Roberta's explanation with a nod. "Are you angry that I glued the table back together for her?"

Roberta smiled. "No. That was probably the best solution for the time being. She can live with a glued table. She still has the nicest dollhouse in New York."

Kyle remained in the kitchen with Roberta, keeping her company while she prepared the salad. He described his drive to the city, and his good fortune in finding a parking space for his truck only half a block from her building. "Maybe I can take Leah out tomorrow so you can work," he proposed. "It's been a long time since I visited the city. We can take in the sights and stay out of your way."

"She'll love that," Roberta predicted. She glanced through the doorway to the living room, where Leah sat in front of her dollhouse, carefully arranging the furniture inside it. Roberta's gaze shifted to the formal dining table in an alcove off the living room. Originally she'd intended to make an elegant dinner that night, setting the long teak table with a linen cloth and matching napkins, china, maybe even cut-crystal candlesticks. But she didn't have the energy to arrange such a festive spread, and it was already well past Leah's usual dinner hour. Roberta gathered her everyday dishes and placed them around the breakfast table. It would be a snug fit for three people, but they could manage it.

Actually, the evening wasn't all that disastrous, she consoled herself. That things hadn't gone smoothly, that she and Leah had argued and dinner was running late, that the fancy meal she had envisioned was failing to materialize—none of that mattered. It was probably just as well that Kyle was being exposed to, if not a typical Friday night at the Frankel house, a Friday night more ordinary than not. If everything had gone perfectly, he would have gotten a false impression of the way things were. One of the purposes of his visit was for him to be enlightened as to what life with Roberta and Leah would be like. Among other things, life with Roberta and Leah would entail witnessing disagreements and spats between mother and daughter, finding the living room less than tidy, eating supper late when Roberta got held up at the office.

Baptism by fire, she decided, wasn't necessarily a bad idea.

"Leah?" she called as she scooped the rice into a serving bowl and set it on a trivet at the center of the table. She located another trivet for the casserole dish and carried it to the table as well. "Dinner's ready."

Leah entered the kitchen, her eyes level with Roberta's waist. "I'm sorry you hurt your knee," she mumbled.

Roberta smiled warmly, although Leah's face was so downcast she couldn't have noticed her mother's loving grin. "I'm sorry your dollhouse table got broken," she said. She squatted down to Leah's height and extended her arms. "Hug?" she asked.

Leah walked to Roberta and accepted the hug. Her face brightening, she climbed onto her chair and reached for the salad bowl. Kyle's gaze shuttled between Leah and Roberta; he was impressed by their seemingly easy reconciliation. Little did he know how much the act of apologizing to her mother had cost a proud child like Leah.

Leah's spirits continued to improve during the meal, and they soared when Kyle told her that he and she would be spending Saturday together out of the apartment so Roberta could work. "Wow!" Leah enthused. "That's great! Where are we going to go?"

"Wherever you'd like," Kyle offered.

Roberta tried to signal him that he shouldn't give Leah too much latitude in planning their outing, but he resolutely ignored her. She nudged him under the table. He cast her a quick look and then grinned smugly and turned back to Leah. "I'll put myself in your hands," he said grandly. "You decide where you'd like to take me."

For a ride, Roberta thought with mild dismay. But what could she do? She'd tried to warn Kyle, and he'd refused to heed her warning. She succumbed to a reluctant smile. Let him learn for himself, she decided. Let him learn everything he can learn about life with Leah.

Indeed, the little girl promptly began to rattle off all the places she could think of to visit with Kyle the following day. "We can go to the Cloisters. Have you ever been to the Cloisters? Aunt Mary took me there right after we moved to New York. Remember, Mommy? Remember when Aunt Mary took me there?"

Taking pity on Kyle, Roberta protested, "Honey, that's as far from SoHo as you can get and still be in Manhattan."

"But it's so neat there," Leah maintained. "It's a museum, Kyle, but it's built like an old castle. What's it called, Mom? An evil castle?"

"Medieval," Roberta assisted.

"Yeah. And then," Leah continued, "we can go on the Staten Island ferry. Have you ever gone on the Staten Island ferry? It's not like a lobster boat, but—"

"Leah," Roberta gently reproached her. "The Staten Island ferry is in the opposite direction from the Cloisters. Maybe you ought to let me map out a reasonable itinerary for you."

"Kyle said wherever I'd like to go," Leah claimed. "I'd like to go on the ferry, okay? 'Cause Kyle likes the water. And on the ferry I don't have to wear that dumb life jacket. And then after the ferry, we could go to the Bronx Zoo."

Roberta laughed. "Leah, it isn't a marathon you're running. You don't have to cover twenty-six miles in one day. More than twenty-six," she added, catching Kyle's perplexed smile. "If you've got a good parking space, Kyle, you'll want to hold on to it. Which means either you'll spend all day tomorrow on the subways and buses, or else you'll let me figure out a saner day for you."

Kyle settled in his chair and gave Roberta a cocky smile. "I don't think that's necessary, Roberta," he contradicted her. "Leah and I can work this out ourselves."

Roberta's eyebrows arched slightly, but she conceded with a shrug. "Suit yourself," she said impassively, thoughts of baptism by fire coursing through her mind again.

Once dinner was done, Leah helped to clear the table without being asked. Roberta suspected that her daughter's uncommon offer of help had arisen solely to impress Kyle, but she accepted Leah's assistance without comment, as if this were normal behavior on Leah's part.

Since it was already nearly eight o'clock by the time the kitchen was clean, Roberta let Leah stay up fifteen minutes past her bedtime. She spent the time showing Kyle the many paintings and pastels that hung on the walls of the living room and hall. "Mommy did these," Leah boasted. "My daddy did this one," she said, pointing to a large cubist oil painting in bright orange, red, yellow and black, depicting dancers in a frenzied celebration. "Mostly he did illustrating, but he also made some paintings like this. Mommy did this one,'' she continued, indicating a watercolor still life that Roberta had always considered trite, but that somehow looked decent framed and hung on a wall. ''I did this one,'' Leah announced, standing boastfully beside a robust maze of crayon lines that Roberta had matted and framed for her.

''So much talent in this family,'' Kyle observed.

''My gramma in California says it's because we live in a loft,'' Leah said.

''And your mommy in New York says it's time to put on your pj's,'' Roberta said, concluding the art tour. Leah seemed ready to object, but Kyle's stern look stifled her, and she trudged to her bedroom to get undressed.

Kyle draped his arm around Roberta, and she rested her head against his shoulder. She was tired. It felt good to lean on him. He kissed her forehead and she smiled. ''She'll be asleep soon,'' Roberta promised.

Kyle seemed about to say something, then stopped himself. Something sexy, Roberta guessed from the smoky glow in his eyes and the seductive arch of his lips. He kissed her, instead.

''Mommy?'' Leah hollered. ''Come tuck me in! Kyle, too!''

''Her highness beckons,'' Roberta muttered, leading Kyle down the hall to Leah's bedroom. The room was spacious and cheerful, with bright flowers painted on one wall, a toy box—whose lid was buried beneath a mountainous heap of stuffed animals—standing against the opposite wall and the lovely rocker Kyle had made for her in one corner. The stuffed giraffe, faded and patched, was cuddled beneath Leah's arm as she climbed into her bed. ''All set?'' Roberta asked.

"I need a story," Leah asserted. "One of Aunt Mary's, okay? Kyle can read it. *Pine Needles*." She named a specific book as Roberta searched through Leah's library, which Leah had moved from the hallway to the floor of her closet. Roberta located the book and handed it to Leah as Kyle balanced his large body on the edge of the mattress. "See?" Leah said, opening the book to the dedication. "See? It says, 'To Leah.' That's me."

Kyle smiled, then read Leah the short tale, which dealt with the adventures of a porcupine named Pine Needles. Leah frequently stopped him to interject some comment on the action, or to embellish the story with an interesting tidbit about its author: "Aunt Mary told me that she got the idea for the turtle from this neighbor of hers who always looks like he's trying to hide his head inside his coat," she reported. "Aunt Mary told me she wrote this part in a moving car, and then she couldn't read what she wrote because the writing got all jumbled up, and she had to write the whole page all over again so she could read it." And finally she added, as Kyle closed the book and stood up, "You read it all right, Kyle, except you went too fast. Mommy makes all the animals talk in different voices when she reads to me. Don't you, Mommy?"

Roberta offered Kyle a placating smile. "I've been at it longer than he has," she reminded Leah. "It takes practice to get all the animals' voices right." She crossed to the nightstand and reached for the lamp.

"Where is Kyle going to sleep tonight?" Leah asked.

Roberta's hand paused on the switch. She cast Kyle a swift look. He appeared resigned to Leah's curiosity. Smiling, Roberta turned back to her daughter. "In my room," she said.

"How come?"

"Because we want to spend some time together."

"I want to spend time with Kyle, too," Leah remarked.

"You'll be spending all day tomorrow with him," Roberta reminded her. "So I'll spend tonight with him. It must feel good to be in such demand," she added, shooting a teasing grin Kyle's way. He looked mildly embarrassed. Roberta turned back to Leah. "Good night, darling," she whispered, kissing the little girl and then turning off the lamp.

She and Kyle left the bedroom and shut the door behind them. They strolled to the living room to fetch his suitcase. Roberta reached for it, but Kyle stayed her, lifting her hand to his shoulder and then wrapping her in his arms. His lips came down upon hers, firm and powerful, and she remembered that there were more important reasons for her to want to marry him than simply to be able to lean on him when she was tired.

Her mouth opened to welcome his tongue, and his fingers plunged into her thick, curly hair, reaching for the nape of her neck and stroking it. Her hands tightened on his shoulders, drawing his body to hers, relishing his warmth and strength.

She would gladly have stood kissing him in the living room forever, but eventually he drew back to catch his breath. He gazed down at her, his lids lowered, his teeth white and even behind his barely parted lips. "Hello," he whispered.

"Hello."

"I don't mean to sound critical," he remarked, "but that's the sort of welcome I was hoping for when I rang your bell a couple of hours ago."

"Oh, sure," Roberta said with a laugh. "I'm supposed to kiss you like that with Little Miss Busybody hanging around, taking notes?"

His hands moved hesitantly through Roberta's hair, then came to rest on her shoulders. "Well, not quite like that, but something a little more affectionate than 'Hi, come on in and join the fray.'"

Roberta's smile grew bittersweet. She lowered her eyes and exhaled. "I tried to tell you last week, Kyle—you've got an unrealistic concept of what my life is like. I would have loved to greet you romantically this evening. I would have loved to come home on time to a neat and orderly house, with Leah sitting on the couch reading Dickens, and Natalie—the baby-sitter—saying, 'Oh, don't bother paying me this week, Mrs. Frankel. It was my pleasure. And I hope you don't mind, but I washed the kitchen floor for you. Leah helped me to wax it.'"

"I get the picture," Kyle muttered.

"Do you want to retract the marriage proposal?"

He propped her chin up with his thumbs so he could see her face. He was laughing. "Don't be silly," he chided her. "Do you think my decision to marry you is contingent on how clean your kitchen floor is?"

"Yours is cleaner than mine," Roberta recalled. "Maybe *I* ought to base my decision to marry you on that."

He brushed her lips with his. "The hell with kitchen floors. There's more to a marriage than that." His voice was husky with longing. His mouth covered hers again, demonstrating specifically what aspect of marriage he was concerned with at that moment.

His kiss was frustratingly brief but full of promise. After releasing Roberta, he lifted his suitcase in one hand and folded the other about her fingers. She ushered him down the hall to her bedroom and closed the door once they were inside.

He scrutinized her bedroom as she'd scrutinized his the previous week. The simple decor of it pleased him. The smooth white walls and high ceilings gave the room a spacious brightness that contrasted nicely with the heavy antique-maple secretary desk and matching dresser. Her double bed featured an arching brass headboard and was decorated with a colorful quilt. A thick Persian rug covered the floor.

Kyle kicked off his shoes and sat on the bed, pulling Roberta between his outstretched legs. He worked open the fastening of her jeans and kissed the skin above her panties. "Kyle," she murmured, combing her fingers through his soft blond hair.

"I missed you," he said.

"It's only been a week," she argued, failing to disguise her delight at his compliment.

He almost told her how achingly empty his bed had seemed without her in it. He almost told her that nothing in his reasonably extensive experience with women had prepared him for what he'd felt with her the night she'd spent with him, and the loss he'd felt after she left. But he wasn't good at putting thoughts like that into words. He could write such things in a letter to Roberta, perhaps, but he couldn't just say them to her face.

"It hasn't been a week," he disputed her. "It's been two and a half hours. I've been missing you ever since I walked through your door."

"Because I didn't give you a warm welcome?" Roberta asked, unbuttoning his shirt.

He nodded and eased her jeans over her hips. "Understand—I *am* being realistic about this marriage, Roberta. But that doesn't mean I have to adore you when you're storming around the kitchen in torn stockings." His tongue ran along the lace-trimmed elastic of her panties, leaving a damp line on the skin of her belly. "I find you much more appealing the way you are now."

She shuddered, her fingers digging into the unyielding muscles of his back. Recognizing the sweet torment he was causing her, he pulled away and slid off his shirt. Roberta ran her hands forward to caress his chest. "If you really want to marry me, you've got to take the bad with the good," she informed him, her voice surprisingly steady despite his having brought his hands back to her hips.

He stroked down her thighs and then up again. "Fair enough," he said, peeling her panties down her long legs and letting them drop to the floor. "I've already taken the bad. Now I deserve the good."

He lifted her to straddle his lap and kissed her. They tumbled down onto the mattress, Kyle's fingers exploring her naked legs and then sliding beneath her shirt, pushing the knit material up and out of his way. Roberta raised her head so he could tug off the shirt. He did away with her bra, then assisted her in removing his slacks.

He knew he was proceeding awfully quickly, but she did nothing to slow him down. Her eagerness thrilled him. "You missed me, too, didn't you?" he deduced, sliding one of his legs between hers and flexing his thigh against her as her fingers probed the muscles of his lower back.

"Yes," she confessed shakily. She'd been too busy all week to be overtly conscious of how much she'd missed Kyle, but now that she was with him, she understood how hollow and lonely her week had been in his absence. She missed his smile, his beautiful eyes, his soft voice. She missed his touch, his agile fingers waltzing over her skin, measuring the fullness of her breasts and the tapering of her waist.

He rolled her onto her back and gazed down at her. His index finger traced the concave line from her lower ribs across her navel to her hips and back up again, its pleas-

antly roughened tip causing her nerve endings to fire errat-
ically beneath her skin.

"Aren't you going to say it?" she breathed.

"Say what?"

"How skinny I am. You say it every time you see me."

"Mm." He leaned back to study her body, then bowed to
kiss the flat expanse of her stomach. "I must be getting used
to you."

"I mean, if you prefer me the other way, I can start
stuffing my face with sweets—"

"Don't you dare," Kyle silenced her.

"I'm partial to chocolate," she added, her voice fading
into a breathless moan as his lips wandered to her thigh. He
nibbled down to her knee, then touched the bandage strip
there with a gentle kiss.

Abruptly he lifted himself from her. He leaned back on
his haunches and stared at her, his expression solemn. "I'm
sorry you had a lousy evening, Roberta," he said.

"It wasn't lousy."

"Typical?"

"Maybe a shade worse than normal," she allowed.
"But—" she smiled "—we're more than making up for that
now."

His eyes met hers. They appeared infinitely soft to her, as
soft and alluring as the dreamlike fog that had descended
upon Kyle and Roberta's world five years ago. She felt her
love for him swell inside her, an actuality, a truth, something she had no choice but to accept. She loved him, and
she could easily endure the lousiest of evenings as long as he
was with her.

She reached for his face, then cupped her hand against the
back of his head and urged him up onto her. He accepted
her invitation by fusing himself to her, filling her, reaching
for her soul with his compelling thrusts.

Her entire body responded, eddies of pleasure rippling through her, increasing in intensity as the motions of their bodies intensified, deepening as Kyle moved deeper and deeper inside Roberta. She bit her lip, but even that couldn't smother the anguished moans of delight that tore from her throat, one after another until the ecstasy building inside her demanded that she surrender. With an exultant cry she did.

Hearing her, feeling her, Kyle raced toward his own climax and groaned as it encompassed him. "Oh, God, Roberta," he gasped, his lips coming to rest near her ear. His tongue darted out to trace the curve of her earlobe, and she moaned again. "I *have* missed you."

"I've missed you, too," she whispered, brushing his mussed hair back from his damp cheeks and brow.

Her hushed tone caused him to raise his head. He peered at her, then at the wall separating Roberta's room from her daughter's. "Can . . . can Leah hear us in here?" he asked.

Roberta had never thought about how soundproof the loft's walls might be. She'd never had to before. "I don't know," she admitted. "She's probably asleep by now. If she isn't, I guess it's too late for us to be worrying about it at this point."

He considered that obvious truth, then sank back down onto the bed beside Roberta. His head settled on the pillow next to hers, and he eased her onto her side to face him. "You're right," he conceded candidly. "This thing is going to take some getting used to."

Roberta's eyes absorbed the sharply chiseled lines of his face, the rugged, clean-shaven jaw she'd become accustomed to, just as he had become accustomed to her lean figure, and the magnificent eyes she'd never forgotten. They were so tender now, so content, that she couldn't imagine them ever becoming hard and cold again.

"You don't have to get used to it," she noted hesitantly. It was her love for him that was forcing her to speak, to give him the opportunity to retreat from a marriage to her if he felt that it would involve a greater adjustment than he wanted to make. "I haven't locked you into any promises yet, Kyle. You're still free to back out."

He frowned, trying to fathom the implications of her statement. "Is that what you want me to do?" he asked.

I want you to love me, she answered silently. But he still hadn't mentioned love, and she just didn't know whether love was any part of what he felt for her, any part at all of what made him want to marry her.

He cared for her, yes, and he missed her; he freely admitted to that. Obviously he desired her. But did he love her? Or did he want to marry her because he was looking for responsibility, or, as he'd said last week, because he hoped to create something meaningful with Roberta and Leah?

"Roberta." He drew a line along her cheek to her temple with his finger, and then followed the slope of her jaw to its gracefully sculpted point beneath her lips. "Tell me what *you* want," he begged her.

"I want—" she sighed "—I want you to be honest with me," she said. "I don't want you to back out, Kyle. But I want you to do what's best for all of us—including yourself. If you decide that this marriage idea isn't panning out the way you thought it would, I want you to tell me. We've got to be honest with each other, all right?"

"Of course." He kissed her, then rolled onto his back and drew her against him, cushioning her head with his shoulder. His fingers wove through her hair, losing themselves in the silky ringlets. "If you want me to be honest, Roberta, then in all honesty, I think you're worrying unnecessarily," he commented. "I enjoyed myself this evening. Leah calmed down, and you kept your wits about you, and then you two made up and it was fantastic. You've got to expect fights every now and then. I'm not afraid of them."

"It's not just fights," Roberta said. "Leah and I don't fight that much. But...it's a very complicated thing, a parent-child relationship. Very delicate."

"And I'm willing to learn. I *want* to learn, Roberta. Don't underestimate me, all right?"

She shifted, angling her head so she could see his face. She hadn't intended her remarks to come across as a put-down, and his grim expression disturbed her. "I'm not underestimating you, Kyle. I know you can handle it if you choose to. I'm only saying, you might find out that it's not what you want at all."

"We'll cross that bridge when we get to it—*if* we get to it," he said, nudging her head back onto his shoulder and stroking his fingers through her hair again.

For a long while neither of them spoke. The only sound was the nearly imperceptible whisper of his hands in her hair. "I've decided to take one of my carpenters out of the workshop so he can help me out with the paperwork at my company," he announced, breaking the silence.

"Oh?" Roberta asked, trying not to sound too surprised. The last thing she'd expected him to mention right then was his work.

He nodded, his chin rubbing gently against the crown of her head. "I'm thinking of grooming him as kind of an operations manager," he elaborated. "Someone to deal with the day-to-day nonsense—inventory, supplies, the first round of complaint calls to my suppliers. I'll still make the major decisions and I'll still oversee the designs themselves. But I've decided I've got to get my hands back on the wood."

"That's probably a good idea," Roberta concurred. In truth, she thought it was a superb idea, but she didn't want to bowl him over with her enthusiasm. "You always did enjoy the actual carpentry work."

He nodded again. "I didn't realize how much I missed it until I began working on that rocker for Leah. No, I take that back," he contradicted himself. "I *did* realize how much I missed it. Almost from the start."

"Then why didn't you get back to it a long time ago?" Roberta asked.

"Because..." He sighed, his fingers meandering in a soothing pattern behind Roberta's ear and down to her throat. "Because I was trying to grow up."

"Grow up?" Roberta blurted out.

He chuckled wryly. "I guess I thought growing up meant I should sit at a desk and make weighty decisions. I'm good at doing that, Roberta. My business is flourishing. I've got architects and interior designers calling me from all over the country, ordering customized pieces. I sit in my glass-enclosed office at the far end of the workshop and dictate letters and push the buttons on my phone and take calls from Venezuela and act very important."

"Whatever gave you the idea that that was the way to grow up?" Roberta asked, raising herself on one elbow and staring down at him.

"Whatever gave you the idea that cutting your hair was a sign of maturity?" he parried her.

"I *had* to cut my hair," she defended herself. "For one thing, I'd never get a job as a commercial artist looking like an out-of-date flower child, and I needed a respectable job to support Leah and myself. For another thing," she continued, "all that hair was a lot of work to shampoo, and it was hot on my neck in the summer. I just outgrew it, I guess."

Kyle contemplated her words, his eyes steady and his smile pensive. "And I thought I should outgrow the out-of-date flower-child carpenter routine," he explained. "Every time I thought of you, Roberta, I thought of how incredibly important it was to be raising a child the way you were. What was I doing that was important? I'd accomplished nothing in my life to match the miracle of making and raising a child." He halted, lost in a private meditation, working through his thoughts. "So I thought if I grew up, stopped spending my mornings repairing old furniture for neighbors and friends, and stopped killing my afternoons paddling about the cove looking for lobsters, maybe I'd accomplish something, too."

"You did," Roberta noted. "You just said that your business is flourishing."

"Making money isn't much of an accomplishment," Kyle opined. "Especially when you forget to keep doing the things that you enjoy most." He peered up at her, smiling hesitantly. "You were right last week, Roberta, nagging me about buying a rowboat. It's crazy for me not to have one. I live near enough the water, and I can certainly afford one. *Not* having a rowboat isn't going to make me a better person."

"And having one *is* going to make you a better person," Roberta added in a quiet but certain tone.

"You made me realize that," he whispered, closing his arms tightly around her. "I appreciate it, Roberta. You're a very perceptive woman, and I appreciate it."

She snuggled up to him and closed her eyes. He appreciated her.

It wasn't love. But perhaps in time appreciation and desire and caring would evolve into love. She could hope for that.

And in the meantime, she'd done something vital for him—she'd shown him that he mustn't give up the simple pleasures of working with wood and boating, both of which meant so much to him. The joy of knowing she had opened his eyes to that truth would satisfy her for now.

Chapter Ten

After devouring a hearty breakfast Saturday morning, Kyle and Leah left the loft for their day on the town. Kyle firmly vetoed Roberta's recommendation that she map out a route for them. He was positive that Leah would take him on a fine tour of the city, he swore.

"Sure," Roberta countered. "Including the outer boroughs, and maybe the suburbs of northern New Jersey."

Unperturbed, Kyle let Leah lead him from the apartment, and Roberta decided not to waste her day worrying about him. He and his young tour guide wouldn't be home until five o'clock, by which time she intended to be done with her lettering samples and ready to go out for dinner. Chinatown wasn't far from her SoHo home. She thought that Kyle would enjoy the quaint Oriental scenery of the neighborhood, to say nothing of the top-notch restaurants in the area.

She felt almost sinfully extravagant having the entire loft—and the entire day—to herself. Even though she had work to do, the freedom to work at her own pace, without a zillion interruptions from Leah, delighted her.

Before knuckling down to her work, she pampered herself with a leisurely bubble bath—a luxury she hadn't enjoyed in months. After soaking her body in the scented froth for thirty hedonistic minutes, she forced herself out of the tub and dressed in a pair of loose-fitting linen slacks and a gauzy blouse. She brewed herself a fresh pot of coffee, poured a cup and retired to the study.

There were many advantages to being married, she mused as she bent over her worktable with her pens. Marriage would provide her with not just the basic pleasure of spending lots of time with someone she loved, but also the chance to let someone else take over the role of parent every now and then. Roberta was used to being the sole adult in Leah's life. It was a fact, not open to argument, so she accepted it without question or quibble. But how nice *not* to be the sole adult in Leah's life, she thought wistfully. How nice to be able to rely on Kyle to entertain Leah for a day. How nice to share the enormous responsibility of parenthood with a willing partner.

She hoped that Kyle was enjoying the change of pace as much as she was. He had implied that living alone and having responsibility for no one other than himself was at least as difficult for him as Roberta's situation was for her. Spending a day romping through New York with Leah might be as much of a treat for Kyle as having the apartment all to herself for a few hours was for Roberta. At least she hoped so.

Without the usual distractions, she was able to work with extraordinary efficiency. By three o'clock she'd created enough lettering variations to satisfy her boss and his client. She flattened the samples between sheets of oaktag and zipped them into her portfolio, then left the study with a happy sigh.

She decided to relax in the living room. She turned on the stereo to a classical music station, free from the worry that Leah, despising the music, would make obnoxious snorting noises until Roberta switched to a livelier broadcast. Curling up on the sofa, she skimmed a few outdated magazines that she hadn't had the time to read when she bought them, and indulged in the sheer bliss of being left alone.

Tossing aside the final magazine in her catch-up pile, she closed her eyes, stretched out on the plump off-white cushions of the couch and considered Kyle's marriage proposal. There were so many good reasons to say yes to him: Leah *did* need a father, and Roberta would benefit from the support and assistance of another adult in raising Leah. Kyle was good-natured, intelligent, kind, generous. He was stunningly attractive and a sublime lover. His profession as a carpenter was closely related to the arts, which Roberta liked.

And even if Kyle didn't love her, he recognized that she was good for him. He'd admitted as much last night, when he'd told her he appreciated her perception about him. He needed someone like her in his life to keep him from losing touch with the simple things he enjoyed—boating and building things out of wood. He needed her to help him retain his perspective.

Then why wasn't she willing to accept all the many advantages of a marriage to Kyle? Why was she holding back, reluctant to agree to his proposal?

It wasn't so much that she was afraid Kyle didn't love her as that *she* loved *him*. She loved him enough to be concerned about whether his marrying her would be the best thing for him. She loved him enough to care about his ability to find satisfaction in a marriage with her. She loved him enough to want only happiness for him, and she wasn't convinced that by marrying her he would find happiness.

Maybe she was underestimating him, as he'd accused her last night. Just because he waxed rhapsodic about the experience of creating and nurturing a child didn't mean that he wasn't aware of the struggles and strains of the job. He could know full well that wood sometimes splintered or cracked, that a carpenter risked cutting himself with his tools or developing blisters from sandpaper, and still adore carpentry. Raising a child was similar, pain mixed in with the pleasure. Maybe Kyle understood that.

Well, she supposed, a long day alone with Leah, and without Roberta close at hand to rescue him if Leah became obstreperous, would probably teach Kyle more than all the pious lectures she could recite about how he wasn't being realistic in his view of the parent-child relationship. Roberta awaited his return with curiosity. And with a mild anxiety. She did hope the day would go well for him. While she wanted what was best for him, she wanted to believe that what was best for him would include marriage to her.

She heard the key in the door announcing Kyle and Leah's return home a few minutes before five. Pulling herself up to sit, she fluffed out her hair with her fingers, then stood up, and strolled to the door to let them in.

"Hi, Mommy!" Leah singsonged, bounding into the living room. She clutched in her fist the string of a buoyant heart-shaped silver balloon, nearly identical to the balloon she'd gotten at the craft fair in Madison the previous weekend. A necklace of clear glass beads hung around her neck. "We had a really neat time! Didn't we, Kyle?"

Roberta turned from Leah to Kyle. After stepping through the doorway and shutting the door, he leaned against the wall as if too fatigued to stand without support. His brow was marked by a deep frown line, his eyelids drooped and the corners of his mouth were definitely slumping downward. The front of his polo shirt was splattered with a brown stain. "What happened to your shirt?" Roberta asked.

"Ask Leah," he grunted, shoving away from the wall and slouching to the sofa. He collapsed onto it and groaned.

Roberta eyed Leah, who shrugged. "I guess I spilled my root beer on Kyle," she said.

"Don't *guess*," Kyle reproached her. "You *did* spill root beer on me."

"Well, it was an accident," Leah asserted, not at all contrite. She skipped around the room, overflowing with energy. "We had a great day, Mommy. We went to South Street Seaport, and there were all these stores there, and Kyle bought me this necklace. Isn't it beautiful?" Before Roberta could compliment her on the beads—or question Kyle about his propensity for spoiling Leah with so many unnecessary gifts—Leah continued. "Then we went to Battery Park and it was really boring. And we went to the top of the World Trade Center and I threw up."

"That sounds like fun," Roberta muttered, trying to catch Kyle's eye. "Just think, Kyle," she teased. "There are worse things than root beer you could have gotten on your shirt."

"Uh-uh, I threw up in the bathroom," Leah assured her mother. "It was too high at the top of the building. It made me sick. So I told Kyle I was going to throw up, and he started running around trying to find a lady to take me into the bathroom. And then he couldn't find one, and he had to come in with me himself. And all these ladies started screaming when he came in, and some of them threw their lipstick at him."

Picturing the scene, Roberta began to giggle. Kyle shot her a scathing look, and she covered her mouth with her hand to keep herself from laughing at what he obviously did not consider even remotely funny. Struggling for sobriety, she asked her daughter, "Did you feel better afterward?"

"Yeah. Kyle said I had to have some ginger ale for my stomach, but I hate ginger ale, so we got root beer instead. I guess I spilled a little on him."

"Don't *guess*," he snarled.

Leah shrugged again. "Then we went to Central Park, and we went to the zoo and stuff. I got this balloon there, because the balloon I got last week is ruined. And then we walked around the park and this guy tried to sell Kyle some sunglasses, and Kyle said he thought the sunglasses were stolen, so we had to pretend we didn't see the guy. So we're walking real fast, and this crazy guy is running after us shouting, 'But they're real good sunglasses, mister, they're polar bears,' or something like that."

"Polar bears?" Roberta asked Kyle.

"Polarized," he mumbled.

"So then we decided to go to the Cloisters, but we got on the wrong subway by mistake, and we ended up by Shea Stadium. I wanted to go in, but Kyle said we couldn't, and he wasn't much of a baseball fan, anyway."

"You don't like baseball?"

Kyle raised his weary eyes to Roberta and grimaced. "Right now I don't like much of anything."

She accepted his statement with a discreet nod and turned back to Leah. "How did you get back to Manhattan from Queens?"

"Through Brooklyn," Leah explained. "Some lady gave us these wrong directions, and we had to get transfers and climb all these stairs, and we rode an elevator train! Mommy, have I ever ridden an elevator train before? I don't remember."

"Elevated," Roberta corrected her. "No, I don't think you have."

Leah gleefully jumped up and down. "I knew it! I knew it! See, Kyle, I told you—it was my first elevator train! And we rode across the bridge, and you could see the Statue of Liberty from the window, and I wanted to take a boat there, but Kyle said it was late and we had to come home. But we got off at the wrong stop, so we wound up walking the rest of the way. It was a great day, Mommy! Wasn't it great, Kyle?"

Roberta glanced compassionately at Kyle. He was hunched over, pinching the bridge of his nose. "You look beat," she observed gently. "Would you like some aspirin?"

"I could use a drink."

"All I have is beer," Roberta reminded him. "You know I don't drink much, so I haven't got anything strong in the house. Would a beer do?"

He considered, then shook his head and stalked to the bathroom. "I'll go with the aspirin," he decided.

Roberta watched him until he vanished into the bathroom. Then she stared at Leah, who was running in a figure-eight route around the living room, trailing her balloon behind her. It was no wonder that Kyle was exhausted, Roberta ruminated. He ought to have been less stubborn and foolhardy and let her plan his day with Leah. Roberta knew how Leah could be, wanting everything, dragging whomever she was with here and there and even to the outer boroughs of Brooklyn and Queens, just as Roberta had warned Kyle she would.

But even with Roberta's warning, Kyle hadn't been adequately prepared for a day with Leah. He didn't know that when Leah got wild, one had to put one's foot down and say, "No. We're *not* going to go to the Cloisters. We are going to visit the South Street Seaport, period." Leah might sulk and whine, but if the adult didn't remain firmly in control, the adult ended up with a whopping headache and a desperate thirst for hard liquor.

After several minutes, Kyle emerged from the bathroom. He'd rinsed his face and combed his hair, but shadows of exhaustion still darkened the skin under his eyes, and his dimples were nowhere in evidence. "How about a beer now?" Roberta asked, moving to his side and ushering him to the sofa as if he were a recovering invalid.

"All right," he said, kicking off his shoes and lifting his feet onto the coffee table. Roberta went to the kitchen and opened a bottle of beer for him. She carried it and a glass to the living room and presented them to Kyle. He ignored the glass and drank some beer straight from the bottle.

Roberta took a seat beside him and patted his hand placatingly. "If you don't want to go to Chinatown for dinner tonight, I understand," she told him. "You look tired."

"I *am* tired," he groaned.

Leah yanked off her beads and twirled them around her finger like a lasso. "I'm not hungry for dinner, anyway," she announced. "I had cotton candy."

"Cotton candy?" Roberta twisted on the sofa and glared at Kyle, her compassion for him in his suffering superseded by her disapproval of his having bought her daughter such useless junk food. "Why in the world did you let her have cotton candy?" she scolded. "That stuff is nothing but sugar, Kyle. Sugar and food coloring. There's not a single worthwhile ingredient in it, and after you gave her root beer—"

"And a chili dog for lunch," Leah added. "And Italian ices for dessert. Pink ones."

Roberta rolled her eyes. "Kyle," she murmured reproachfully.

"The root beer," he explained in a taut voice, "was because she threw up. The chili dog was because I told her to order a hot dog but while I was pulling out my wallet she asked the vendor to throw some chili on it. The Italian ices were because it was hot."

"And the cotton candy?" Roberta prodded him.

He shuddered and issued a dismal sigh. "The cotton candy," he muttered beneath his breath, "was part of a deal Leah and I made."

"What deal?"

He glowered briefly at Leah, then took another long, bracing drink of his beer. "The deal," he said, addressing the bottle, "was that if I bought her cotton candy she'd stop singing repulsive songs about eating decayed gopher's meat for lunch or about a corpse invaded by worms who play pinochle on its snout. In fact, for the price of one portion of cotton candy, Leah promised not to sing any song with the words 'green' or 'slime' in it."

Roberta nodded. Leah was currently at an age where she found songs containing such disgusting imagery utterly hilarious. When Leah embarked on one of her gross-out medleys, Roberta knew how to tune her out. Apparently Kyle didn't. "Poor Kyle," she said, patting his arm. "Rough day, huh?"

"Climbing Mount Everest would have been easy in comparison," he complained.

"Mount Everest?" Leah stopped twirling her necklace and flopped onto the floor at Kyle's feet. "Where's that?"

"Someplace far away," he snapped. "Maybe we ought to send you there."

"Now, Kyle," Roberta tried to calm him. "Don't bite Leah's head off. I know you're tired, but—" at his plaintive look, she smiled "—you should have let me organize your day. It wouldn't have been nearly as tiring." Gazing at his clouded eyes, she flashed on a picture of him invading a public ladies' rest room with a chalky-faced, nauseated little girl in tow and being barraged by hurled tubes of lipstick from the shrieking women within. She began to giggle again.

Kyle scowled and shrugged his arm free of her hand. "I'm glad you find this so amusing," he spat out.

"Oh, Kyle, I'm sorry," she said, sniffling back her laughter. She stood up resolutely. "Well, maybe you guys have been stuffing your faces with junk all day, but I haven't and I'm hungry. So here's what we're going to do: I'll go down to the deli on the corner and buy some cold cuts and hard rolls. We'll have sandwiches for supper, all right?"

"Wow!" Leah cheered. "Sounds great!" Kyle's only response was to drain his beer bottle.

"As a matter of fact," Roberta said, her gaze taking in Kyle's forlorn demeanor, "Leah, you can come with me to the deli. We'll let Kyle have a few minutes of peace and quiet, okay? He needs it."

"Okay," Leah agreed, racing to the door while Roberta hurried to her bedroom to get her purse. She pocketed the spare key she'd given Kyle for the day and swung the door wide. "We'll be back in a little while," she promised him before urging Leah ahead of her out of the apartment.

On the way to the deli, Leah regaled Roberta with more details of her day. She claimed to have dragged Kyle into countless shops at the South Street Seaport. "It was funny, Mommy," she noted astutely. "Kyle was in a much better mood there. That's where he bought me my necklace. He got kind of grouchy later. How come, do you think?"

"I think you tired him out," Roberta replied, holding the deli door open for Leah and following her inside.

"Do you think he doesn't like me anymore?" Leah asked, her small, pretty face registering deep concern.

"I think—" Roberta strove for honesty "—I think that right now you aren't his favorite person in the world. I'm sure he'll forgive you in time."

Leah absorbed Roberta's assessment of Kyle's feelings, her lips set in a solemn line. "Am I *your* favorite person?" she asked hopefully.

"You are my favorite little girl in the world," Roberta assured her.

Mollified, Leah raced to the glass counter and squawked, "Potato salad, Mommy! Let's get potato salad!"

A quart of potato salad, a pound each of sliced turkey breast and sliced roast beef and half a dozen hard rolls later, Roberta and Leah returned to the loft. In their absence, Kyle had showered and changed into a clean shirt. He appeared a bit more refreshed, and he exerted himself to be pleasant, though Roberta could tell he was still awfully tired.

"You did just fine for your rookie run," she tried to bolster him during a brief moment when Leah left them alone in the kitchen to clean up. "Don't take it so hard."

Kyle finished off the remains of his second beer. "I consider myself lucky that I survived," he commented, setting his empty bottle on the counter. "You know, Roberta, this city is filled with joggers. Even today, when it was hot and muggy outside, we kept seeing joggers racing along the sidewalks, sweat dripping from their faces, gasping for breath, looking as if they were about to drop. And I kept staring at those guys and thinking, 'You think *you've* got it tough? You think *you're* getting a workout?' Jogging in August has to be easier than what I went through today."

"What you went through is a lot like jogging," Roberta remarked. "Both activities require stamina. It takes time and practice to build up your strength."

Kyle nodded grimly. "I don't feel very strong at all right now."

Roberta kissed his cheek. "As you said, you survived," she pointed out. "It could have been worse."

"Kyle!" Leah called from the living room. "Kyle, will you play Candy Land with me?"

"Candy Land?" he asked Roberta nervously.

"It's a game," she told him. "A classic. I played it when I was a kid, too."

"I don't think I can handle it," he muttered.

Roberta chuckled and nudged him toward the living room. "It's a board game," she informed him. "You play it sitting down. Go on, play with Leah while I finish cleaning up in here."

After she was through in the kitchen, she joined Kyle and Leah for a second game of Candy Land. Kyle clearly found the simple game boring, but he politely played until Leah's bedtime arrived. He seemed as thrilled as Leah was disconsolate about her having to go to bed.

As on the previous night, Leah insisted on Kyle's reading her a bedtime story. She interrupted him numerous times, demonstrating for him the expressive way she wanted him to depict the various animals' voices in the story. "Owls hoot," she explained to him. "You should make Dr. Fowl-Owl hoot when he speaks." She illustrated by hooting several times. "And bears growl, Kyle. You know how to growl. Remember how you growled like a bear when we got lost in Queens and that man we asked for directions in the station didn't speak English? Remember? You asked him how to get to Manhattan and he started talking in some funny language—"

"It wasn't a funny language," Kyle cut her off, his tone dry and remonstrative. "It was Greek. Plato spoke Greek. Socrates spoke Greek. The *Iliad* was written in Greek."

"Oh," Leah said, unimpressed. "How long are you going to be a grouch, Kyle? Will you stop being a grouch tomorrow?"

He drew in a sharp breath, then forced a smile. "I need a good night's sleep as much as you do, Leah," he declared. "Enough of Mr. Fowl-Owl."

"*Dr.* Fowl-Owl," Leah corrected him.

"Right." He clapped the book shut and set it on the dresser. "Good night, Leah," he said as he stood up.

"Good night, Kyle. Good night, Mommy."

Roberta kissed Leah and clicked off the lamp. She and Kyle left Leah's room and moved directly to the master bedroom next door. Kyle flopped onto the bed and pulled Roberta down to sit beside him. "I think I struck out today," he said in a critique of his first major solo outing with Leah.

Roberta ruffled her fingers consolingly through his hair. "And she's worried about having struck out with you, Kyle. I'd say, all in all, it was probably a draw."

Kyle took her hand in his and studied it, running his thumbs over her knuckles and tracing her slender fingers. "You were right, Roberta," he confessed. "Playing Daddy for a frisky little girl isn't as easy as I thought it would be." He eyed Roberta with a mixture of condemnation and admiration. "How come you make it look so easy?"

"I've had five years of practice," Roberta reminded him.

He shook his head. "It takes more than practice," he asserted. "It takes talent. I—I don't think I've got it."

His blunt self-criticism surprised her. "It doesn't take talent," she gently disputed him. "Millions of people become parents every year. They aren't especially talented."

"And I bet most of them aren't much good as parents, either," Kyle countered. "You're a good parent, Roberta, and that's something rare. I must have been crazy to think I could be one, too."

"Don't be so hard on yourself," Roberta soothed him. She leaned over and kissed his lips. "Stay right here," she whispered before rising from the bed. "I'll be back in a few minutes, and I'm going to put your whole dismal day behind you."

He attempted a smile. Roberta kissed him again, then left the bedroom.

Kyle definitely needed to have his spirits restored, and his ego. With that goal in mind, she shut herself into the bathroom, undressed and splashed a lightly scented cologne behind her ears and between her breasts. Then she slipped on the lace-trimmed silk kimono Mary had given her a few years ago. Roberta rarely had any use for it; after moving back to New York she'd hung it in the storage closet outside the bathroom and forgotten about it.

But tonight it would be put to good use, she decided. Pirouetting in front of the full-length mirror attached to the bathroom door, she studied the diaphanous garment with its suggestive translucence and its delicate touches of lace. It looked lovely on her, and as soon as she'd tied it shut she glided back to the bedroom, determined to make Kyle forget all about his miserable day.

She slid onto the bed beside him and kissed him. He groaned and rolled away. She sat up, frowned and studied his heavy body, his arm slung over his face, his breathing slow and even. He was fast asleep.

Her mouth shaped a tender smile. Parenting was without question exhausting; she'd had more than enough experience to prove that. She only hoped that when Kyle woke up he wouldn't be as hard on himself as he'd been a few minutes ago.

She removed his clothing, careful not to awaken him, and then slid the lightweight quilt out from under his body and drew it up over him. After removing her kimono, she joined him beneath the blanket and turned off the bedside lamp.

Having had a relatively placid day herself, she wasn't sleepy. She lay awake beside Kyle, listening to him breathe, trying to imagine how he must have felt during his various mishaps and travails with Leah during the day.

To a certain extent, what had happened today was his own fault. He should have listened to her; he should have heeded her warnings and let her plan his outing with Leah. But the real problem lay much deeper than Leah's rambunctiousness and Kyle's failure to control her.

The real problem, as Roberta analyzed it, was that Kyle had expected something substantially different from what had actually occurred. He had expected fathering to come as naturally to him as mothering seemed to come to her. It was his totally unrealistic ideas of what being a parent was all about that left him so disappointed by the reality of it.

Roberta wondered whether, after his misadventures with Leah today, he would seriously rethink his decision to marry her. She hoped he would. She wanted him to give the situation the most intense and thorough consideration before he committed himself to her. If their marriage was not going to be what he was expecting—and it was fast becoming clear to Roberta that it wasn't—she wanted him to recognize that and to make his mind up before it was too late. She didn't want him to feel obliged to marry her, and then to chafe at the constraints of his built-in family and resent her for sticking him with something that fell far short of his imaginings.

He shouldn't have proposed to her in the first place, she pondered. He'd jumped the gun; he'd raised the question prematurely. He should have allowed for a normal, natural courtship, a weekend here and a weekend there, allowing Roberta and him to take their time in learning about each other.

Yet that would have seemed artificial, since she and Kyle already knew so much about each other. A marriage after five years of a long-distance but intimate friendship didn't exactly qualify as a rush-rush wedding.

On the other hand, everything they knew about each other simply wasn't enough. Letters could only approximate the truth. As Kyle had pointed out, Roberta had never written to him about Leah's frequent misbehavior or about her own frustrations and doubts as a mother. She'd written to him only about the wonderful things, and that was what had shaped his concept of life with Leah.

Roberta supposed she and Kyle could retreat, if necessary. They could back off from his proposal and start all over again, approaching each other in a more traditional way, with dinners at restaurants, tickets to concerts, Sunday afternoons with Leah. That was the way that Roberta had imagined her social life would develop once she began dating.

But it would be next to impossible for her and Kyle to engage in a pleasant, relaxed courtship when they both knew that it had begun with a marriage proposal. The notion of marriage would loom above them, around them, and either they'd spend all their energy trying to be oblivious of it, or else they'd go ahead and get married just so they wouldn't have the issue hanging over their heads.

Roberta couldn't possibly resolve the problem by herself. All she knew was that she loved Kyle and she wanted him to be happy. With that basic understanding to comfort her, she drifted off to sleep.

She awoke the following morning to feel Kyle's hand moving over the smooth skin of her back. She twisted to face him, and he covered her mouth with his own, taking full possession of it. She groaned happily, her arms rising to circle his shoulders, her body rapidly following her mind into consciousness.

Kyle slid his mouth from hers, nipped her chin and then leaned back on his pillow. "I'm sorry about last night," he whispered.

"Sorry about what?"

"Falling asleep on you." His index finger drew a line from her throat to her navel, and he bent forward to kiss the hollow between her breasts. "You smell so good, Roberta."

She recalled her preparations for him the previous night, the sexy robe and the splash of cologne. But if she told him about that, he'd feel even worse for having fallen asleep so early. "You smell good, too," she said.

"I smell like root beer," he argued, smiling roguishly. "I was so tired last night I don't even remember getting undressed."

"I undressed you," Roberta told him. "You were even more tired than you think."

His hand reached her hip and molded to its womanly curve. "Oh, Roberta." He sighed, then slid his fingers forward to touch the soft hair below her belly. "How could you undress me and let me miss all the fun by sleeping through it? You should have pinched me until I woke up."

"You're up now," Roberta said.

Kyle laughed and shifted his body closer to her, letting her feel his full arousal. She smiled when she realized her unintended pun. But before she could apologize for it, Kyle was kissing her again and stroking her. His hand ignited her with its gentle caresses, and his chest moved over her breasts, stimulating her nipples with the sensuous texture of his chest hair.

A low moan of pleasure gathered in Roberta's throat, but Kyle's kiss prevented it from escaping. Suffering from the dazzling frustration of wanting to express herself, she used her hands to speak, instead, tensing them over his shoulders and then drawing them the length of his back to his buttocks. She dug her fingertips into the muscled flesh and he filled her mouth with his own agonized groan.

The sudden explosion jolted them apart. It came from the direction of the living room, a rumbling *kaboom!* "What the hell was that?" Kyle gasped, wrestling with his erratic breath.

Roberta strained to listen and heard maniacal laughter. "The TV," she told him, her chest heaving as spasmodically as his. "Leah's watching cartoons."

"Cartoons?" Kyle snorted. "It sounds like World War Three in there."

"I know," Roberta lamented. "They make such violent cartoons these days." As if on cue, they heard a chain of smaller explosions and more crazed, nasal laughter from the television.

Kyle took a moment to recover his control over himself. "Not exactly romantic background music," he muttered as the explosion sounds were replaced by a bouncy jingle. "Isn't it a little early for her to be up?"

Roberta grinned. "Leah's too young to understand the concept of sleeping late on weekends," she noted. "Only those of us who have to be up early every weekday realize how important it is to sleep in on Sundays. Maybe in another week, after she starts school, she'll start sleeping late, too."

Kyle gradually became inured to the cartoon babble filtering through the closed bedroom door. He set his hand free on Roberta's body again and overwhelmed her mouth with another consuming kiss.

Concentrating fully on Kyle and the sensations he was creating within her, Roberta lost all consciousness of the television noises from the other room. Her body instinctively began to rock against his fingers, and her hands floated the length of his torso again, this time sliding forward to his chest, his belly and lower, seeking to arouse him as he was arousing her. He moaned softly, then slid half on top of her, replacing his fingers with his body and moving rhythmically against her eager flesh.

"Kyle," she breathed, her fingers fanning his sides and gripping him. Her long night of wanting him was finally going to be satisfied. "Kyle, please..."

He rose fully onto her. Her legs parted for him, her arms tightened around him, her body opened in welcome.

And then came three sharp knocks on the door. "Mommy? Mommy, I'm starving!"

Kyle literally froze in her arms, his body becoming motionless and cold. Roberta stroked her hands up and down his back, hoping to thaw him. "I'm not up yet, Leah," she called toward the door.

"But I'm *starving*!" Leah insisted.

Roberta took a deep breath, hoping to clear the passionate hoarseness out of her voice. "Leah, honey, why don't you just eat some Cheerios from the box?"

"I don't want Cheerios from the box," Leah replied from the other side of the door. "I want pancakes. It's Sunday."

"Then you'll have to wait awhile," Roberta called to her. "Either eat the Cheerios or don't eat anything. I'll come out when I'm ready."

"What about Kyle? Will he make me pancakes?" Leah demanded to know.

A muscle in Kyle's jaw tensed visibly. Roberta rubbed it with her thumb. "Kyle will come out when I come out," she called to the door. "Now go munch on some Cheerios and watch TV for a while, all right?"

They listened to the sound of Leah padding barefoot down the hall to the living room. Roberta filled her hands with Kyle's face and raised herself away from the pillow to kiss him. She combed her fingers through his hair and smiled at his sour expression. "It's not the end of the world," she murmured.

"It's the end of something," he complained. He eased off Roberta and slid her into the cradle of his arm, cuddling her body to his. She covered him with her hand, but her gentle caresses had no effect on him. "Forget it," he grunted, pulling her hand away. "I think I've lost the spirit of this thing right now."

She nodded and let her hand come to rest on his stomach. He hugged her tightly, but his eyes gazed past her at the wall. He looked miserable.

"If I hadn't conked out so early last night..." he muttered apologetically.

"It isn't important, Kyle," she whispered. "Really, I don't care. It's not important to me."

"It's damned important to me," he said, then drew in a sharp breath and loosened his hold on her. He rolled onto his back and stared at the ceiling. "Oh, God," he whispered. "That was a terrible thing to say."

Roberta studied him, wishing she could do something to assuage his anger, trying to ignore the ache his words had caused within her. She didn't know whether what hurt her was his obvious pain or his brutal words. Was sex the most important thing going on between them? Was that why he'd asked her to marry him? Was that why he was so distraught now?

At least he'd admitted that what he'd said wasn't exactly consoling. Friday night, she'd asked him to be honest with her, and his blunt comment proved that he was being honest with her. "If that's how you feel, Kyle, there's nothing wrong with saying it," she said, forgiving him as best she could.

"I've never been like that, so—so intent on sex," he said falteringly. "But damn it, this whole weekend... It just hasn't gone the way I pictured it, and then this, even this." He dared to look at her, his eyes troubled, clouded. "After last weekend, Roberta, I was sure of this between us. I knew that no matter what else, what we had going for us in bed would be good. And now—" he exhaled slowly, bitterly "—it's not."

"Kyle." Roberta raised herself on her elbow and urged his face to hers. "It *is* good. Just holding you is good. Feeling you next to me is good." His scowl implied that he wasn't convinced. "Why do you always have to expect so much?" she challenged him, her tone tinged with exasperation at his inability to accept what had happened with equanimity, as she had. "Why?"

His eyes journeyed across her face, memorizing its lines and angles, the soft dark wisps of her lashes, the faint creases time had etched at the outer corners of her eyes. "Because I *want* so much," he said quietly.

"You want more than you've found here this weekend, don't you?" she guessed, her voice much steadier than her nerves.

He considered her statement, then shook his head. "I don't know, Roberta. Maybe I've found more than I want."

"You don't—" she swallowed the hitch in her voice "—you don't have to marry me, Kyle."

He lapsed into silence. His gaze drifted past her again, then refocused on her face, just inches from his. "I asked you to marry me," he declared.

That wasn't what she'd wanted to hear. She'd wanted him to say that he *did* have to marry her because, no matter what

else, he loved her and nothing, not even Leah and her rau-
cous television cartoons, could change that basic fact.

But he didn't say that, and Roberta did her best to conceal her dejection. "We can pretend you didn't ask me to
marry you," she offered, recalling what she'd contemplated last night. If they could backtrack, if they could have
an ordinary courtship, maybe in time marriage would seem
more plausible, more natural. "We can pretend the subject
never came up."

"Is that what you want?" Kyle asked, his eyes hardening
to the color of flint.

"I want—" she sighed "—I want what's best for you."

"Well, damn it, what do you want?" he snapped. "I
asked you to marry me, and you say, 'Let's pretend you
didn't ask.' That's not an answer, Roberta. Don't keep
throwing this thing in my lap. I asked you to marry me. You
make up your own mind."

He seemed much more infuriated with her than in love
with her. She could write off his mood as a result of disappointment, a man's sensitivity about an anatomical short-
circuit . . . but no. There was more to his attitude than that.
He seemed unsure of himself and of what he wanted. So he
was issuing an ultimatum: the decision concerning their
marriage was to be hers.

"No, Kyle," Roberta said. "My answer is no."

Chapter Eleven

Kyle leaned his forearms on the railing of the deck and watched the fireflies blinking their luminous tails at the edge of the woods surrounding the yard. The evanescent sparks of light cut through the descending gloom, a reminder to him that, even in the darkness, life existed. He wondered whether Leah had ever seen fireflies before, whether she had ever collected a swarm of fireflies inside a jar hoping that they would illuminate the night like a light bulb. Someday he would have to collect fireflies with her.

No. That was behind him now.

"Hey, Kyle, are you gonna finish your beer?" Jerry called to him from one of the canvas chairs. "I mean, if you are, I'll go get another, but you've hardly touched yours, and—"

"Help yourself," Kyle welcomed his friend. "I'm really not thirsty."

"You're really not thirsty; you're really not hungry," Jerry mused. "It's been almost a week now. What the hell did she do to you, anyway?"

Kyle turned his back to the woods and rested his hips against the railing. Jerry had already appropriated Kyle's bottle of beer and was balancing it on one knee. "She said no," Kyle answered. "I told you that."

"When Ursula turned you down, you were relieved," Jerry reminded Kyle. "Why is it that I don't sense any relief this time around?"

Kyle ignored his friend's inane comparison. When he'd asked Ursula to marry him, he had known that she would refuse; he'd known she didn't have the same dreams he had. He'd have been shocked if Ursula had agreed to marry him and had broken into an elated smile and cried, "Oh, yes, Kyle, let's. Let's have a child. Let's settle down and make a true commitment to each other." It hadn't been in Ursula to want commitment.

But it *was* in Roberta. She had already made commitments in her life, and she thrived within them. A fear of committing herself to Kyle or a distrust of his commitment to her—that wasn't why she'd said no.

He had mentally relived countless times already the last morning they'd spent together. But he drifted into another rerun of it, torturing himself with it the way one sometimes can't keep from touching a bruise again and again, wincing with fresh pain each time, but unable to stop.

They had been subdued over breakfast. Leah had worn over her cotton pajamas the bead necklace Kyle had given her, and she'd chattered gaily about the resemblance between her pancakes and bunny rabbits. But her animated conversation couldn't overcome the palpable chill that had wrapped around Kyle and Roberta as they sipped their coffee and picked at their food.

Once they were done with breakfast, Kyle had packed his small bag and taken his leave. He'd given Leah an affectionate hug, and then Roberta had accompanied him downstairs to his truck. He'd tossed his suitcase onto the passenger seat, slammed the door shut and turned to face her.

"Kyle," she murmured, her gaze even with his chin. "I said no before, but…but that doesn't mean I don't care for you."

"I know that," he said quietly.

She lifted her eyes timidly to his. "It also doesn't mean that marriage would be out of the question for us forever." His emotionless expression prompted her to inquire, "Or does it?"

He considered his answer carefully. "Roberta, something special happened to us. But maybe…maybe we're just responding to a memory of it. I don't know anymore. I'd like to get married. I'd like to think I'm ready for that kind of commitment. And I thought…I thought, since you and I have a special relationship—"

"We do, Kyle," Roberta insisted.

"Yes, but maybe you're right. Maybe I don't understand the realities here. There was nothing at all sacred about my time with Leah yesterday. She drove me crazy, and I didn't handle it well. And this morning, too." He twirled his finger through a loose curl beside Roberta's ear. "You believe I need to rethink the whole idea, don't you?" he guessed.

Roberta nodded.

"Protecting me from my own stupidity, I suppose," he grunted.

"Protecting myself," Roberta countered. "I don't want to marry someone who's looking for a pretty Norman Rockwell world and finds himself stuck in a nutty Marc Chagall world instead. I love Marc Chagall's paintings, Kyle, but they're full of flying horses and upside-down cows and cheerful fiddlers floating through yellow skies. That's what life is like with a five-year-old child, and if I forced you into that world—" she sighed "—you might hate me forever."

Kyle gazed down at Roberta for a long, intense moment. "I may hate myself for letting you say no," he whispered. He kissed her gently, then climbed into his truck. "Take care, Roberta," he murmured before closing the door and revving the engine.

Roberta hadn't waited around to see him drive off. She hadn't even waved. She had simply marched back into her building and let the door swing shut behind her.

He knew why she'd said no. Groping his way back into the present, he raked his fingers through his dense, sandy-colored hair and smiled sadly. "I failed, Jerry," he said. "That's what it's all about. I failed."

"What do you mean?" Jerry asked, curious.

What Kyle *didn't* mean was what had happened in bed. That sort of failure was unpleasant, no question about it. At the time it had seemed more than unpleasant—incredibly disappointing, perhaps a bit ego-puncturing. But Kyle wasn't the first man in the world who'd lost his concentration, and he wouldn't be the last.

His failure had occurred afterward, though. God, what had he said to Roberta? Horrible things about how important sex was to him, about how the best thing he and Roberta had going for them was their sexual compatibility, and now they didn't even have that. He couldn't remember the specific words; all he could remember was Roberta's wounded expression. And her decision to say no.

He failed afterward, and he failed even more devastatingly before that wretched Sunday morning. "Last weekend was a kind of test for me," he explained to Jerry, watching with detached fascination as his beer vanished down his friend's throat. "I flunked it with flying colors."

"What is this, Wesleyan? They took away your Phi Beta Kappa key? You're three credits shy of graduating, and Roberta's gonna withhold your diploma?" Jerry snorted.

"Love isn't a test, Kyle. It's a feeling. Since when do people get graded on feelings?"

"It's more than a feeling," Kyle argued. "That's one thing I've learned from Roberta. I aced the feeling part of the test, Jerry, but I failed the reality."

"This sounds heavy," Jerry said ominously. "Will I need another beer?"

"If you drink another beer, I'm not going to let you drive home," Kyle alerted him. "And since I don't want you spending the night here, you're going to sip what you've got slowly and then switch to water."

Jerry subsided in his chair and struck an attentive pose. "All right, Mother Temperance. Explain reality to me, one philosopher to another."

Kyle took a moment to sort his thoughts. "Reality... reality is wearing a shirt that smells of root beer. Or sour milk, if you're a mother. Reality is being chided by a snot-nosed five-year-old kid for not hooting like an owl. Reality is being lost in Brooklyn and having to listen to a song about the decomposition of corpses for the seventeenth time." He shook his head and laughed. When he described his weekend that way, it sounded perversely funny.

Jerry laughed, too. "If that's reality, I can see why so many people escape it with drugs."

"It's more than that," Kyle continued, his voice low and reflective. "It's ... it's listening to the snot-nosed five-year-old kid sing about decomposed corpses, and then smiling and hugging her and saying, 'I love you, anyway.'"

"Is that the part you failed?" Jerry guessed.

Kyle nodded grimly and turned away. A cluster of fireflies flashed their tails all at once, creating a dazzling effect in the thickening night, like sparks rising from a camp fire. All day today, all day yesterday—ever since he'd arrived home Sunday—he'd been tempted to turn the truck around and speed back to New York, to gather Leah into his arms and say, "You're a snot-nosed five-year-old kid and I love you, anyway."

But he'd refrained. He didn't trust himself. Sunday afternoon he might hug her, and then Sunday evening she'd spill something else on him or throw a tantrum or commit any other number of heinous acts he knew she was fully capable of, and everything would fall apart again. Kyle wasn't as strong as Roberta. He wasn't as forgiving. He would only fail again.

"And that's why Roberta showed you the door? Because her kid was obnoxious and you couldn't take it?"

"She said no to spare me from my own stupidity," Kyle explained. He understood Roberta's decision. It hurt like the devil, but he understood that she'd refused him for his own sake.

"So why aren't you grateful? Why don't you thank your lucky stars that she's saved you from a fate worse than death, and let me have Linda set you up with a friend?"

"I thought you weren't talking to Linda," Kyle remarked. The last time he'd spoken to Jerry, Jerry and his on-again-off-again girlfriend were definitely off.

"We aren't talking," Jerry confirmed. "We've discovered we get along much better that way."

"Terrific," Kyle grunted. "I'll thank you to tell her—in sign language or whatever system you're using at the moment—that I don't want to meet any of her friends."

"What do you want?" Jerry asked.

I want to be as strong as Roberta, Kyle replied silently. "Some time alone," he said aloud.

"You've got it," Jerry magnanimously offered. He drained the beer bottle, stood and loped off the deck. "Call me when you feel like talking some more," he shouted over his shoulder just before he disappeared around the side of the house.

Kyle remained on the deck for a long time, watching the fireflies, listening to the crickets. Had Leah ever heard crickets? Did she think the sounds of night were limited to taxis honking and municipal buses wheezing and an occasional police siren wailing in the distance? Even if Roberta wouldn't marry Kyle, her daughter needed country living. Crickets, fireflies, someone to take her out on the Sound in a rowboat, to explain to her how lobster traps work, to appraise her sand castles with an objective eye.

It was only a matter of minutes before he was standing barefoot on the beach, staring out at the black water of the Sound and remembering. Here, alone on the sand with the sky stretched endlessly above him, glittering with stars in the absence of a moon, Kyle listened to the steady rush of the waves. Two night songs Leah had to hear: crickets and tides.

Hypnotized by the music of the surf, he forgot the melody of the jingle about decomposing corpses. He forgot the lyrics. He forgot every other sound in the universe but one: Leah's intoxicating laughter in the borrowed rowboat when Kyle had deliberately splashed a handful of water in her face.

And then he remembered another sound even more beautiful than Leah's laughter: the sound of Roberta whispering his name in love.

THE NEXT DAY he bought a boat. He found it at a flea market, an old, splintery dinghy that needed some tender loving care and cost next to nothing. He'd have the whole Labor Day weekend to work on it. Better to sand and refinish a rowboat than to mope on the deck, opening bottles of beer and then losing his interest in their contents after the second sip.

He dragged a pair of sawhorses outside from the rear of his garage and set them up in the backyard. Then he descended to the cellar to fetch his power sander and planer. Nearly half of his basement was devoted to a workshop he used far too seldom. He stared at the neatly organized tools, the spotless workbench, the clean floor. A few scraps of maple were stacked against a wall next to his firewood, remnants of the child-size rocking chair he'd constructed not long ago. Closing his eyes, he pictured Leah rocking blissfully in her chair. Why couldn't he remember the song about corpses?

The sun beat down on his head as he shaved several scaly layers of paint from the rowboat, which he'd balanced across the sawhorses. He could almost feel his hair being bleached by the scorching rays. By noon his shirt was drenched, and he removed it. Still, he didn't stop working on the boat. It felt too good to sweat, to feel his shoulders toast to a dark brown, to scrape his palms against the time-roughened wood of the boat. It felt too good to stop.

He worked on the boat throughout the weekend. He was almost reluctant to leave the boat to put in time at his job after the extended holiday weekend, even though he knew he'd have an hour or so every afternoon to plunge into woodworking with his employees while Bob Neilson oversaw his paperwork in the glass-walled office at the end of the workshop. The imported West Indian mahogany that was gradually being shaped into a dining room set was vastly superior to the rough pine of Kyle's dinghy, but he'd still rather be working on the boat. When he worked on the boat, he remembered Leah's laughter.

In bed at night he remembered, too. Not Leah, neither her laughter nor her ghastly cartoons and her demands for pancakes. He remembered Roberta. He remembered the skin of her abdomen, with its faint pale ripples along her

pelvis, proof of the wonders her body had achieved. He remembered her breasts, so warm and full in his hands, and
her legs, legs that had once gotten so tangled up beneath her
that she couldn't stand without Kyle's assistance, but that
were now capable of holding his body inescapably to her
own, imprisoning him inside her, inside heaven. He remembered her face, her dense lashes, her expressive eyes,
the fine lines emanating from their outer edges, giving them
extra character. He had never seen her cry except from
happiness, he realized. And from onions. Even those tears
had been beautiful.

He remembered the way she'd smelled the last time they
were together. It was a distant fragrance, something flowery but not particularly sweet, blended with her own musky
aroma. He remembered lying beside her and hearing her say,
"Holding you is good. Feeling you next to me is good."

And then her accusation, "Why do you have to expect so
much?"

She was right, as always. He had expected perfection. He
had expected his life to be elevated, exalted, turned into
something quasi-holy by marrying Roberta. But neither she
nor her daughter were sacred. Leah could be a brat. Roberta could tear a stocking on a broken toy and curse. They
were no more perfect than Kyle was. The only difference
between them and him was that they knew how to forget the
bad stuff and remember only the good.

Why had he let Roberta say no? Why had he let her protect him from his own stupidity? Why, when she'd said there
was still a chance for their future, had he been afraid to believe her?

It was only by chance that he happened to drive to his
house during the afternoon on Thursday. One of his stain
suppliers had mistakenly sent him some polyurethane that

he hadn't ordered, and rather than return the entire shipment, Kyle set aside a few gallons to use on his boat. He
drove his Saab home at lunchtime in order to pick up his
truck. Although he was reasonably sure the cans wouldn't
leak, he didn't want to take the risk of transporting the
polyurethane in his new car.

It was only by chance, then, that he picked up his mail at
an hour when the post office was still open.

He recognized the envelope, the loose, looping hand-
writing. He almost forgot about exchanging his car for his
truck as he tore open the envelope and shook out the letter.

"Dear Kyle," it began. "I thought you might want to
hear about Leah's first day of school."

"Oh, God," he whispered to himself. There was nothing, nothing in the universe he wanted to hear about more
than Leah's first day of school.

He slumped to the ground beside his roadside mailbox
and devoured the letter. Roberta described how pretty Leah
had looked in a new dress embellished with the bead necklace Kyle had given her. She wrote about how eagerly Leah
had raced up the stairs of the school building and inside,
how fond she seemed to be of her teacher, how although she
claimed to be the only child in the full-day kindergarten, if
not the entire school, who didn't own a set of pencils with
her name stamped into them in gold letters, she was still the
best reader and writer in her class, and her brand-new pencil case was the envy of many of her classmates. He continued reading:

I think she'll adjust to school well, Kyle. I know *I'll*
adjust to her being in school instead of ransacking the
apartment with the baby-sitter. I am so proud of her,
Kyle, and I knew you'd want to hear about it.

My job is keeping me busy, as usual. The Labor Day weekend was a needed break for me.

I hope you're doing well.

Sincerely, Roberta.

Sincerely.

Kyle reread the letter, searching it for the merest clue of her feelings. Nothing. The letter had no more passion in it than every letter she'd ever written to him before. For five years he'd been receiving such letters from her, filled with news about Leah and a brief mention of Roberta's work, signed "Sincerely."

What was she trying to tell him? That they could be pen pals again? Pen pals and nothing more?

Or that they could still have each other? That if Kyle accepted the reality of their friendship, their affection, their trust, they could recapture the special closeness that had sustained them both for five years?

He scrambled into his truck and headed straight to the post office. He was lucky to find a few sheets of his office stationery in the cab of the truck, or he would have had nothing to write on. He penned his brief message, sealed it and for the second time in his life, mailed a letter special delivery.

"POSTAL CARRIER," a man's voice crackled through the building's intercom. "I've got a special delivery letter for Roberta Frankel that's got to be signed for."

It was Friday evening. Roberta and Leah had arrived at the loft less than fifteen minutes before—just long enough for Roberta to have changed from her poplin business suit to a pair of jeans and a cotton shirt. "I'll be down in a minute," she said into the intercom before slipping the earpiece onto its hook and grabbing her keys. "I'll be right back," she told Leah. "Stay out of trouble."

Riding downstairs in the elevator, she tried to guess who would have sent her a special delivery letter. The only other special delivery letter she'd ever gotten in her life had been from Kyle, just before she'd moved back to New York, asking her to call him as soon as she was settled in her new home so they could arrange a get-together.

She hoped that the letter awaiting her this time would lead to a happier conclusion.

Through the building's locked glass door she spotted the postman, dressed in uniform. He held a letter up to the glass for her, and she cracked open the door and signed the form confirming her receipt of the letter. As soon as the postman was gone, she slid her finger under the envelope flap and shook out the letter.

All it said was: "Damn it, Roberta, marry me."

No signature. None was necessary.

Not sure what to think, she read the sentence over and over as she rode the elevator upstairs to her apartment. "Damn it, Roberta, marry me."

By the time she'd let herself inside the loft, she had made up her mind as to a course of action. "Leah, how would you like to spend the weekend with Aunt Mary?" she asked.

"In the city?" Leah asked.

"You know she closed up her summer house last weekend," Roberta said, speaking rapidly, her mouth trying to keep up with her racing thoughts. "I have to call her and see if it'll be a problem for her. If it isn't, would you like to stay with her? Mommy has to go out of town this weekend." There was no way Roberta would consider bringing Leah with her. She hadn't any idea what would happen once she saw Kyle, but whatever did happen, it would have to happen between the two of them alone, without Leah to run circles around them or spill soda pop on their clothing.

Mary immediately agreed to take Leah for the weekend. "Actually, this will work out perfectly," she told Roberta. "I've outlined a new book, and I'd like to try it out on Leah before I continue work on it. Leah's not only my biggest fan—she's my most dependable critic."

Upon hearing Mary's flattering words about her, Leah readily agreed to spend the weekend with Mary.

Saturday morning Roberta dropped Leah off at Mary's Greenwich Village apartment, then took the subway uptown to Grand Central Station and caught a train to New Haven. She supposed she should have telephoned Kyle first. But if she had, she wouldn't have known what to say, other than "I'm coming." She didn't want to give him the opportunity to say, "Don't come unless your answer is yes."

She wanted to believe her answer would be yes. But she wasn't certain. She had to see him first. She had to see what had occurred to inspire him to propose again, not in person and not on the phone, but by letter.

She wondered if he'd sent her his letter after receiving hers. Maybe he'd read her unemotional note about Leah and figured that she had chosen to resume the postal relationship they'd had before. But if that was the case, he wouldn't have asked her to marry him. If he honestly wanted her to marry him, why in the world would he write it?

Why wouldn't he? Of course he'd propose by letter. In the past he'd always used letters to express the things that mattered most to him. His letters had communicated his innermost feelings, his disappointments and desires, his satisfaction with his work and his longing to return to his Connecticut home. It was from his letters that Roberta had learned how much he loved working with wood. It was from his letters that she'd come to understand how important helping with Leah's birth had been to him and how significant a part of his life she still was. Perhaps he felt that his verbal marriage proposal hadn't been as effective as a written one would be.

And so he'd written, "Damn it, Roberta, marry me." Nothing abstract, nothing tentative, no room for misinterpretation. *Damn it, Roberta, marry me.*

The train arrived in New Haven shortly after noon, and Roberta hailed a cab to drive her to Madison. She didn't allow herself to consider the possibility that Kyle wouldn't be home. If he wasn't, she'd wait for him. If he was gone overnight, she'd wait until tomorrow.

Still, she was relieved when she spotted his battered blue truck parked in his driveway. She paid the cabdriver, lifted her overnight bag from the seat next to her, and hurried to the front door. She rang the bell and waited. No answer.

He wouldn't have left his truck in the driveway if he wasn't home, she mused. At the very least, he would have locked it inside the garage. If he hadn't heard the doorbell, it was probably because he wasn't indoors. Setting her bag on the front step, she roamed around the house to the backyard.

Kyle was standing with his back to her in the middle of the lawn, appraising a small wooden rowboat balanced on two sawhorses. An electric sander rested on the birchwood deck, and a toolbox stood on the grass at Kyle's feet. He wore stained dungarees and a blue work shirt with its sleeves rolled up.

Roberta approached, her footsteps muffled by the plush grass. Several feet from him, she stopped. "Hello," she said.

He jumped, then spun around. His eyes widened with surprise. "Roberta," he said, as if he wanted to ascertain that he wasn't dreaming.

"It's me," she confirmed.

He reached for a convenient rag and wiped his hands on it. Two long strides carried him to her side. "What are you doing here?" he asked, bewildered.

"I got your letter," she replied, peeking past him at the boat. "Is that yours?"

He glanced over his shoulder and nodded. "As you can see, it needs some work. It's seaworthy but pretty splintery. I've scraped and sanded it. Now it needs a few layers of polyurethane."

"Why didn't you just get an aluminum boat?" Roberta asked. "Aren't they much easier to maintain?"

Kyle's eyes momentarily narrowed on her, and then he smiled almost bashfully. "I don't know how to work with aluminum," he reminded her. "Wood is my specialty. This boat may be more work, but it'll also be more fun."

"I see your point," Roberta concurred.

They stood awkwardly for several moments, neither sure what to do. Finally Kyle cupped his hands about Roberta's shoulders and touched her lips with a light kiss. "Do you have an answer for me?" he asked.

It felt so good to be with him, to feel his hands on her, and his lips. She arched her arms around him and hugged him, then broke away. She mustn't let her love for him run away with her. She had to make certain of Kyle's feelings first. "Do you have some answers for me?" she countered.

Frowning slightly, he led her to the deck. They sat on the canvas chairs by the parsons table, and Kyle folded one of Roberta's hands inside his. "Fire away," he invited her.

"Do you..." She took a deep breath for courage, then asked, "Do you love me, Kyle?"

He appeared startled. "What do you mean, do I love you? I asked you to marry me, didn't I?"

"But you've never said you loved me, Kyle. Never once."

His jaw flexed, and he tightened his hold on her hand. "Yes," he said, "I love you."

"Why?" She had to be certain. "Why do you love me?"

"You came all this way just to fish for compliments?" Kyle joked.

Roberta's solemn expression stifled his laughter. He lifted her hand to his mouth and kissed it, then let it rest in his lap. "I love you because you're the strongest woman I've ever met. I've known that since the day we met, Roberta. You're strong and brave. Devoted. Much more sensible than I am, and much more clear-sighted." His smile faded and he raised his eyes to her. "You're beautiful and talented. And...and you've got so much love inside you, it's hard not to love you."

She hadn't realized how nervous she was about what he'd say, but slowly she felt her anxiety drain away, easing from her shoulders and back, leaving behind a sweet warmth. "Why haven't you ever said any of this before?" she asked him.

His gaze dropped to her hand. "Because I didn't recognize it before," he admitted. "I didn't recognize it until after you said no to me."

Roberta's brow dipped in a scowl, deepening the tiny creases at the bridge of her nose. "Then why... why, if you didn't even realize that you loved me, did you propose to me?"

"Oh, Roberta, isn't it obvious?" He groaned at his own past foolishness. "I longed for everything you had, everything you stood for—not just love, but family love, maternal love, that all-embracing love that forgets the bad stuff and remembers only the good. I admired you, Roberta, and I thought you'd be good for me. But I didn't understand..."

He exhaled, his eyes drifting to the boat and beyond it to the trees bordering the yard. "Ever since I left New York, I've been reliving the weekend we spent together," he continued. "I kept going over it again and again in my mind. And a funny thing happened," he confessed. "After a while, I couldn't really remember how furious I was with Leah when she dragged me into the public ladies' room, or sang me those horrible songs. Instead, I kept remembering how her eyes lit up when I bought her that necklace, and how cute she sounded when she burst into giggles at the end of one of her disgusting lyrics. I tried to remember—"

His voice broke for a second, and he cleared his throat. "I tried to remember how frustrated I was Sunday morning, when I wanted you so much and I couldn't make love to you. I tried to remember, but all I could remember was how wonderful you felt in my arms and how delicious you smelled and how calm you were when I was ready to boil over."

His gaze traveled back to her. His eyes were soft and shimmering, his smile tentative. "I came back to Madison not knowing what to do. So I bought this boat. I worked on scraping off the old paint. I started sanding it. And I thought, *This is what Roberta would have me do.* You know me better than I know myself, Roberta. I've got to have you in my life." He smiled hesitantly, but his eyes were solemn. "That's what love is all about, isn't it?"

Her smile was also hesitant. "It's also about taking the bad with the good," she reminded him. "If we get married, there are no guarantees that Leah isn't going to drag you into public ladies' rooms again and sing her disgusting songs and drive you up the wall."

Kyle nodded. "And I'll get angry and I'll be a grouch—wasn't that her word for me?—and then a day or two will pass and I'll forget the bad and remember the good. When

I left you, Roberta, I didn't know that I was capable of doing that. But now I've done it, so I know that I can." He slid off his chair and dropped to his knees before Roberta. "I didn't do this right the first time, so let me do it right now. Will you marry me, Roberta?"

Roberta leaned forward and touched her lips to his golden hair. "If you want to know the truth, Kyle, my favorite of your proposals was the one I got last night. You know: 'Damn it, Roberta—'"

He laughed. "Maybe not romantic, but it was effective. You're here, aren't you?"

"Yes, I'm here," she whispered, angling his mouth to hers and kissing him deeply. "I'm here and I'll marry you," she breathed when the kiss ended.

"Will Leah mind?" he asked.

"Not a chance," Roberta promised. "She misses you, Kyle. She's been wearing the necklace you gave her all the time. But I wrote to you about that."

"Yes." He rose to his feet. "I got your letter." He fell silent for a moment, then cocked his head as he appraised her. "Did you really mean that?"

"Mean what?"

"*Sincerely*. Why did you write that, Roberta? *How* could you write it?"

"I meant it," she swore. She stood before him and rested her head on his shoulder, hiding her face against his neck. "Kyle, it was devastating enough to think I'd lost you as a lover. But to lose you as a friend, too—I couldn't give up everything. I couldn't give up my closest confidant."

"Yes, but *sincerely*?" he pressed her.

She dared to peer up at him. His eyes captured hers and held them. "I was afraid to write 'love,'" she admitted. "I thought it might scare you away."

"After I scared so easily in New York, I can see why you were afraid," he granted frankly. He combed his fingers through the soft curls framing her face. "I got your letter, Roberta, and it proved to me once again that you're much stronger than I am."

"Stronger?" she echoed, incredulous. "Oh, Kyle, if I were strong, I would have gotten on the phone and told you I loved you, and that of course I wanted to marry you, and that I had said no too soon, that I underestimated you, that I misjudged you—"

"Misjudged me? Your judgment of me has always been right on target. I behaved abominably that morning. And the worst of it was that after I'd behaved so abominably, I put you on the spot about the whole marriage issue." He cringed as he recalled the morning in question. "How could you have said anything but no?"

"If I were as strong as you think I am," Roberta murmured, "I would have realized that you were feeling badly and that you didn't mean what you said. I would have had enough faith in you to know that you *would* forget the bad stuff in time and remember the good. That would have been the strong thing to do," she admitted.

"You've disillusioned me about breast-feeding, Roberta," he scolded her gently. "Are you going to disillusion me about your strength, too?"

She laughed meekly. "If you want to know the truth, Kyle, I thought you were the strong one here. If I marry you, I'm going to lean on you sometimes and depend on you and be just as weak as I want to be. I'm tired of being strong all the time."

"Uh-oh," Kyle grumbled. "It sounds to me like Leah may be stronger than the both of us put together. We could be facing big trouble here."

"To say nothing of the fact that I squeeze the toothpaste tube from the middle and you squeeze it from the end," Roberta reminded him. "But I'm not saying no this time. You could have gotten rid of me when I said no, but you blew it and proposed again. Now you're stuck with me."

"What a depressing thought," Kyle whispered before giving her a contented kiss. "How long are you planning to stay?" he asked. "Is Leah with Mary?"

Roberta took Kyle's hand. "Leah's with Mary—in New York. And I've got a suitcase with me. I left it by the front door."

"I like the way this weekend is shaping up," Kyle said, smiling sensuously as he led Roberta through the house to fetch her overnight bag from the front step. "I guess we ought to telephone Leah and tell her we're getting married," he mused, lifting the bag and carrying it inside.

Roberta gave him a loving look, her eyes glowing enchantingly. "We can call her later."

Kyle had no difficulty reading the longing in her gaze, a longing as imperative as his own. "Definitely later," he concurred before ushering her down the hall to his bedroom.

Epilogue

Roberta sat on one of the canvas chairs, a sketch pad open on her knees and her bare feet propped up on the deck railing. Having her legs extended at that sloping angle caused the hem of her denim jumper to ride daringly up her thighs, but there was nobody, other than a few chattering squirrels romping along the edge of the woods to notice her unladylike position. She set the brown pastel stick in its slot in the box beside her on the parsons table and lifted a peach-colored pastel stick. She blended it with the brown shadow she'd just drawn to create a contoured effect.

The June Saturday afternoon was mild, but her ponytail drooped low and sat warmly on her neck. She tossed the pastel stick into the box and reached behind her to refasten the barrette in her hair, which now fell an inch or so past her shoulders. She couldn't imagine ever letting it grow down to her waist again, but Kyle claimed he liked it long, so Roberta had compromised with him on it.

As she unclipped the barrette, her hands were unexpectedly captured by the strong, callused fingers she knew so well. She twisted around in her chair and found Kyle standing behind her, holding the barrette and grinning. "Sneak!" she scolded him. "When did you get back?"

"Two and a half seconds ago," he told her, gazing over her shoulder to examine the sketch she'd been working on. "What the hell is that?" he asked.

"My feet."

"I know it's your feet," he said, frowning. "Roberta, when I told you to quit the job at the agency and do art full-time for a while, I didn't think you were going to be frittering away your talents on...on drawing feet, of all things."

Roberta sniffed indignantly. "It happens to be an excellent rendering," she defended her creation. "Besides, in another two months I'm not going to be able to see my feet anymore. I'll need this to remember what they look like."

Kyle laughed and reached beneath her knees, swinging her legs off the railing. "Just do me a favor and don't hang that picture over the dining room table," he warned her. "I don't want to have to look at an artistic enlargement of your knobby toes while I'm eating dinner."

"Knobby?" Roberta erupted. "You think my toes are *knobby*?"

Kyle ignored her fury. He calmly checked his wristwatch, then pulled her out of the chair. "I've now been home a total of three minutes, which means we've got all of one hour and fifty-seven minutes before Mary and Alvin bring Leah back. I suggest that we don't waste any more time discussing the shape of your toes."

"Right," Roberta heartily agreed. She set her pad on the table with her pastels and let Kyle lead her into the house. "Did Alvin mind having Leah with them this afternoon?" she asked as they sidestepped the checkerboard, the Raggedy Ann doll and the baseball glove Leah had left scattered about the living room floor. "After all, he and Mary are newlyweds. Maybe he doesn't want to be spending his first post-honeymoon weekend with a pint-sized chaperon."

"You know Mary," Kyle said with a snort. "True love is swell, but when it comes time to outline a new book, she isn't going to trust the plot analysis and critique to some retired stockbroker she happens to have gotten married to. Leah's her expert."

Roberta nodded. She crossed the threshold to the bedroom ahead of Kyle, and as soon as they reached the bed she turned in his arms to face him. He kissed her profoundly. "Did I happen to mention that you're looking gorgeous today?" he whispered as his fingers dug into her hair and pulled it back from her face.

"I look like a hippopotamus," she argued, her hands moving down the front of his shirt and opening the buttons.

"Oh, a hippopotamus, is it?" he said with a chuckle. "I was thinking you looked more like a walrus." He slid the jumper up over her gently rounding belly, then stroked the tautly stretched skin above her panties.

"You really know how to turn a woman on," she said, but she didn't sound nearly as sarcastic as she'd intended. Kyle *did* know how to turn a woman on; he was proving it with his fingers, which had drifted down to arch around her bottom, his thumbs sliding beneath the elastic of her panties. She sucked in her breath and forced her trembling hands to open his jeans.

Their motions became more frantic as they hastily completed undressing each other. They were racing not against the clock but against their own desire—and they were losing the race. Kyle barely had a chance to kiss Roberta's heavy breasts, to caress her thighs, to unlock her body with his magic touch before she was urging him onto her, into her.

He groaned softly as their bodies became one. He didn't move, only held her to him, his heartbeat pounding fiercely against her soft skin, his hands tight in her hair. "How are you?" he finally breathed.

She sighed, then opened her eyes. "Actually, Kyle, you're kind of smashing down in to my stomach."

He groaned again, this time in frustration, although a begrudging smile cut dimples into his cheeks. "Maybe your stomach is kind of smashing up into me," he observed.

"Either way, I can't breathe."

"Hard to satisfy, aren't you?" he complained good-naturedly as he withdrew from her. He glared at her protruding abdomen for a minute. "It's one thing for them to get in the way and spoil things *after* they're born," he remarked. "But *before* they're born?"

"Being a good parent means being flexible and open-minded," Roberta lectured him.

He rolled his eyes in pretended annoyance. Roberta's abrupt shove, which landed him on his back, caught him unprepared, but before he could question her, she was straddling him, lowering herself onto him.

His hands caught her hips and guided her. A husky growl of delight emerged from him as he arched up from the mattress to accommodate the new position. God bless Roberta's magnificently troublesome shape, he thought hazily as the muscles in his back and legs drove him up into her. There was a great deal to be said for flexibility and open-mindedness.

Roberta closed her eyes in order to savor fully the sensation of Kyle's movements inside her. She heard her own voice, distant and tremulous, shaping his name. It seemed impossible that a man could make her feel so desirable, even when she was five months along and looking...all right, not like a hippo, not like a walrus, but definitely like a five-months' pregnant woman.

A woman—that was what she was right now. A woman in the throes of love, a woman whose lover—whose husband—knew how to satisfy her body and to celebrate it, no matter what it looked like. His thrusts grew more forceful, more demanding. She tensed her knees around his hips and tucked her toes under his flexing thighs. Maybe he considered her toes knobby, she mused, but the pressure of them against his skin obviously excited him.

His changing tempo, his uncompromising surges, his powerful love left her helpless before her own response. Her body closed around him and then opened, closed and opened, a torrent of unspeakable pleasure pulsing through her. She shuddered in blissful surrender, then sank fully onto him to absorb his own ferocious climax within her.

"Roberta," he whispered, weak but sated, as she rested on top of him. "If this keeps getting better and better, we're going to be having one hell of a good time when we're seventy."

"Mm," she agreed, kissing the underside of his chin. "I can hardly wait."

He laughed, then grunted and recoiled beneath her. "Ow! Your belly button is assaulting me!"

Giggling, Roberta shifted off him. The fetus had evidently decided that now was the time to perform a vigorous aerobics workout. "Don't complain to me," Roberta chided Kyle. "It's *your* child."

"Mine?" He pointed accusingly at her swollen abdomen. "In other words, you had nothing to do with this?"

"You were the one who was agitating for another child," she maintained. "As I remember it, you got me all distracted so I didn't even know what you were up to."

"Is that what you call it?" he asked, grinning seductively and running his hand between her legs. "Distracted?"

"It *is* rather distracting," she whispered, shivering with pleasure at the gentle friction of his fingers against her sensitive flesh.

Kyle let his hand remain where it was as he lowered his lips to her belly. "Hey, you in there," he murmured. "You don't kick me, and I won't kick you, all right? Have we got a deal?" He pressed his ear against the roundness and listened. "What?" he exclaimed, scowling at Roberta's belly. He confronted Roberta. "It says it wants lobster for dinner."

Roberta shrugged. "I guess we'll have to go to a restaurant, then," she noted. "You have yet to pull anything other than seaweed out of that trap of yours."

Kyle feigned indignation. "Leah and I are working on something," he asserted. "A new strategy. It's Leah's idea—she recommends that we try baiting the trap with peanut-butter-and-jelly sandwiches. We're going to row out tomorrow and give it a try."

Roberta chuckled. "Meanwhile, I can always eat lobster at a restaurant."

"Haven't you got any faith in me?" Kyle asked.

She curled her hand around the back of his neck and drew his mouth to hers. "None whatsoever," she said, sighing, before losing herself in his kiss, losing herself in the boundless faith she had for her savior, her knight in shining armor, her confidant, her husband, her strength. Her man.

Harlequin American Romance

COMING NEXT MONTH

#153 SHADOWS by Stella Cameron

Leah knew she was gambling her future on a man she'd met only once, but Guy had offered his help one lonely night. When she arrived on his doorstep, she understood that Guy was bound to help her. Leah saw, too, that the feelings she'd harbored for him would have to be forgotten. But how could that be, when those feelings were all she had left?

#154 MACKENZIE'S LADY by Dallas Schulze

It began so innocently, as a quest for a friend's stolen watch, but Holly was quickly subjected to the horrors of multiple propositions, a barroom brawl and a dubious rescue by an unsavory character named Mackenzie. She yearned for home—for safety—but with Mac still on her heels, she feared how the adventure would end.

#155 MINOR MIRACLES by Rebecca Flanders

Leslie watched the demonstration of supernatural strength as Michael Bradshaw melted iron chains, boiled water and caused disconnected phones to ring—using nothing more than the power of his mind. She was trained to seek rational explanations, but when his topaz eyes smiled at her through the two-way mirror, she could only wonder: exactly what was Michael Bradshaw?

#156 HEAVEN SHARED by Cathy Gillen Thacker

For years the Cavanaughs dreamed of having a baby, but it never happened. Then the fertility pills paid off. Ellie's pregnancy seemed to occur at the wrong time: her law career was taking off and Neil was busier than ever at the hospital. Could they expect a second miracle—could they expect the baby to sort out their tangled lives?

Take 4 books & a surprise gift FREE

SPECIAL LIMITED-TIME OFFER

Mail to   **Harlequin Reader Service**®

In the U.S.   In Canada
901 Fuhrmann Blvd.   P.O. Box 2800, Station "A"
P.O. Box 1394   5170 Yonge Street
Buffalo, N.Y. 14240-1394   Willowdale, Ontario M2N 6J3

YES! Please send me 4 free Harlequin American Romance® novels and my free surprise gift. Then send me 4 brand-new novels as they come off the presses. Bill me at the low price of $2.25 each —a 11% saving off the retail price. There are no shipping, handling or other hidden costs. There is no minimum number of books I must purchase. I can always return a shipment and cancel at any time. Even if I never buy another book from Harlequin, the 4 free novels and the surprise gift are mine to keep forever.

154-BPA-BP6S

	(PLEASE PRINT)
Name	

Address		Apt. No.

City	State/Prov.	Zip/Postal Code

One of America's best-selling romance authors writes
her most thrilling novel!

TWIST OF FATE

JAYNE ANN KRENTZ

Hannah inherited the anthropological papers that could
bring her instant fame. But will she risk her life and give
up the man she loves to follow the family tradition?

Available in June at your favorite retail outlet, or reserve your copy for
May shipping by sending your name, address, and zip or postal code
along with a check or money order for $4.70 (includes 75¢ for postage
and handling) payable to Worldwide Library Reader Service to:

((•)) WORLDWIDE LIBRARY®

BPA—TOF-H-1